POLLY SHARPE

The Royal Mouser

kindle direct publishing

For my family – you are all a glorious inspiration every day.

Contents

1

PROLOGUE

How Things Used to Be.

Sunday 19 June 2016, Anmer Hall, Norfolk.
The atmosphere between the Duke and Duchess of Cambridge was strained as they dressed.

French lace tickled the Georgian sash windows of the expansive attic bedroom at Anmer Hall, teasing the morning sun as it streamed in over Norfolk fields and through clematis leaves. The four-poster bed, a wedding present from Charles, wallowed on squat, bronze legs in dappled, aquarium light like an ancient narwhal of maritime legend. Rumpled Egyptian cotton sheets, awaiting a pummelling from domestic hands, roiled across the mattress and cascaded onto Persian carpet. A lost ear pod lay like a pearl in the folds.

Princess Diana's favourite Eames chair stood proudly in the reading nook, surrounded by first editions and Richard and Judy book-club recommendations. On it sat a cushion with a crocheted spaniel's face. A pair of toddler's swimming goggles hung over the handle of an antique armoire; bottle-green coveralls and helicopter manuals spilled over William's side of the bed.

"Babe, what's wrong?" Kate, fresh from a purified rainfall shower, hoisted her towel, peered into the vanity unit mirror, put a swoop of eyeliner over each upper lid and gave William her full attention.

"It's nothing."

"Clearly, it isn't." Kate pushed William's under-flight-suit cotton onesie off his pillow, briefly considering how it might look with heels, and sat down.

William felt in his bedside table drawer for his lucky gold Duke of Edinburgh badge and squeezed it as his eyes misted.

"I've a technical inspection this morning, then a practice flight to the Scillies. I hate working on Sundays. Also, I can't stop thinking about Granny ticking me off on the balcony at Trooping of the Colour last week. And those horrible press reports about you being in love with Harry. I feel totally out of control and I hate it."

Kate sensed that a joke about taking control of William's gear stick could wait. She looked at him kindly.

"Harry and I like having a laugh. I know you're not a fan, but H is always up for watching *Made in Chelsea.*"

"I don't see the point of reality TV," William muttered. "It's bad enough watching *Game of Thrones.*"

Kate stood up, slipped out of the towel and into her Monday knickers.

"The thing is... I hate to say this, babe, but you're becoming a bit..." she whispered, "boring."

William's lip curled. He kicked Kate's copy of *Runner's World* across the bedroom floor. It slid under a solid gold antique stool and came to rest against Lupo, who was lying on his back in a pool of sunlight with George's crocheted spaniel cushion in his mouth, dreaming of the nappy he had pilfered from Charlotte's bedroom and stashed behind the model train depot.

"Why don't you go and play with the children for a bit before you go to work? Harold is taking them..."... Kate paused.

William frowned. "*Where's* he taking them?"

Kate looked down and fiddled with a cuticle.

"The new children's mud enclosure at Glastonbury before it opens next weekend."

"Oh, great," William said. "How am I supposed to compete with that?" He paced the floor, growling softly. "I'm trying *really* hard to be current and cool. I'm on the cover of bloody *Attitude* magazine; I wore that headband for mental health, even though it brought attention to my crown."

"... or lack of," muttered Kate, pulling on skinny jeans.

"I'm flying to France, via the Scillies today and I just haven't got time for this."

William marched along the corridor, kicking small toys through the banisters as he went. With a satisfying thunk, they each hit the wall and bounced down the stairs. Watching a Lego parachutist tumble into a Farrow and Ball abyss gave him an idea. He entered the bright, airy playroom, with its floor-to-ceiling toy cupboards and faux-fur quiet corner. A train track ran in spirals around the perimeter of the room, with to-scale Eurostars, Shinkansen and South West Railway models lined up in a depot the size of a large dog kennel. William's eye was drawn to a quivering by the window and he waited for his three-year-old son to emerge from behind the curtains.

"George!"

"Pops!"

George's blonde mop slithered silkily between his father's fingers as he succumbed to the usual hair tousle.

"Do you want to come flying?" William asked, with all the enthusiasm of a man offering to take his child to work.

"Yessss!!" said George.

"This might be the last chance we have to see France while we're still part of the EU. How about it? A trip in the helicopter with your old Dad?"

"Eee-Uwww!" shrieked George, running towards William.

"Well, yes," William caught him expertly. "I'm glad you feel so passionately. We must remain neutral, of course, but personally, I think..."

"Lottie's nappy stinks!" George waved Lupo's buried treasure in front of William's nose.

"NO, Georgie." William plucked it from George's fingers. Nanny had gone to find new batteries for the baby monitor, so he took a deep breath, steeled his nerves and dropped it into the nappy bin all by himself. "No time for larking about. If we're to cross the Channel," he said, buoyed by his own resourcefulness, "we must get a wiggle on."

George stood on his Peter Rabbit rug, treading old Play-Doh lumps in more firmly as he thought. He picked up a discarded, two-handled beaker, sucked thoughtfully and dropped it again. After a moment or two, he disappeared into the walk-in dressing up room and returned carrying two black and white striped, cashmere beanie hats. He grinned.

"French!"

"Oh, you rascal!" said William affectionately. But, since the son had got his hat on, William donned one too and thought this might be one instance when forgetting about heirs and graces and letting go might be fun.

2

CHAPTER ONE

Tuesday 2 May 2023, Elderfield, West Sussex.

Tess Oates fell onto the kitchen floor and surrendered to Rowley's tongue.

Outside, the birds warbled petulantly in the afternoon's relentless heat. Inside was cool and quiet, oiled by Dan's mellifluous mumble seeping through the ceiling. Tess pictured her husband sitting cross-legged on the stripped-bare IKEA double bed upstairs, tapping away at his pillow-balanced laptop screen as urine-stained sheets lay in a foetid bundle in the hallway. Jack's bed-wetting had relapsed to a nightly occurrence. She focused on the damp patch above the window: recent dry weather had dried it to near-invisibility but the patch of mould in the corner would need another scrub. Rowley grunted with pleasure, blissfully using Tess' feet as a salt lick. It was four weeks until the summer half-term. Tess wasn't sure she'd make it.

She pulled herself up and heard Dan say,

"I've been making notes and I'd like to talk you through the first twelve bullet points."

It was his turn to get the children.

"Shall we go get Mollie and Jack?" she asked Rowley, pointlessly.

Rowley stretched, shook himself and lay down. It was supper time. Brown, curly hairs settled on Tess's charity shop shorts: acceptable for a bottom-heavy forty-year-old with flats but, if her boss Enid Saunders' expression was anything to go by, not for much longer. Tess remembered with a wince the afternoon's painful sign-off process for a prospective new university logo: Enid had refused to entertain the idea that the initialism for Craworth University of Nautical Technology, written in a rectangular design might be misconstrued. Then again, the same issue applied every time she had to shorten their own trust name to its initials: The Wenceslas Academy Trust and Enid didn't seem to care. White wine whispered from the fridge.

Tess hauled herself up and fed Rowley, forcing herself to resist alcohol until after-school 'Owls' club pick-up. She could almost hear the ice cracking and feel the day's fire-fighting fading with each sip. Almost.

The church bell down the road chimed five o'clock. Tess fetched Rowley's lead and wedged a tennis ball between his jaws: he was useless at retrieving but liked the mouth feel. The walk up Love Lane to Elderfield Junior School was short and pretty, with neat, boxy council-owned houses lining the road like mushrooms in the sun. Occasional patches of mowed front lawn and potted geraniums belied the privation within. If Tess looked carefully, she could see the torn blinds and gaffer-taped holes in the window frames of number eleven. At number nine, the cracked windshield of the Bindmans' rusting Honda Accord glinted in the sunlight. At number seven, she paused to stroke

Billy, the tailless tabby. Rowley bared well-ground teeth and cowered at her ankles. She turned the corner, hastily skipped over a burst of feathers from a recently deceased pigeon and reached the school gate.

She hesitated as her phone rang with an unknown number. Jack appeared at the six-foot high hall window, screwed his nose up and stuck out his tongue. They had discussed this behaviour before. Tess gave him a thumbs down, shook her head, mouthed, 'disappointed' and took the call.

"Tess Oates? This is Caroline Bouch*aay*." The accent sliced through Tess like dental floss. "Director of External Relations at Oscar's."

Rowley yawned and dropped his tennis ball, which rolled under a parked car. Jack banged on the window, slipped off his vantage point with a muffled cry and disappeared. Tess turned her back and covered her left ear to concentrate.

"I'll cut to the chase. We were *so* very impressed with the film you produced for The Wenceslas Academy, we want to invite you to Oscar's for a chemistry-meet. We've restructured our comms team and are embarking on a new strategy. We think you could be *just* the person to lead our video marketing. Obviously, it's a competitive brief..." Caroline breezily promised further details by email and rang off.

Swallowing hard, Tess side-stepped a discarded Hula Hoops packet and sat down on the curb. Oscar's. An elite private school in Berkshire, for Sheikh princes and multi-millionaires. Lacrosse, Latin and Lamborghinis. With, no doubt, a stonking great marketing budget. A bit different from Elderfield Primary with its classes of thirty-two children bouncing off the leaky ceilings and dependable *Shrek* screenings if a cover teacher failed to show. She sucked her split ends.

Mollie's voice trilled through the school's front door letterbox, "Muh-uhm – number one, you're late. Number two, come and see our marble run!"

Tess gave up on the tennis ball and tied Rowley to a lamppost.

"This could be it," she whispered into his fringe. "Oscar's is where the Prince and Princess of Wales's children go. This might be my big chance to escape Enid's clutches and put an end to Ofsted compliance website pages and sponsored trampolining press releases. I could hand Enid my resignation and finally go freelance." She imagined Enid's face as she opened the envelope, her tight lips disappearing under the pressure of suppressed rage. For a minute she was happier than she'd been all day.

Climbing the steps to release her children from after-school club, she allowed the fantasies to go further: ringing a silver doorbell and seeing double oak doors open, revealing her immaculate, straw-boatered brood emerging between planters of fragrant spring blooms, clutching leather satchels and chattering excitedly about their day of cello playing and polo. And surely working for Oscar's, freelance or not, might mean she would be given a juicy fee discount? She made a face as she remembered her principles. The country was in enough of a mess without more class divide. State education was the way forward! Although, who could blame her for wanting Mollie and Jack to have opportunities she never had? Mollie might rub shoulders with future Booker Prize winners and Jack would almost certainly become a world-class environmental engineer. She could dream, couldn't she? They'd thank her further down the track for her brilliant foresight. They might even buy her a house, like rock stars did for their mums. Also, whilst she would never admit it, she wouldn't mind rubbing shoulders with a Royal or two.

Jack shot through the door like a bullet train.

"Me and Rob have formed a club. It's called the 'F word' club..."

"Rob and I," Tess said automatically. "And that's a *bad* name."

"Mu-hum, it means the 'Friday play date club! It's only for year three!"

"What do you do?"

Jack gave the lost property box at the bottom of the steps a kick. A water bottle flew out of his bag, hitting Mollie on the leg before rolling down the steps. Mollie shoved Jack, who fell into Rowley – his lead straining as he lunged joyfully towards the children.

Jack said proudly: "We pick up logs and put them in a different place."

The sun shone brightly. Tess wondered how long Oscar's' after-school club hours were. She unhooked Rowley, picked up Jack's water bottle from the gutter and trudged back down the road to the fridge.

3

CHAPTER TWO

Monday 8 May 2023, Elderfield, West Sussex.

"Tracy picks Rowley up at eleven thirty," Tess yelled at Dan, who was shaving in the shower, "and don't forget a tennis ball. She has her own poo bags."

She squeezed along the side of the bed to the shared wardrobe and carefully removed her new maroon viscose top from the hanger. It crackled as she smoothed it between the folds of a towel. More fashionable luggage would be nice; since their honeymoon in Bristol, the ancient pull-ons had only been used for hide-and-seek.

Jack wandered into the bedroom, naked from the waist down. He dropped a library book titled: *Astronomy - everything a kid should know* on the bed, picked up a mascara and daubed his upper face. Tess observed with the helpless detachment of one watching flood waters rise.

"Is Pluto a dorf planet?"

"Yes."

"Why?"

"It's smaller than the rest."

"Like me?" His eyes were hypnotic, even crusted with black grease and sleepy dust. Tess wrapped her arms around his clammy bottom and hoisted him into the air.

"Yep. Did you do a wee in your bed last night, darling?"

Jack looked down. "No, on my Lego level crossing. It was a strong and powerful one." He clocked the pile of clothes. "Where are you going?"

"Berkshire, remember?" sang Mollie, skipping into the bedroom like a neon-trousered Dick Whittington. She flung a floral drawstring bag on the bed, blew hair out of her eyes and started to rearrange Tess's packing.

"It's INSET day! I'm going with Mum and you're bike riding with Dad."

The pitch with Caroline Bouchet had gone well. So well, Tess had been offered a preliminary visit to Oscar's. The sumptuous 'school with a heart' where young children learned the joys of outdoor education on the land and water. The problem was how she was going to keep it from Enid.

"We want to demonstrate a real sense of *community engagement*."

Caroline's voice had oozed confidence. Tess imagined her lying on a matching linen bed set, surrounded by Pomeranians.

"We were so impressed with your films for, ah, The Wenceslas Academy and Elderfield Primary and, of course, with all your ideas, especially the concept of the children doing a river clean and water quality sampling..." she had paused, as though trying to summon an impossible image. "*Absolutely* something we would never have come up with ourselves, ha! Bloody brilliant. *Loved* it. And so we'd like to see if you're a, ah, *good fit*."

Mollie held out photocopies of the itinerary she had written for the trip. At nine years old, her organisational skills no longer surprised Tess. It was titled, 'Posh trip to Berkshire with Mum.' She'd listed, 'posh wellies, cake, Pokemon cards (good ones).' Tess laid the papers carefully in the pleather folder, bought especially for the project.

Dan came in from the bathroom, rubbing hand cream into his cuticles. A wet curl had escaped his flannel turban. His chest glowed and he smelled of lemon. He sat down at Tess's dressing table and started picking at his eyebrows.

"I hope the sun shines for you. Don't forget to change at Basingstoke."

"I know," said Tess, trying to sound light. "Don't worry."

A juicy-marrowed bone of contention in the shape of un- fulfilled dreams hovered above the couple like a drone. Dan stared gloomily at the folder.

"Are you sure Jack and I can't come?"

"It'll be good for you to have some one-on-one bonding," said Tess, more forcefully than intended, knowing that al- though they'd have a great time whizzing around on bikes, it could then mean several hours of distraction from *Minecraft* and falling asleep on the sofa reading train magazines to Jack until his eyes twitched.

"They shoot some of *Saturday Night Disco* near Wokingham. I thought we could have a look..." he tailed off before saying sheepishly, "... and Sam Price is playing at The Lane."

Tess's hands squeezed each other's fingers. The packing had taken its toll; the last time she'd needed an overnight bag was for a hospital stay after Jack scalded himself on a museum floor light.

"Oscar's is nowhere near Wokingham."

"Shame."

"Let it go, Dan," Tess said gently.

Her thoughts swam back to carefree student nights at the Angel Comedy Club. Sam Price had been in Tess and Dan's year. He and Dan had toured the pubs of Bristol with jokes about car parks, but Sam was now a successful stand-up comic who had carved out a niche on perky quips, while Dan dreamed of the spotlight and played the occasional pub, but spent most of his time testing firewalls on dodgy hips.

"Jack and I could still tag along?"

Mollie looked at him with undisguised pity.

"Dad, let it *go*."

Dan dropped his towel, revealing pants with cheese and pint glasses. Mollie's eyes rolled backwards into their sockets and she retreated to her room.

4

CHAPTER THREE

Monday 8 May 2023, Windsor, Berkshire.

The Princess of Wales - Catherine to her public, Kate to select friends - glanced warily at the gorgeous, green-edged chrysanthemum cutting she had brought down the M4 on her lap, all the way from Kensington Palace. It was named after her daughter, Charlotte. She was given the plant six years ago by a Dutch floral company after the Chelsea Flower Show and, back then, she was determined to plant it herself and watch it bloom. Well, it certainly had. Now, as the family grew steadily into their Windsor home, it was time to watch it thrive again in the fertile soils of Berkshire.

Charlotte herself was in full throttle, hurtling around the garden on a souped-up John Deere go kart, with her four-year-old brother, Louis balanced on the bonnet, as she dealt with the pain of a recently stubbed toe by yodelling *Jerusalem* out of tune. Both children were off school, in the last eight hours of quarantine, following a vomiting bug.

"Gosh," said William, as he prepared pork balls for an impromptu barbecue. The sausage meat had come from his

14

favourite West London deli, couriered that morning. Bowls of kimchi and thrice-cooked chips, as well as perspiring jugs of lemonade studded the snow-white tablecloths next to him. Tabitha, the family's working Cocker, drooled silently by his ankle. "What's that?"

"Princess Charlotte, babe," said Kate patiently, not sure whether he was referring to the cries or the chrys.

"Well, I wish she would shut up. Her birthday was last week. There's no excuse for such a racket."

They paused, heads on one side, listening to their daughter's anguish as she ripped the edge of the kitchen garden to shreds.

"Should we move her to the spare plot?" asked William, hopefully. "It's really quite distracting." He wished George were there to take Charlotte's mind off the pain; he was good in a crisis.

Kate frowned. "Think of Harry: we've vowed never to use that word around her. Too insensitive - and the fallout could be dangerous."

"Fine. Has Nanny clocked on yet?"

Kate nodded. Nanny no longer lived in, which meant the family enjoyed far more privacy even if it had taken some time for William to realise he had to make his own glass of midnight milk.

"Has she tried Calpol?"

"I think so."

"A wet paper towel?"

"Yes."

"Pa's agricultural speech recordings?"

Kate looked at him hard.

"Nanny's tried nearly everything, but she said she might have a little trick left up her sleeve." Kate blew gently on her silk gardening glove as a little spider edged towards her elbow. What a beautiful wallpaper pattern a spider and a chrysanthemum would make, she thought. Perfect for bathroom number nine in Windsor Castle. (It paid to plan ahead). The delicate legs stretching deep into the heart of the bloom...

Nanny, a robust, Spanish lady with a bun like a stale chocolate muffin and slab-heels, appeared round the corner looking serious.

"The toe ... it hurts her so much. But," she said, looking down at the spider, now crawling across the table in front of Kate, "with your help, we may nip this in the bud."

Nanny divulged that she was gifted with a secret family skill she had, so far, not needed to employ with the Wales family.

"My grandmother made blankets from spider silk," she confided. "And the spiders only come from the finest roses and chrysanthemums. Just like these," she pointed delightedly at the bloom Kate held. Five tiny arachnids moved across its petals.

Louis came over for a look.

"Spidey spiders!" he said, before bonking Tabitha sharply on the nose.

"*Don't* hurt Tab," warned William. "Her bite's worse than your shark."

Louis glanced over towards the swimming pool. The Wales siblings had been permitted to keep a Lantern shark in the deep end after David Attenborough's last visit. He looked down, wishing George were there and not at some stupid school lacrosse match. "Sorry, Pops."

Nanny broke the tension by sweeping some spiders into Kate's gardening clutch bag, on top of Tabitha's gravy bones.

"Can you catch some more?" she asked Kate. "I will ring my mother about instructions for the blanket. I'm sure I can whip one up. Five hundred should do it. Then tomorrow, the princess should sleep well, and her toe will feel better."

Louis brightened. He wasn't sure how they would go about extracting whatever was needed from spiders to make silk, but he was pretty sure he'd enjoy it.

From across the garden, Charlotte's yells grew stronger.

"Of course," said Kate hastily, peeling petals. "Anything to help. Cries-and-the-mum, hey, babe?"

She looked at William for appreciation, but he had turned his attention back to his balls. Charlotte began singing Lizzo at the top of her voice. Missing George, who knew how to handle situations like this, and feeling sad that her favourite ear defenders had been chewed that morning by Tabitha, she started searching for spiders to help make Charlotte's web.

CHAPTER FOUR

Tuesday 9 May 2023, Oscar's School, Berkshire.

After checking into a five-star hotel, filling out a mountain of forms and freshening up in a bathroom bigger than their kitchen, Mollie and Tess tripped lightly down the beige marble staircase to a waiting car.

The balmy air smelled of apple blossom, blackthorn and newly mown grass. Narrow country lanes lined with vigorously blooming cow parsley twisted this way and that. A heated encounter with a tractor left them so hot and sticky, they finished two big complementary bottles of Evian, which Tess guessed cost more than a week's packed lunches.

Finally, a discreet, blue sign appeared, stencilled with a single word: Oscar's. The wild hedgerows gave way to perfectly pruned silver birch. Tess felt in the front pocket of her rucksack for a hair brush. Mollie winked and stuck her head out of the window, breathing cow dung and ozone.

They clambered out of the car and found Caroline waiting in the reception area. The vast entrance to the Oscar's riverboat club soaked up any sound their shoes might have made into dense seagrass matting. Black and white framed photographs of small flotillas with even smaller helmsmen scooting upriver scattered the walls.

Mollie beamed.

"It's lovely to be here," she said, stretching out her hand. "I'm Mollie. And before you ask, I'm nine."

Caroline's lipstick glittered. The corners of her eyes suggested invisible support as she smiled with just the bottom of her face.

"How utterly gorgeous to see you both," her voice trickled downwards, like a mountain stream. "We're just in time to see the children launch their boats. Follow me."

She led the way across a glistening green field, ripe with a rare breed of cow. A sheepdog eyed the trio cautiously from a distance, ran up, lay down, and scampered away again. At the corner, they plunged into a leafy, emerald sanctuary, where the sun was briefly defeated in its attempts to fry exposed skin.

"D'you think we'll be able to have a go at sailing?" Mollie asked, slapping at a mosquito.

"You're not insured," Caroline shrugged. "But you're welcome to paddle."

Emerging from the tree tunnel's limpid shadows, Tess inhaled a fresh breeze, cut with the tang of ice-lollies. The pearlescent path in front of them evoked a flash of bathroom cleaning guilt. Her brow prickled with heat as she squinted towards a low, olive-green hut, bordered with flags, flapping like soon-to-be landed fish. Only on television had she seen sun-bleached pontoons like the one before them, freckled with wet footprints and encircled with fronds of waterlilies – lush and resplendent as the new velvet cushions she coveted in *Homes and Gardens.*

The river air reminded her of the stream in Elderfield; the one with shopping trollies and old trainers – but this river was majestic, alive. The smell of expensive sun cream and light sweat drifted up from small boys and girls, darting up and down like tropical fish to coil ropes into neat worm casts – children like Mollie and Jack but shinier, almost 4D – with tidy haircuts and no second-hand polo shirts between them. She had seen these types of children before, of course - on stage at the local theatre group, giving the impression of confidence. However, this was real life. She looked at the rope worm casts and thought how it might feel to stamp on them.

Dragonflies zoomed among the reeds like tiny drones. Fat, white rowing dinghies slapped playfully at the water. Further downstream, rough, woven tubs like upturned beetles bobbed drunkenly under dripping willows, soothed by the white noise of the weir.

"*Coracles,*" said Caroline, loudly.

"I know," said Tess. "I've read Enid Blyton."

Beside her, Mollie danced on the spot, hugging a soft rabbit to her chest with one hand and waving to a tall, blonde boy on the pontoon below with the other.

Caroline gasped and pushed them both behind a nearby shower block.

"You absolutely *mustn't* attempt to make contact with *Prince George,*" she gasped.

"But I *know* him," protested Mollie. "From TV. He had supper with President Obama in his dressing gown," she wiped the sweat from her face with her rabbit, "watched the Wimbledon final and got told off by his sister at the Queen's funeral."

Caroline gave a wobbly laugh.

"It's more than my job's worth to give - ah, any of our students special treatment. It's all in the NDAs."

"Well, that's ridiculous," said Mollie, firmly. We're not babies. I can make friends," she insisted, "with *anyone*."

"I don't doubt it," muttered Caroline, seeing her entire career hinging on maintaining Oscar's' most prestigious client's privacy. She said so to Mollie, who held a forefinger up to her cheek and pushed her bottom lip out.

"Sad."

Mollie escaped the shower block corner and disappeared towards the group of small sailors, a red rucksack bouncing on her shoulders and bits of plait plastered to her neck like small, brown lightning bolts.

Awkwardness enveloped Tess like an ice bath. The last time she was asked to leave an establishment had been for rude dancing on a party boat on the Solent over twenty years ago. She zipped and unzipped her pleather folder. Inside, nestled amongst the itineraries and hotel information lay her secret weapon.

6

CHAPTER FIVE

Mollie passed groups of children in short, black wetsuits, calling happily to each other: "Monty, you left your sunnies in my sail bag!" "Hebe, wait for me!" "Can I be in Jolyon's crew?"

"*May* I..." tutted Mollie under her breath. She found George behind a boat shed, drawing circles in the dusty earth with a stick. His ice-white shirt hurt her eyes and the origami creases running down its Aertex sleeves were like the paper aeroplanes she made Jack. Sitting down next to him, she tucked the rabbit back into her rucksack, produced a David Walliams book and a pencil and started scribbling in the margins. George put down the stick and started raking his thick fringe rhythmically with dirty fingers.

"I've read that one," he said after a while.

Mollie glanced across, shading her eyes.

"I didn't expect you to say you'd applied the theory of Deconstruction to it."

"Is that what you're doing?"

"Yep."

They sat together in silence, listening for the inevitable shouts of grown-up panic. Mollie's scratching continued.

"The teachers know this is my safe space. It's where I come when I can't cope."

Mollie nodded. "It must be awful having everything because you're rich and going to be king."

George got up. He thrashed at an overhanging willow branch and stared coldly at Mollie. "If you're another sarcastic bully, you can get lost. I can put you on the list for execution."

Mollie smiled benignly. "Of course you can't."

An insect hummed busily between them. A high, bubbling sound could be heard, like the water feature section at a garden centre. As the children of Oscar's flowed down to the water's edge, George flinched as though physically smitten.

"Anyway," said Mollie, "it's quite bullying to threaten me with execution." She mimed chopping off her head. "I'd only come and haunt you afterwards. I'd love to glide through doors and make things move in Buckingham Palace."

George glared. Didn't this girl know anything? "Stop it, you sound like Charlotte. She's always banging about, making noise at home. Anyway, we don't live in Buckingham Palace, Grandpa Wales does."

Mollie snorted. "I thought Louis was the loud one."

George sniffed. "They're both ear-piercing."

"Let me know where they work then," Mollie said. "I've been dying to wear proper earrings for ages. I bet Mum would let me if it was being done by royalty."

George glared again, but his mouth bent into a wonky smile. "What are you drawing?"

"My Lantern shark's pool at home."

It was Mollie's turn to boil. "Err… you know it's *cruel* to keep sharks in captivity? Especially Lantern sharks. They're pelagic!"

"We look after it," George huffed. He didn't know what 'pelagic' meant but it sounded regal. His eyes narrowed. "What's your name? And what year are you in? I haven't seen you before."

Mollie thought quickly. With Tess's opportunity hanging in the balance, she knew she had to be clever.

"I'm Mollie," she said simply.

"Mollificent Weatherby-Good?" George frowned. "But she's in Charlotte's year."

From somewhere between the trees floated a growing and strident cacophony of voices. Mollie bristled. "They'll be on us in a sec. Oh, ok - Mollie Oates," she breathed. "And I'm not actually at Oscar's. I've come up with my mum to see if they want her to make a video of your school. We've got an INSET day today, so I don't have to go in and I'm here because I'm really good at projects. Especially scripts and speeches. I helped my mum do the video at my school, Elderfield Primary. I'm the best in the cartoon club so I drew what they should film." She watched a tear slide off George's nose and splash onto his sandals. "Err... what's the matter?"

He sniffed, then said in a small voice, "my lacrosse team lost."

Mollie lay her pencil carefully down, its lead on a leaf. George's back crumpled with a sob. She put her arm tentatively around his shoulders and squeezed. She thought hard. Even for a prince, his explanation seemed unlikely.

"Lacrosse sounds like a sad sport," she said, brightly. "It's even got 'loss' in it. Why don't you play football?" George glowered. "Or just sit at home on your iPad like normal kids?"

"There's no-one to play football with in Windsor except Charlotte and Louis," he said in a small voice. "Lottie's better than me and the kids in the park don't want me to join in because they think I'm having private football lessons, so I'm going to be really good. But I'm not! Good, I mean. And I only have lessons when the helicopter's available to take me to Madrid."

Mollie took his face in her hands. It was as soft as a foxglove.

"You are *Prince George*," she insisted. "Be proud of it. But I don't think that's the problem. I think you're fed up because you can't express yourself very clearly and you think no-one's listening anyway."

George's face flushed the colour of a ripe peach. After several seconds, he sniffed.

"What's an INSET day?"

"It's when teachers get a day off to train and eat flapjacks and children stay at home."

"Lucky," George said. He sniffed again. "Tell me more about your school."

Mollie talked animatedly about the roller-coaster that was life at Elderfield Primary. George's mouth watered as she described the delights of free school meals. To have such limited choice at lunch time - no more deliberations over slow-roasted lamb or jewelled couscous. How delightfully easy it sounded!

"GEORGE!"

The sound erupted from the nettles around the corner from the shed. Caroline's glistening forehead hove into view above the undergrowth.

George stared at his new friend, his eyes opaque with desperation.

"Will you help me?" he hissed.

"What do you mean?"

He led her around to the back of the shed. The river noise faded and George's face clouded.

"I need help with," he lowered his voice and paused. "Speaking."

Mollie studied him for a beat before deciding he wasn't joking. "But you're going to be *king*."

"Stop saying that!"

Flecks of spit flew. Mollie held up her David Walliams in defence.

"I don't need a reminder! And I don't mean help with talking to people like you. Or at home. I mean at school. And in public. I can't..." he looked down and the sandals took another drenching. "I just can't... seem to..."

"GEORGE!!"

A short, nut-brown man, arms like bulging Christmas stockings and 'Staff' in capital letters stretched tight across his chest appeared with Caroline. They pushed their way through the nettles, panting like a pair of hot Labradors. Caroline's silky blouse was sweat-stained and covered in sticky willies.

"Come on, Your Royal Highness." Gruffly, nut-brown led George away. Caroline looked as if she was going to say something explosive to Mollie, then thought better of it.

"Your mother's coming," she growled, "and neither of us are impressed."

Watching George stumble off, Mollie thought she had never seen such a painful sight. No other children seemed to be interested in his whereabouts - or perhaps they had been told not to be - and the look he shot over his shoulder was worse than Jack's face after the family's iPad screen cracked. She picked up George's stick and wondered if she could sell it on eBay.

"Why does George seem so sad?"

Caroline looked pious. "I'm not at liberty to say."

"Is he ill?"

"He's... he suffers from a, a..."

"Speech impediment?"

Caroline looked put out. "I speak perfectly well, thank you." Her squeezed lips reminded Mollie of the tied end of a balloon. "Well, if you must know, George has selective mutism. He won't – or can't - talk to anyone at school."

"But he's just been telling me all sorts of things!"

"Oh, *you're* safe," scoffed Caroline. "It's only teachers, an audience and people he knows he *should* be friends with that make him freeze."

"That's a relief." Mollie smiled beatifically. She refused to give this wannabe headmistress the satisfaction of seeing her insulted. A hand grabbed her arm.

"I've been looking all over for you!" Tess tightened her grip. Caroline drained her Dior water bottle and patted her mouth. Her crystal-toned sunglasses were black holes. "Where have you been?"

Mollie admitted to telling the future king to pull his socks up.

She followed her mother back through the willows and behind the stable boxes, where black stallions nodded like pendulums, their velvet noses soothing jangled nerves all round. Caroline explained that, under the circumstances, they would have to reconsider the film-making commission.

"And why is that?" asked Tess.

"Because, clearly, you have no idea how the upper half

live," Caroline purred, "and your daughter is something of a liability."

"What about the storyboard?" Mollie protested. "Mum, show her!"

Tess produced the secret weapon from her folder and spread it out on a tack store. Crudely drawn stick girls and boys with representative icons, caged within outlined squares denoted frolics a-plenty at Oscar's. There was a climbing wall, a ballerina, a bike and a tennis racket.

"What's *that*?" asked Caroline, pointing to what looked like a duck.

"A swan," said Tess plainly. "We filmed magpies at Elderfield, but I thought at Oscar's we would need to be more... *diverse*."

"Wait..." Caroline's lips pursed. "Are you saying your *daughter* wrote this treatment?"

Tess bristled. "Not at all. Mollie has a good feel for what students enjoy most at school and how to talk to people. She drew the storyboard for Elderfield Primary and I thought it would be a good experience for her to come and see what Oscar's has to offer. I translate into a script once the story has been established. We're a little team."

Tess and Mollie locked eyes and nudged shoulders.

"Outrageous," fumed Caroline. "I brought you here in good faith," she glared at Tess.

Sensing it was time to depart before they were expelled, Mollie held up her pencil for quiet. She looked at Tess's shoulders and said: "we ought to go and put some sunscreen on, Mum."

Tess looked at her gratefully. Anything to get out of this place. Nut-brown came charging up to them. "The eagle has landed. It's a closed book," he said officiously to Caroline.

"Neither of those expressions makes sense if you mean what I think you mean," retorted Mollie, "which is that poor old George has been cast once again into his wilderness of silence."

They walked through the fields, back to the reception area and congregated on the visitor's drive. Once she'd reached the safety of gravel, the wind went out of Caroline's sails.

"I'm jolly sorry it all seems to have ended like this," she said stiffly. "I just don't think you're quite what we're looking for. I hope you can understand. We'll be in touch about the NDAs and whatnot. Do have a safe journey back."

Mollie and Tess said goodbye, used the receptionist's Montblanc fountain pen to leave a sad face in the visitor's book, climbed into the waiting car and left.

CHAPTER SIX

Tuesday 9 May 2023, Elderfield, West Sussex.

Dan was eating porridge and scrolling the Met Office app. The afternoon weather was perfect for a spring bike ride across the village. He imagined the number of work emails he'd received by now would already be into double figures but he'd promised himself he wouldn't check them. He was mildly annoyed that both Tess and he had had to take a day off for the children's INSET, but he hoped she was getting on well at the posh school, he really did.

Jack sat beside him, secretly spooning porridge into Rowley's waiting jaws. He preferred his mother's - she added cinnamon and chocolate buttons. On the kitchen floor stood Jack's bike, a hand-me-down from Mollie, upturned onto its handlebars. Dan looked at it mournfully.

"Your tires were fine last weekend," he said. "What happened?"

He got down to investigate.

Jack shrugged, knowing full well what had happened. It involved a kitchen knife. He said nothing.

"Helloooo?" bellowed Arran through the letterbox. "Where are you, you old sod?"

Arran Bindman's friendship with Dan stretched back thirty-five years, beginning in an inner-city Brixton primary school. After a couple of decades of transient living, Arran and his family had moved counties to settle two doors away from the Oates. Arran had seen Dan naked, drunk, weeping and singing. Their sons were born in adjacent hospital beds and he'd watched Dan hold Robert as lovingly as he'd held Jack. He'd never seen him lying on his back with a dog's head between his legs, fixing a bicycle before, but there was a first time for everything.

"Hand me that valve cap, will you?" asked Dan. "Rowley, *geddoff.*"

Jack, who had gone outside into the back garden with Robert, didn't answer the door. Arran had let himself in and now dropped to the floor. "Might as well warm up if you're busy." His press-ups incited Rowley, whose humping eventually forced him to give up and make coffee. Tire fixed, the men sat and drank while they caught their breath.

"Any more gigs?" Arran asked.

"The Swan at the end of the month," Dan said. "I've got some new material. It's about the recession."

"Sounds hopeful." Arran liked to be supportive.

"Not really," Dan said.

"Hit me."

"What do you call Bob the Builder during a recession?"

"I don't know."

"Bob."

"Nice." Arran nodded approvingly. "Can't wait." He moved swiftly on: "speaking of builders," we've had our bricks nicked over the weekend. Bloody scavs."

"Things are bad," agreed Dan. "Our Aldi shop only stretched to five days last week. We ate noodles all weekend. Thank god we don't have to turn on the heating." He paused. "Actually, that would make a good joke, if I say, 'We should get a dog and call it Noodles,' and then I say, 'My wife says, 'don't be silly, we eat noodles,' and then I say, 'if it gets bad enough, ok then."

Arran narrowed his eyes. They sipped in silence until Robert shot through the door, brandishing a plant cane. He was as white as a sheet.

"Malcolm just hit Jack on the back with this!"

"Who's Malcolm?" asked Arran.

"Malcolm Swift, the bully! From school."

Dan had been quite enjoying the day, though he would have preferred to be living it up in a classy hotel in Berkshire, making full use of the breakfast buffet and gym. At least he was going to spend some quality time with some of the most important men in his life.

Since his father died, Dan had visited his mother in London every other weekend and listened to the reasons why she hoped he was happy, despite his appalling childhood. Dan disagreed. They'd had a rough time of it, that was true; growing up in a one-bedroomed flat in the outer reaches of Brixton, sirens wailing every night, dodging the piles of nitrous oxide bullets on the crumbling pavements outside the school gates, like slalom skiers.

It had all been fairly grim until he'd had the courage to apply for a Saturday warm-up slot at a new satellite TV channel in the '90s. His good manners had clinched the win. Mediocre fame had ensued. Once, when a Britpop star had arrived, still drunk, at the studio and urinated in the corridor outside the communal dressing room, Dan had politely explained the health and safety policy and pointed down the corridor to the loos. The Britpop star had ogled him.

"Are you taking the piss?" she'd demanded, then laughed and choked at her own wit. Dan had quickly incorporated the anecdote into his repertoire that day – using no names, of course.

If there was one thing he wouldn't tolerate, it was bullies. He stood up and strode outside.

"Excuse me, you forgot something," he yelled through the washing line's drying laundry, waving the cane at Malcolm's departing back. The boy slowed his scooter and turned.

"You can have it!" yelled Malcolm, and zoomed off around the corner.

Robert and Jack emerged from behind a duvet cover.

"Little toad," muttered Dan.

"When I finally get a motocross bike I'll run him down," Jack clenched his small fists.

The group stacked the dishwasher, packed up and left. A mile down the road, Arran and Robert in front, Dan pulled up to Jack.

"What was all that about?" he asked.

"Malcolm's a big fat poo face."

"Why is he so mean?"

Jack shrugged. "He just doesn't like me."

"You know you can always come to me and I'll try to help?"

Jack's face clouded. "No offence, Dad, but you just tell jokes and make it worse. It's not like you're famous or anything, otherwise it might be ok."

Dan imagined Malcolm's garden cane piercing his heart. Just

ahead of them lay a wasteland of scrubby ground, forced into undulating dirt hills. Robert and Arran skidded in and started whooping up and down the bumps. Jack cast an apologetic look at his father and joined them.

Dan vowed then to make Jack proud. And Mollie and Tess, for that matter. And that little toad Malcolm would see who got the last laugh.

CHAPTER SEVEN

Monday 15 May 2023, Windsor, Berkshire.
Kate was in the kitchen making a green morning smoothie. Tabitha finished her chicken liver pate, bared small, sharp teeth in a smile and bowed graciously before her mistress. Kate nodded absently and sucked spirulina off a spoon. She tiptoed across the marble floor to peer over George's shoulder. The numbers on his exercise book page spun before her eyes.

"Is that maths?" she asked.

"Higher," he muttered.

"Is that maths?" she repeated, raising her voice by an octave.

William, sitting at the top of the table, snorted into his coffee. He needed some light relief. He'd been up most of the night worrying about the state of the monarchy and the direction of his environmental awards. It was all very well having a big, annual international event, but as well as large, global countries, the need to impress the importance of inventiveness and responsibility on local people in his own country had become abundantly clear. Last year, he and Kate had visited a factory in Stockport, making electric motors. They had been floored by the ingenuity of the designers, the cost-efficiency of the materials and the cleanliness of the bathrooms. But William's lips trembled as he recalled the single-use plastics in the canteen, the hundreds of PCs left on standby at hot desks and the thousands of disposable plastic shoe coverings in the enormous bins behind the building.

After sleepless nights wondering what his grandmother and mother would do if she were alive and his father would do if he were allowed to campaign, he had taken it upon himself to launch the local 'Briti-shot' awards: local awards for local people in the UK. The ceremony was two weeks away and they were light years away from agreeing a winner. There were too many great contenders.

Charlotte chewed a pencil and looked up from her books. She was hoping for an A that week in science, for a project on the moon. The face-to-face interview with Neil Armstrong's son would help. She began to daydream about standing up in front of the class to share her findings.

"Have you finished your homework?" asked Kate.

"No. Jinx!" shouted George and Charlotte at the same time.

"No 'jinx-ing' at the table or there'll be no home cinema for a week," Will threatened his children.

"Sorry, Pops. Jinx!" they whispered.

Kate rested her chin on William's head. It was warm and smelt of leather and his very own Duchy honey scalp cream. It reminded her of visits to her grandmother-in-law's stables, where she would help in looking after the horses. She wanted to assist Nanny, but could not bring herself to touch the breakfast plates, covered as they were in congealed egg and smashed avocado. She wanted to help William with his local environment dilemma but he refused to listen to her brilliant ideas about a sustainable wallpaper design competition. She wanted to help George with his confidence but in truth, she still wasn't a hugely confident public speaker herself and, more importantly, she was fed up with making suggestions, only to be rejected, and coming last in the pecking order of the family's needs. She was desperate for something that would get her creative juices going, whilst still being involved in 'the important stuff.'

Kate went upstairs to her dressing room and practised saying, 'I say, I have a thought – could someone please listen to me?' in the mirror. She pursed her lips. She sounded needy. She tried, "guys, listen up. I've got a wizard plan," but that didn't work. She marched downstairs and said, "I know exactly what you must do."

Charlotte and Will looked up. Charlotte yawned. Kate sipped green liquid and savoured her moment.

"Local awards," she announced, "for local people need a bit of spark behind the scenes, babe. I've some marvellous ideas for the Green Room decor. And for you, darling, a play date with a *positive* influence," she said, directing the latter comment towards George. "But not your cousins," she added. Mia and Savannah were inclined to bring their iPads over and introduce George, Charlotte and Louis to video games with dark swamps and slimy creatures. They reminded Kate of tricky visits to America and challenging family dynamics.

"Jolly good plan. Although we'll have to check to see what Camilla's organised," William pondered. "She's taking this Queen's Consort title pretty seriously."

Camilla's revamp of Windsor Castle had been unexpected. Acres of Designer's Guild fabric and gallons of paint had arrived one day in the middle of Sunday lunch. Camilla had picked up the carving knife and quietly snuck off to strip the sofas. It was shortly after this that her penchant for Bauhaus was exposed. Two weeks later, the armchairs were smooth and geometric and every trace of floral abundance pruned and discarded. King Charles was putting on a brave face, though he missed his pouffes. Once the final Turkish rug had been rehomed, she'd taken it a step further and offered her services to William for the Briti-shot awards.

"Fine," Kate said boldly. She moved to George and bent at the knees and waist, like Nanny had taught her. "Whom would you like to invite over, George?"

George summoned every ounce of bravery within his small frame. "Mollie," he breathed.

Kate was confused. She looked down at George's work. Instead of fractions, he'd written, 'Mollie Wales' in tiny letters in the margin.

"How strange to find someone with the same surname as you! Is she from school?" asked Kate, hopefully.

George shook his head, crossed out 'Wales' with big, black slashes, and admitted the real story. He glossed over the part where he was marched away, saying only that he didn't think Mollie would visit Oscar's again. "And so I don't think I'll find another friend like that," he said, quietly. "Because she was a real person, who goes to a real school and eats real school puddings. They're called Angel Delight."

Kate bristled. It wasn't uncommon for George to meet a commoner, but it was unheard of for him to show this level of passion for a peasant.

"You're a real person, George," she soothed, pointing to the fridge. "You've got the ski instructor certificates to prove it."

Louis bounded in and tried to straddle Tabitha, who snarled and ran away to gnaw her golden frisbee. She was a hopeless retriever but she liked the mouth feel.

William was now making himself an espresso for the road before heading to a homeless charity, trying desperately to remember where he'd left his favourite trainers. His aide, an earnest, slim man called Parth, knocked quietly on the back door and slipped into the kitchen.

"Sir," he said, stepping neatly over Louis, who was lying on the floor, face down, "we should get going."

Kate pointed William towards his trainers. She was annoyed that she was going to have to ask an awkward question of Parth, but she couldn't bear to see George upset for another minute.

"Could we possibly ask you a favour?"

Parth knew he had to answer carefully. He glanced at William, who nodded permission. He glanced at Kate, and was dazzled by her perfectly uneven smile.

Kate said dramatically, so that George could hear, "our boy is in need of genuine friendship. He yearns for the company of a young girl he met last week."

Parth nodded, his hazel eyes shining like chocolate ganache.

"Could you find this young girl, Parth?"

Parth agreed that he could. Will downed a second espresso and turned to his family. Charlotte's eyes reminded him of his late grandmother. George's lips reminded him of his mother. Louis' behaviour reminded him of the Jungle Book, but he tried not to mention it too often.

"Let it be so, Parth," he said, magnanimously, and left for Shelter.

39

CHAPTER EIGHT

Monday 15 May 2023, Elderfield, West Sussex.

Tess came out of the staff room at St. Wenceslas Academy, staggering under the weight of three pull-up banners in black canvas cases. She put her head down, pushed through the milling crowds of teenagers in the corridor - ducking rucksacks like a rabbit in a storm - and landed in the office she shared with her boss, Enid Saunders.

"Oh, so you *are* under there. That colour is excellent on you, I must say." Enid smirked and lifted the lid on a plastic snack pot. She selected an almond, popped it in her mouth and turned back to her laptop. There was a soft 'click' and Mozart's *Requiem* buzzed tinnily from a pair of foam Walkman headphones.

Tess sighed with relief. She could now store the banners safely without further comment. She propped them in a corner and settled at her own desk.

Enid's head swivelled like an owl's. "Let's see them, then."

Tess froze. Slowly, she unzipped the first case and unrolled the banner.

'Ambiton, Respect, Heart,' read the slogan beneath a group of smiling sixth formers who had followed the photographer's brief superbly and looked delighted to be pointing at a Bunsen burner, while showing their teeth.

"Aren't there two 'i's in 'ambition?" queried Enid.

Tess's heart rate slowed. *Not again.* At least this time the typo wasn't plastered across a 48-sheet billboard at Elderfield train station. She forced herself to look and relief flooded her bloodstream like engine coolant. There was a wrinkle in the canvas. 'Ambition, Respect, Heart'. The banner was perfect.

"Yes," she breathed, happily. "There are."

Enid and Tess tapped away next to each other. Tess tried to ignore the dark classical music emanating from Enid's ebony pixie crop. Little love was lost between the two women. Enid resented Tess's naturally coloured hair, nuclear family unit and strong physique. Working at The Wenceslas Academy Trust as 'Media, marketing, PR, Ops and event director' took its toll. From redesigning prospectuses to publicising exam results for the average-achieving group of sixteen primary and secondary schools, there was always too much to do. Not to mention the fact she was going through the menopause. Enid had lived without a partner for the greater part of her life and, after eight years of writing blog posts on behalf of head teachers, she simply couldn't be bothered any more.

"St. Cuthbert's got the Ofsted call this morning," Enid said, "the two-day inspection starts tomorrow."

"What are they expecting the judgement to be?" asked Tess, politely. "By the way, the Staff Awards proposal is done."

"Requires Improvement," said Enid.

Tess's lip wobbled. She'd tried hard with the proposal. Then realisation dawned: Enid meant St. Cuthbert's.

Enid swept the snack pot into a drawer and banged it shut. She sprinkled her throat with the last drops of rooibos tea and lifted the headphones a fraction. "I'm off to speak to the Director of SEND about 'well done' cards," she said, importantly. "Write the draft Ofsted press release by lunch, please." The door slammed and Tess breathed again.

Seconds later, Enid returned. "Forgot my phone," she said, stretching over Tess's desk. Her sleeve brushed a pen to the floor. Huffing, she reached down to retrieve it. In Tess's open handbag, she spied a small, blue business card upon which glittered the words, 'Oscar's' and 'Director of External Relations'.

Tess saw Enid look up from the floor. She was vaguely aware that there seemed to be more malice in her eyes than usual, but she was lost in a world of Ofsted acronyms. She steered her eyes back to the screen. After a quick, cold smile, Enid left the office.

Tess noticed her bag was open and zipped it shut. She decided to make coffee. For some reason, there was fear in her heart. Again.

Rowley was lying in a state of bewilderment in the corner of the kitchen. Around him, the family screeched with excitement. Dan peered at a letter on the table. He read aloud: *"If you're unable to attend this play date, please contact us as soon as possible. If your passes have already been dispatched, for security reasons you will then need to return these to the address above."*

Mollie stuttered, "I can't believe it, I can't believe it." Jack, wrapped in Rowley's blanket, squirmed on the kitchen floor in ecstasy.

Tess, wearing penguin pyjamas with two missing buttons,

bit her fist and paced the lino. Dan handed Tess the letter, saying, "Never in a million years would I have dreamt this would happen. Never. My mum will have a fit when I tell her."

Tess cleared a pile of folded laundry from a stool and sat down. She'd arrived home, disconsolate after a day on the battlefield with Enid, to an envelope thicker and creamier than fresh milk. She'd opened it and had to sit down on the doorstep. The contents were harder to digest than a lottery win.

She read the letter for the seventh time.

Adelaide Cottage

Windsor

Berkshire

SL4 2JQ

Dear Mollie

I wanted to express my thanks, following your amazing efforts with my son, George, earlier this month at his school.

George, Charlotte, Louis, William and I are all inspired by kind people like you, who are confident and generous enough to make friends with anyone.

I know your efforts have been hugely appreciated by George and we are all so proud of what you have achieved.

I hope you will be able to join us in our Windsor home for a play date with George on 20 May, at 4pm.

We would also be delighted if Mollie's younger brother could come. Charlotte's Russian lesson has been cancelled and she is at a loose end.

Please bring swimming costumes.

Yours,

Catherine (Princess)

PS your security passes have been dispatched. Please follow

the instructions to the letter (no pun intended ;)).

The winky smiley face was a shame, Tess thought.

Rowley wondered what on earth the fuss was all about. He heard the words, 'play date' and shuddered: those never ended well. He crawled under the kitchen table. After a short sleep, he barked to be let out and ran around the block to clear his head. He stopped in front of a house four doors down and stared into the window, then chased his own tail for three revolutions. Kayoss, an Icelandic Sheepdog with a rust-coloured coat and a cheeky smile wuffed appreciation for Rowley's athleticism through the glass. This cheered him up. He sprinted down the road after a squirrel, ate a small, dried fragment of bird excrement and felt much better.

10

CHAPTER NINE

Saturday 20 May 2023, Windsor, Berkshire.

It was Kate's first time using the new oven. A KitchenAid was one thing; a Professional Series range cooker was another. She much preferred Anmer Hall's Aga. Something was missing but she couldn't put her finger on it. She fiddled with some knobs. Tabitha yawned and stretched from her privileged position on the sofa, pink pads wobbling in the sunshine.

Kate remembered what was wrong at precisely the same time as Louis came out of the pantry licking his fingers, closely followed by a cloud of flour dust. She'd forgotten to make any scones.

Louis shouted, "When are they gettin' 'ere?"

Kate yanked him into the middle of the kitchen and said: "Louis, when they *do* arrive, please speak properly."

Louis said, "Yes, Mar-mee. When are they *arrivin'*?"

George and Charlotte came into the room, carrying iPads. George was crying. Charlotte hissed, "I told you not to use 'Prince' in your Roblox username."

"What's the matter?" asked Kate.

"Someone messaged me to say they thought Prince George is a cissy," sniffed George.

George did seem to be a tiny bit more *sensitive* than usual just at the moment, thought Kate. She felt the usual maternal guilt tugging at her heart. She drew her son to her chest: poor George.

Charlotte switched her iPad off and began to practise ballet positions. She said, "Aren't they terribly late?"

Kate glanced at her Rolex. "Two minutes. But they have to get through security."

"Can we go and greet them at the Rule Britannia gates?" asked George.

Kate nodded and watched them sprint away, Louis lolloping down the drive like a happy puppy. She turned to the oven and cursed it silently, then summoned Anastasia, her Lady-in-Waiting.

"Can Fortnum deliver within the hour?" she asked. She supposed it wouldn't do to receive guests without providing afternoon tea. This would be the perfect opportunity to use some of the two-fridges-worth of her father-in-law's strawberry jam. She didn't have the energy to worry about it not being home-made. Anastasia smiled. She had seen this coming and ordered a cream tea special. Thank heavens for online shopping.

The Oates children shouted to Tess: "Prince Louis is coming to meet us!"

Tess, who was gaping at the manicured lawns, rose buds that looked Photoshopped onto lush, jade stems and the fresh-as-a-daisy paintwork on the intricate and gleaming gates, looked up. Hurtling towards them, with his eyes closed, was the fourth-in-line to the throne of the United Kingdom.

Tess yelled, "watch out!" but it was too late. Louis stumbled on a gold swan statuette, flew through the air and landed hard on his kneecaps on the shingle.

Tess ran in what felt like slow motion towards the slumped heap. Behind Louis, George and Charlotte locked eyes with Mollie and Jack and grimaced. Charlotte shouted grumpily, "he's always doing that."

"Does it hurt?" asked Tess, over Louis's screams.

Jack said: "I think it does."

Tess watched Kate come running out of the house. She was dumbstruck. That hair. Those legs. Even under an apron, she could tell that Kate's thighs would be at home on an Olympic running track. She was like a thoroughbred racehorse, midway through its first race, several lengths ahead of the rest of the field.

"Can you stand, Louis?" Kate asked.

Mollie giggled and said, "The monkey impression was a bit inappropriate but I'm sure we can put up with him, Your Royal Highness."

Kate flashed Mollie a dazzling smile. Someone who loved wordplay too! She relaxed a little.

George tugged shyly at his mother's hand. "Can we go swimming, Mama?"

Jack glanced at Mollie warily. As if reading his mind, Charlotte said, "we set our shark free at the weekend. George insisted for some reason." She smirked. Her forefingers and thumbs formed a heart shape in the middle of her chest, too fleetingly for anyone to notice except Mollie.

Kate nodded and messaged Nanny to accompany them. Tess watched her children run away with George and Charlotte and felt light-headed. Was this real? She looked at Louis, whose nose was bubbling like a fountain, snot mixing with royal blood as he wiped his hand across his knee. His sun hat lay upside-down, the name label proudly displaying, 'Louis Wales'. They were the same mail order stickers she used for Mollie and Jack. Thank heavens for online shopping. Tess vaguely remembered a history lesson about Louis Mountbatten, who was responsible for a great deal of kerfuffle over the royal family's surname. Mountbatten-Windsor was settled on by the late Queen, for those who did not 'enjoy' the title of Royal Highness. What a pain to have to think about what you were called and when.

Kate remained stooped over her youngest child. She hesitated. Should she ask Louis a question in front of a complete stranger, and risk a typically LouLou answer? She came to her senses. She was, after all, famous across the world for her skills with young children. And his mother. This was no time to dither. She took Louis's hands in her porcelain fingers and said: "What on earth were you doing, my darling?"

"I wanted to see if I could run with my eyes closed."

"And what did you conclude?"

Louis's chin dropped.

Kate muttered placatory remarks and absently hummed a line from *Golden Slumbers*. Tess bit the inside of her cheeks and went inside with Kate and Louis. To be helpful, she told them of the time Jack cracked his first adult tooth in half on the gum line by mistake, using suction from a Calpol stick.

"We were waiting for seven hours in A&E and left at three in the morning, after being told there were five more people in front of us than there were when we arrived."

Kate played for time. "Really. What hospital was that?" Her

mind raced – the situation sounded diabolical and surely could not be true. Why, in the Lindo Wing when she had given birth to all three of her children, there were five people to every new mother. And that was just the chefs. Her head ached. Should she say anything further? Being political was not allowed - being political was not allowed. But this was appalling.

Tess, who had thought Kate had said, 'rarely', bristled and said: "It's quite common. The NHS is on its knees. It's killing us."

Louis groaned. His knees were killing him.

Nanny swept in, pulled Louis to her bosom and swept out again. Louis's wails trailed away down the hall like the ghost of Christmas past. Kate and Tess were alone. Tess glanced around the room, her throat drying rapidly. Her fingers itched with awkwardness. She knocked a maple cutting board sharply with her knuckles for something to do.

"Nice and solid. Although I prefer rubber."

"Me too," said Kate, with feeling, "but I like a good, thick chopper."

The two women's eyes met for a split second; long enough for them to know they would not be bored with each other.

Kate said: "I've heard a lot about you from George."

Tess refrained from saying she had heard a lot about Kate from copies of *Hello*. "I didn't get the Oscar's film job by the way," she said. "Mollie and George ran away and I think that sealed the deal - or rather, unstuck the envelope - for me."

What AM I talking about? She thought,

Kate's eyebrows rose like the softest of soufflés. She had been trained to show an interest, however perplexing, in subjects. "I'm afraid it's been a while since I opened my own correspondence. Is it *very* difficult?"

"Could we start again?" asked Tess. "I'm feeling rather nervous."

Kate smiled and led Tess through the kitchen-diner, along a herringbone floored hallway lined with works by modern artists Tess knew she should recognise, and into the smallest of her sitting rooms. Overstuffed cushions stood to attention like Grenadier Guards under the watchful glow of an army of table lamps. Polished wood shone reassuringly from doors and bureaus. Outside the window, a fountain trickled melodically somewhere just out of sight and the golden light warmed a lawn filled with footballs, Nerf guns and skateboards.

"My father-in-law says all you really need is an excellent view and an even better bottle." Kate leant down and extracted two Waterford wine glasses and a bottle of Chateau-Neuf-du-Pape from under the sofa. The afternoon tea faded like a distant memory. Anastasia could have it for herself. She pressed a button on a side table and a blind moved smoothly down in front of the window. It was painted on the inside with a repeat pattern of six-inch portraits of Kate.

"What do you think?" she said bashfully. She felt a territorial love for the picture, having been eight months pregnant with George at the time. (She hadn't had to take any hair supplements back then. And those diamond earrings really *were* the bomb). But, she wondered, would Tess appreciate the design?

Tess took in the hundreds of swollen tummies of the future Queen, marching geometrically across the wall in front of her. Swathed in emerald silk, they reminded her of rolling, lush countryside. She pictured the design in her bedroom at home. It would complement the damp patches on the ceiling beautifully.

"D'you know, I think it would make good wallpaper." She accepted a full glass and settled back, feeling her cheeks flush as ruby as the wine.

Kate dropped her stemware on the ivory carpet. Before Tess could react, Anastasia appeared with salt and a bottle of Vanish. When the clean-up was completed, Kate gazed at Tess in surprised rapture.

"It's already in print," she said in a low whisper. "I'm considering selling it on Etsy."

Tess's glass fell to the floor. This time, Anastasia made a faint clicking sound with her tongue as she scrubbed.

"It's called, 'Safety-in-numbers,'" Kate said. "With hyphens." She sniffed. "It's the last time I knew for sure that George was truly protected."

Tess nodded. She understood. The women drank the rest of the bottle and shared pregnancy stories. Shouts and splashes, studded with Nanny's thunderous growls and Tabitha's yelps floated over the wall outside as the children bonded in the swimming pool.

Charlotte performed a triple somersault dive from the 10m board, hauled herself onto an inflatable flamingo and paddled it towards Jack. "What stage of swimming are you in?" she demanded.

"Four."

"I'm in stage seven," she said proudly. "The swim cap's silver. So it helps with imagining my future."

Louis appeared, wearing patterned elephant trunks. His knee was bandaged. He raised his hands to the air and roared: "I just passed stage three!" Nanny's hand guided him down the step into ten centimetres of water, where he sluiced his shoulders with tepid chlorine and shivered with delight.

Jack was impressed, both with Louis and Charlotte. He turned to the young Princess. "Can you do butterfly stroke?" Charlotte nodded solemnly. "I'm practically the best in the whole of Oscar's. Race?"

Jack slipped carefully off his crocodile ride-on with a squeak. The turquoise water closed over his head. He looked up through his goggles at the cling-filmy sky and panicked for a moment, before remembering he was in the shallow end. He stood up, lost a two-length freestyle contest to Charlotte, and then accepted a challenge to a handstand competition.

Mollie trod water with George in the deep end. She told him he was lucky to have his own swimming pool and that she was glad he'd freed the Lantern shark.

"I miss him, though," George admitted. "He was good to talk to." His fingers skimmed lightly across the surface of the water, trailing small bubbles.

"Do you like living in Windsor?"

"Of course," said George, quickly. "But we don't invite people here very often."

Mollie chattered about the birthday parties George could hold. "You've enough space for a bike track. You could even have a bouncy castle."

George looked at her blankly. "Why would I want to do that when I've got real ones?"

They clung to the edge of the pool chatting for a while before clambering out for a tour of the garden. The Nerf guns, footballs and skateboards had been cleared away by invisible hands. They shivered under towels as fluffy as candyfloss, jumping up and down on the grass to warm up.

"Where do you think our mums are?"

"Drinking wine," said George, confidently.

Together, they crept around the corner of the vast stone wall. Twenty feet away, a rectangle of light shone like an amber mirror. The children settled themselves in the flowerbed underneath the windowsill and listened.

"... to be frank, George is a bit of a loner," Kate was saying.

"He's got a lot on his shoulders," Tess said kindly.

"We've had a talk. William and I discussed it and we thought his teen years should be a time for him to explore his own interests, rather than be confused about expectations. And so we've decided not to tell him about his destiny until he's at least twenty."

There was a long pause. Mollie looked at George with anguish. "Don't tell me *I was the first person* to tell you you're going to be king?" she hissed.

George put his fingers to his lips. "Wait."

A dignified snuffle emanated from behind the open window. Kate's voice tinkled, "only joking! He knows all about it. It's a cross to bear, that's for sure, but I have every faith in our little PG Tips."

Mollie hit George on the arm. She studied his hair, eyes, neck, chest and legs. "You look normal," she said, "and your Mum obviously thinks you can cope with the crown."

George said he did his best, but the last time he had tried to give a presentation at school, the teacher had told him to wear a VR headset and forget the crowds. Mollie laughed: "Did it make it easier?"

George shrugged. "Not really."

"What were you looking at?"

"The fall of Pompeii."

"We're doing that at school!"

"So are we!"

They grinned at each other.

"I think it's horrible we don't recognise those who died," said Mollie, with feeling. Too many animals had perished. It wasn't so much the people she felt for, but those poor donkeys, dogs and cockerels.

"Pretty cool the way their brains turned to glass," said George. He told Mollie his teacher had shown them a glossy sample of brain matter from a skull inside a boat house. "Imagine your skull exploding and your brain crystallising, all in fifteen minutes. How cool."

"That's what happens to me in times tables tests."

"Oh, I can help you with those," George said breezily.

They gurned at each other shyly, then hurried indoors to the spa. George showed Mollie how to turn the Jacuzzi on and they sat companionably for a while, before putting their clothes back on and joining the others for kale and cauliflower macaroni cheese.

CHAPTER TEN

Saturday 20 May 2023, Windsor, Berkshire.

King Charles was in bed at Windsor Castle, dreaming that the plants in the Duchy Nursery had changed into toddlers. Everywhere, small children climbed pergolas or knocked over fruit tree saplings. A tiny, ginger-haired child plucked a sunflower seed and stuffed it up her nose. Charles snorted and turned over. It was too late now: the Duchy was firmly in William's hands.

"I say," said Camilla, elbowing him roughly as she blew wetly on freshly painted fingernails. "It's nearly four o'clock. Aren't you meant to be doing the rounds with William?"

'Doing one's rounds' was an affectionate term for knighting practice, inspired by the 'Knights of the Round Table'. Prince Phillip had made it up after a footman had a quiet word with him about saying he was off to, 'practise touching people on the shoulder with one's sword.'

Charles opened one eye and looked at his love. Beautiful nails. She was wearing that colour he adored: Pearly Queen. Afternoon naps were the best. He rolled out of bed and switched on the Teasmade. Despite the staff, he favoured old school discomfort.

William let himself in through the back door and shouted greetings. They met outside and made their way, as was tradition, to the centre of the largest maze, where Parth waited with props.

William ran his plastic sword along the top of the hedges. Box leaves skittered overhead like locusts. "Who's on the list today?" he asked.

Charles stroked his chin. "Let's have... Piers Morgan... and that redhead from the state banquet last week."

Parth looked away and coughed.

"Only joking. We'll stick with the usual."

William cleared his throat. Charles became serious and dropped his head. Parth took his cue and mumbled, "... to receive the order of Knighthood, Sir Ed Sheeran."

William nodded his chin minutely and took six small steps forward, quivering with excitement. He beamed at his father and tapped him lightly once on each shoulder. He accepted a hardback book from Parth, roughly the size of a medal box.

"... and a little something to go with it. It's a brooch."

Parth coughed the words, "Grand Cross," into his hand.

"Sorry," said William. A little something to go with it: the Order of the British Empire: The Grand Cross."

Charles smiled widely. "Thank you so much, Your Majesty."

Now came the tricky part. William knew small talk was vital. The obvious option was to admire the number of records produced but that wouldn't move the monarchy forwards, for goodness sake. He understood his public. They wanted insight. He looked Charles in the eye and said: "so Harry, whose body were you thinking about when you wrote 'Shape of You?'"

Parth's coughing got worse. He stepped backwards into the hedge. In his experience, it was better to remain in the shade.

Charles studied his son. "Brave move."

"Thanks, Pops."

"Sadly, I don't think it quite hits the nail for the situation but there's still time."

William shrugged. "I'll get there."

"You will."

William smiled proudly. He was born to do this.

They ran through some old favourites: Barbara Windsor (familiar surnames could throw one), Bill Gates, Michael Caine and Julie Andrews. With each touch of the sword, William's confidence flourished. When it was time for Charles to become Liz Taylor, Parth asked to be excused to check on the Briti-shot Awards arrangements.

William gladly obliged: he wanted to be alone with his father. George was playing on his mind and taking up valuable thinking time. Advice was needed.

Charles took a wrong turn out of the centre of the maze, cupped his hands around his mouth and yelled, "any gardeners out there? We could do with a hand."

"But I know the way," protested William.

"A father does his best to guide his child through life's crunchers," said Charles, steering them towards another dead end.

"Which brings me to my next question," said William - rather cleverly, he thought. "Georgie is having a crisis of confidence."

"The talking thing again?"

William nodded, stabbing the ground with his sword.

Charles walked briskly around three corners before reaching

his point of origin and saying, "We ought to get him up at your Awards night. Just the thing: cold turkey, take the plunge. Have you got someone for the warm-up session?"

"No," admitted William. "I'd rather thought you might say a few words, given that you're the King."

"Pfft," Charles said. "Nope."

William tried not to feel deflated. "Ah. Um. No. I suppose you can't campaign any longer, of course... What would George say about local environmental initiatives?"

Charles shrugged. He remembered Nanny giving Anne and him a small allotment at Balmoral for rhubarb and beans. He loved rhubarb. Tart but sweet, rather like that redhead...

"Dad??"

"Something about his little vegetable patch in Norfolk?"

"He doesn't grow food at Anmer, he moves animal feed around and looks after the guinea fowl."

Charles looked pleased. "A little speech about chicks. I'll look forward to it."

Parth, who had hurried back to deliver news of the Oates' arrival, winced.

William considered when to break the news to the family about George's new role. Not today, he decided. This play date seemed to mean quite a lot to Georgie; why spoil it? There would be plenty of time - well, four days - for George to get used to the idea, the speech writers to do their magic and to help him rehearse. And even if George wasn't delighted, how hard could it be? William had already decided to bring Charlotte to the event, so there would be plenty of support. It was bound to be a success... *bound* to. He felt a familiar icy tickle down his back. If only they could decide on a winner. There had been a tie the last time the judges voted. The trouble was the calibre of the finalists was so goddamn high. A nice problem to have, William reminded himself.

The men reached safety and parted ways. William headed towards his Land Rover and pulled out his phone. He found the list of finalists on an email and read them again.

Scent to Heaven: organic, lavender-infused body bags.

Spitting Water: alpaca swimming school.

Bio Balls for Bouncers: biodegradable tennis balls for dogs.

The Uniform Unicorn: a nationwide network of second-hand school uniform shops.

Bug Butter: like peanut butter but made from insects[1].

The judging panel, which comprised some of the most eminent environmental experts of the time as well as William himself, had concluded that Scent from Heaven and Bio Balls should share the top spot. The problem was, there could be only one winner and the inventor of Bio Balls - though a clear champion in Williams' mind - was Kate's brother, James. Nepotism was, of course, out of the question. No; the real question was, given Parth's proven wonders of discretion, were Bio Balls to win, could they keep the founder's identity a secret?

He arrived home, still vaguely rattled. The first thing to strike him was the smell. In all his long years of fatherhood, he had not returned home to the aroma that floated through the hallway, enticing him into the kitchen.

"Is that..?" he wondered.

It wasn't.

Given the sweet, sharp tang of citrus in the air, William had

---

[1]   Available online only, since Brexit regulations made it illegal to sell in shops.

hoped to find one of his late grandmother's favourite puddings, lemon posset, bubbling away. Instead he was confronted with two extra children than he was used to, and what must be thirty spent lemons, with jugs of weak citric acid lined up along the table.

"Pops, look at this!"

Charlotte, her tongue peeping sideways, dipped a paintbrush into a jug and carefully traced a heart on a piece of white paper. She held it up with pride.

William squinted, wondering if his eyesight had deteriorated further. There was nothing there.

"Now, watch this!"

She hopped off the kitchen bench and thrust the paper into the new oven. Kate, who was nowhere to be seen, did not leap forward to prevent a first-degree burn. Which meant it was up to William to intervene.

"Where's Nanny?" he demanded. "And Mummy?"

Mollie looked up from her invisible painting. "She's dead."

William dropped his phone.

"I mean, *your* Mummy's dead," said Mollie. "I'm so sorry, by the way."

"Thank you."

Louis, who was colouring his hair with lemon juice, whispered, "We love you, Granny Diana."

"Was the car going *very* fast?" asked Jack.

This must be like teaching in one of those city state schools, thought William, feeling ten eyes boring into him. Where on earth was Kate?

"Look, Pops." Charlotte snatched something from the oven, stood under William's nose and held up her sheet of paper. In the middle of the page was a light brown heart. "Invisible ink!"

"Babe? Is that you?" Kate, followed by a dumpy woman William took to be Tess, entered the kitchen. They swayed towards the nearest kitchen island, as if recently disembarked from a vessel. Anastasia rushed forward with a tray of crystal water tumblers.

"Mama!" yelled Louis, lowering a jug of neat lemon juice from his lips.

"LouLou," Kate said fondly. "Are you having fun?"

"*You* clearly are," said William, tightly.

Kate introduced Tess, who attempted a small curtsy but tripped over Tabitha, sprawling languidly across the floor. Anastasia offered Tess a small leather sofa and a cashmere blanket. Tess curled up and closed her eyes gratefully, praying she wouldn't be sick.

William muttered, "may I have a word?"

Since he rarely used 'that look', Kate delivered a charming apology and left the children and Tess with Anastasia, giving instructions to break out the Fortnum cream tea for pudding.

William and Kate reached the bottom of the main staircase and sat down. Kate wrapped an arm casually around a bannister as a precautionary measure against a strange dizziness that wouldn't go away. William looked down and fiddled with Kate's engagement ring as he proposed the idea of George warming up for the Briti-shots. Only when Kate failed to utter her usual demure consent did he raise his eyes to look at her.

"I think it's an absolutely superrrb suggestion," she said, gazing at him with shining eyes. "But let's tell Georgie now, while Mollie's here. He thinks the complete world of her."

George was summoned. He turned pale but took the news on the chin. "As you wish," he muttered, and disappeared.

"He's been watching *The Princess Bride* again, hasn't he?"
Kate nodded.

"We'd better get back to the fray." Will's eyes lingered on
Kate's wine-stained lips. "Fancy a game of 'Never Have I Ever'
later?"

Kate twinkled and kissed him gently. She nodded towards
the enormous hallway window, which looked out towards the
Secret Garden. "Your place or mine?"

It was a legitimate question. Outside, beyond the Kitchen
Garden - where carefully tended radishes, onions, raspberries
and potatoes jostled cheerfully for space - rose a pale, stone
wall with a door to which only Kate and William held a key. No
staff had ever seen what lay within. Known only as the Secret
Garden, William and Kate had worked hard to lay the entirely
private area with a patchwork of low-maintenance AstroTurf,
hiding offcuts taken from the children's all-weather pitch in
Isfahan rugs. The space contained two garden offices, each
housing a double bed of a slightly different size. The offices
were named after the beds.

"Let's meet in the Super King," whispered William, "as I
believe the Queen's covered in wallpaper samples. See you
there once we've shown the Oates around?"

Kate giggled. "You keep telling me I can't have another baby
because you've finished sowing your oats around!"

William tickled her in the ribs until they fell off the bottom
step. Parth appeared with Anastasia and they turned their
backs discreetly until they could be sure all clothing was back
intact. Parth suspected it wouldn't be long before they headed
off to the Secret Garden. He could always tell when things were
turning frisky. As long as they didn't expect him to bid the
Oates farewell. They seemed a perfectly nice family but, well,

so *ordinary.*

12

CHAPTER ELEVEN

Sunday 21 May 2023, Elderfield, West Sussex.

Sausages hissed and spat like angry snakes in the sun. Squashed paper cups leaking cherryade rolled gently on the parched grass. Flies idled on the coleslaw. Rowley lay under a bench, biding his time.

Dan, walking into the Bindman's tiny back garden from the kitchen, misjudged the effort required to open a can of beer. His plate wobbled and slipped onto the grass with a dull clatter. A burger escaped its bun and plunged headlong into Rowley's waiting jaws. Patience always pays, thought Rowley. Patience always pays. Unless someone gave a 'stay' command in the High Street and went into a shop. Then it was better to open your mouth and howl.

The Bindmans had opened the barbecue season in Elderfield. Arran had a particularly moist leg of lamb he had picked up from Lidl for a song and was itching to grill. Having successfully cooked the standard meaty offerings, this joint was to be the main event. As Beyonce warbled from the bluetooth speaker, he sprung up and down on his toes in time to the music, waving his tongs to the beat.

"Where are the girls?" asked Dan, stabbing a second burger from the grill.

Arran nodded towards the house. "Putting the world to rights."

Inside the kitchen, Tess and JoJo Bindman pored over phones and indulged in making up humble brags about their children.

"This is Jack after colouring his hair with orange highlighter. It took a week to wash out, his hair's so thick."

"This is Robert with the 'Man of the Match' trophy. So embarrassing; he's not even in the regular team."

"Mollie's exhausted; she's reading until midnight – I just can't get her to put *Great Expectations* down."

They smiled at one another. Tess leant up and wiped a smear of ketchup from JoJo's chin. She loved this, but her mind was back in Windsor, replaying what she could remember of the extraordinary play date, over and over. Keeping it a secret was killing her. JoJo got up to get more crisps. Tess had one of her looks; she needed space, and salt.

JoJo and Tess had not sparked an immediate connection. Their friendship had been a slow burn: six feet tall and in the permanent grip of athleisure wear, JoJo was intimidatingly strong. Not toned strong; *strong* strong. JoJo had been irritatingly insistent with her invitations to her boot camp 'to help wake up the tired bits' and Tess, whose last dalliance with exercise had been a trial pregnancy yoga class before children in which she circled her big toes for thirty seconds and fell asleep, had flatly refused for months – until one day she ran out of excuses.

Strangely, despite her best attempts to hate it, she didn't. There were women who reminded her of Enid there, but who smiled. They helped her imagine her boss might have a human side after all. Tess enjoyed the squats, the lunges and the interval training. She even tolerated burpees. Because JoJo made it fun. Her awesome body belied a nature soft as a tumble-dried kitten. She chose music from 1980s rom-coms and cried her eyes out when *Flashdance* came on. Importantly, she kept up a wicked and witty repertoire throughout her workouts, leaving Tess no time to dwell on the pain of the exercise - or her day in the office.

Mollie and Jack were having an argument on the front path. Jack wanted to know why he wasn't allowed to tell Robert about the trip to Windsor. The word 'idiot' was mentioned. Mollie accused Jack of having a memory like a goldfish.

"We signed an agreement with that man Parth that we wouldn't share details," she growled.

"Wha's that you won't share details abou'?" shouted Pearl Whitehead, as she climbed out of her Citroen 2CV and swung a seal-sized raffia bag over her arm. Her skirts billowed as she walked along the pavement and braids hung down her back like new bicycle chains. Her dress sense was remarked upon daily by the Elderfield Junior staff, student and parent bodies. As Head Teacher, she was often stopped in the street by six-year-olds wanting to feel the gold embroidery along her sleeves. She had ears like the proverbial bat.

"Where's ya mammy?"

"Inside," said Mollie, smiling angelically. "And don't worry about the details, Mrs Whitehead. It's a family secret."

Pearl frowned. "You know we don' like to use tha' word 'secret'. 'Surprise' is fine but 'secrets' can be tricky."

"You're telling me," grinned Mollie.

Robert joined Jack. For Christmas and birthday, he'd been

given a hoverboard. Jack was bitterly envious. It played music, turned into a hover kart and made you four inches taller. He was granted a go, started well, lost his balance and fell hard onto his elbow. Undaunted, he picked himself up and tried again. This time, his knee bore the brunt. Robert took the opportunity to pretend to be an F1 first-aider and bundled Jack up with an armful of kitchen roll.

Pearl went inside and joined Tess and JoJo at the table. The stigma of fraternising with her students' parents had never worried her. In Madagascar, her place of birth, community was all that mattered. Boundaries were made to be blurred, in Pearl's world. Except when it came to looking after children.

She sank into a chair and yawned.

"I wish you'd give yourself time to rest," said Tess. "I bet INSET day was full on - did you put any time aside to just chill? You look like a tranquilised bloodhound."

"Nah, INSET days are for workin' *hard,* darlin'," said Pearl, with feeling. "Year five and six residentials nex' week. I'm men' ta be in Bracklesham Bay wi' sixty chidden, showin' a damn councillor aroun' an' interviewin' parent governors at the same time."

"How are you so interminably optimistic?" asked Tess. "And why is your diary such a mess?"

Pearl shrugged. "We do it for the children."

The ninth of ten children, Pearl had wanted to be a Head Teacher since she sat, as a six-year-old, at the front of the classroom in the tiny bush village of Agnena singing along to the hand washing song and felt a strong urge to encourage better enunciation. The settlement in the forests of South East Madagascar was home to a few hundred people: family units living in one-room wooden shacks, twelve people to a room.

Then, one day, when Pearl was eighteen, she fell in love with a bright, skinny English graduate volunteer called Jacob Whitehead. Theirs was a story of forty-degree heat - inside and out. Language didn't matter. Via the mediums of guitar, moonlight swims, capoeira and factor 50 sun cream massage, Jacob and Pearl stayed up late and rose early. After two months, when Jacob had finished a placement building latrines to feel worthy, Pearl went back with him to the UK and they moved into a damp flat in Portsmouth.

A couple of decades, two PGCEs and thousands spent on air tickets to and from Madagascar to keep up with Pearl's family later, the couple had married and risen through the ranks to become formidable UK Head Teachers - at the same school. Pearl and Jacob referred to themselves openly as 'the black and white Heads' and, amongst many hundreds of primary aged children, Mollie and Jack had benefited from their co-steerage. Whilst Jacob was serious and calm, it was his yin to Pearl's firm but quirky yang that kept Elderfield Primary on the straight and narrow, and in the category of Ofsted Outstanding. Sadly, Jacob's death eighteen months previously of a stroke meant Pearl was still bereft, though the Oates and Bindmans did their best to keep her spirits up.

Dan excused himself and sat next to Pearl.

"When's your AirBnB free next?" he asked, hopefully. "It's all a bit crowded at home."

Pearl looked him straight in the eye. "The website give' ya dates," she said. She liked Dan. She knew he was looking for a rehearsal space for his routine and had her annexe in mind, which she had spent hours painstakingly renovating since Jacob's death, to pimp out on AirBnB. She also knew Dan was not a paying customer and would mess up her towels.

"You can come and practice here if you like," JoJo offered. She used the tiny box room at the back of the Bindmans' three-bed semi for video conference classes. "I've got my barre up but I can easily lower it for you."

"I'll try not to take that as an insult," Dan said. He met JoJo's eye, which - to his surprise - winked. Blushing, he looked away, then followed her up the stairs, trying to avert his gaze from her Lycra-ed bottom. *Great*, he thought. The last thing he needed was a sudden, irrational, lust for his best friend's wife. He studied the carpet pattern, stopping abruptly as the concentric pattern reminded him of undulating buttocks.

Rowley plundered the snack table when no one was looking. He ate a bowlful of tortilla chips, had a long drink of water and was settling down to doze on Pearl's skirts when his ears pricked up at the mention of his name.

"... *nothing* like Rowley," whispered Tess to Pearl. "This one was clean, a manageable size and smelled divine."

"*Whose* dog are you talkin' about?" asked Pearl. She had been half-listening to Tess wax lyrical about a beautiful Cocker whose breed she was considering saving up for, "because Rowley's getting on a bit," and half thinking about the assembly she was delivering on Vikings.

Rowley flinched. He was only ten, for heaven's sake. Hardly a geriatric. He heard Tess clear her throat; her voice became conspiratorial.

"You mustn't breathe *a word* of this to anyone."

"Aw', you know me. Confidentiality is my middle name."

"Well...." Rowley could hear the pride in Tess's voice as she told Pearl about the family's Windsor adventure.

"Man," said Pearl when Tess had finished. "*Maaan*." She whistled slowly. "Was their kitchen *enorme*?"

"An archipelago of kitchen islands and a cooker bigger than our bedroom. There was a boot room JUST for boots, and..."

Jack ran in panting, cheeks like plum tomatoes. "Would you rather have a head instead of your feet or a foot instead of your head?"

Without missing a beat, Tess said, "Head instead of feet."

Jack ran away.

"... and a separate dog's wash room."

Rowley nudged Tess's knee with a sock he had found under a tea towel. She extracted it from his molars with surgical precision, tousling his wiry head. At the same time, her phone pinged with a flash SMS.

URGENT REQUEST FROM HIS ROYAL HIGHNESS. PLEASE CONTACT ME AT MY PRIVATE EMAIL: parthtogreatness@gmail.com OR CALL +44 7890 123456.

Tess dropped the sock. Rowley snatched it and bolted as fast as his arthritis allowed, nearly knocking over Dan, who had made it back downstairs.

"Just have to make a call," said Tess, and disappeared.

Pearl held her breath and waited for the beans to be spilled. She didn't have to wait long. Minutes later, Tess returned from outside the front door. She was trembling.

"It's the Briti-shots. We've been asked to go to Buckingham Palace by William's aide..."

Dan was vaguely disappointed. He'd been to Buckingham Palace on a school trip and it had smelt of old people. Where was the personal invitation to Balmoral? The request to join the Wales's skiing? The family pass to Wimbledon?

"... if Mollie would help George with his speech."

Pearl clapped her hands. Dan cheered up slightly. Mollie was awfully talented and it was a huge compliment for her to have been asked. "She must do a talk in assembly about it next week," said Pearl with relief, imagining a boatload of Vikings slipping off her conscience into the water and rowing away.

Tess sought out Mollie and insisted they take Rowley around the block with Pearl. When they were out of earshot, Tess brought Mollie up to speed.

"I mean," she said, "we'll be staying in one of the finest hotels in London for the night. And you'd probably get your name on the Awards programme."

"Dunno," said Mollie, as she scratched a mosquito bite on her elbow, "do I have to share a room with Jack? And what else do I get out of it? I mean, I like George and all that but shouldn't I be *paid* or something?"

"Could they call an award afta' Elderfield Primary?" asked Pearl.

"Not unless you sponsor it," said Mollie, "which would be weird."

Pearl extracted a biro from the folds of her skirt and did some calculations on her wrist. "The school's only £15k in deficit," she said cheerily. "We could use some of the money raised from last year's fireworks."

"How much was that again?"

"£209," said Pearl.

"I don't think payment or sponsorship is on the cards, but it should be a nice evening out," said Tess, already worrying about the family's wardrobe. Could they downgrade the hotel and use some of the cash for clothes?

As they headed back towards the Bindman's house, from inside the garage came the sound of Jack and Robert banging the empty beer keg, as the two boys practised pit stop changes for their F1 futures.

CHAPTER TWELVE

Thursday 25 May 2023, Kensington Palace, London.

Anastasia travelled to London by train. The green landscape of Windsor and Eton flashed past in a blur as she cracked the back of a new James Paterson and settled into the primary coloured diamonds of her second class seat. Luckily, there was a direct line to Waterloo, where she could - if she was fast - pop into Smiths to grab a KitKat before catching the tube to Queensway. The Royal Family did not approve of this means of travel but it was not altogether forbidden. Cheap-ish (she expensed it back, of course) and with the thrill of knowing she was sharing air with Real People, she loved being privy to the public's paperbacks, picnics and problems and relished the chance of an hour or so of normality. Though sometimes she wondered how her employers would cope with taking public transport regularly.

It would never happen. The Range Rovers, helicopters and RAF Voyagers frequented by Kate and William and paid for by the taxpayer were unlikely to disappear soon, thought Anastasia, despite the odd appearance of the family on commercial flights and William's professed love of rhinos, electric vehicles and environmental awards.

She got off the tube, walked to Kensington Palace, made her way through security, sweeping up a parcel for the Wales's from the lobby – marked safe with a green stamp of approval – and let herself into Apartment 1A. Despite her privileged job, Anastasia was poor. Rents in London forbade her indulging in so much as a trip to a supermarket with more than four letters in its name. Orla ran towards her and leapt up at the package which was tucked under Anastasia's arm. Anastasia surrendered it and Orla ripped at the paper, pinning it with her front paws and devouring the contents.

"Was that from Heston Blumenthal?" asked William suspiciously, appearing suddenly from behind a wall.

Anastasia sighed, searched through the fleshy contents of the present for a message and concluded that it was.

"There goes my meat fruit," William said, sadly. "I asked him to send it – it's one of his most famous signature dishes: looks convincingly like tangerines but really," he whispered, conspiratorially, "it's meat."

Anastasia didn't know how much it would cost to send a piece of fake fruit that was actually meat through the post. She supposed it might depend on whether it was spam or fillet steak. She nodded in a manner she hoped could be described as sympathetic.

Since George and Charlotte had become vegetarian following the Oates' visit, William's gastronomic life in Windsor had nosedived. The usual culinary fireworks he enjoyed had vanished and his taste buds felt dull; as if swathed in an old net curtain. Bacon at breakfast was off the cards. Foie gras? Forget it. And supper? Friday night wagyu beef mince spag bol had been replaced with vegetable lasagne. At least both Kate and he liked sushi.

Kate stood in the panic room and surveyed the CCTV monitors as she often did when she needed time alone. The moving images of William and Anastasia brought her some comfort. William leaned gauchely against a door frame, whilst Anastasia stood with ankles crossed, ripped parcel paper dangling from her fingers. They were behaving exactly as she would expect, although she was cross about Orla's manners. The dog had been tutored in servitude since the day it was born, for heaven's sake; why was she such a disaster? She frowned. Imagine if one got into the habit of ripping open the daily packages from Roksanda et al. It wouldn't do at all. She made a mental note to speak to someone about more training.

When Anastasia had vanished from view, Kate exited the panic room and hurried along the hallway. She bumped into the King, who was pacing the floor with his back to her. How funny he looks, thought Kate, with his sloping shoulders and big nose. Then stopped, as she realised he was measuring the length of the runner with his strides.

"Camilla's just popped out," said Charles. "She's asked me to see if our old rugs would fit in here. Save the taxpayers and all that."

Oh bloody hell, thought Kate, who hadn't known Camilla had popped in. "How kind. But we only had the herringbone laid last year. She seems awfully tired," she added. "I do hope the refurbishments aren't taking too great a toll?"

Charles slowed and faced her.

"It has given her," he said frankly, "a new lease of life. She wouldn't give up this hobby for the world. Now she's finished at Windsor, she's experimenting here. William said you wouldn't mind."

Kate looked beyond Charles and saw her very own sitting room, the furniture draped in dust sheets. Many of the dust sheets were made of pure silk that Kate identified as coming from her own airing cupboard. Nobody appeared to have thought to mention it to her. She felt her blood rise. She hadn't slept well; she had dreamt about Louis being swept out to sea off Holkham beach. She twitched at the recollection. His cashmere jumper had been ruined.

"Have you seen William?"

Charles shook his head. "He was muttering about being hungry a while ago. I think he's gone to see Parth about later. He seems terribly worried about tonight."

And well he might be, thought Kate. With the Briti-shot Awards live, televised final in a matter of hours, William had until lunch time to approve the judges' final choice. She would be glad when the night was over: she had a private appointment for bikini fittings the next day. Mustique was only six weeks away. She could practically taste the pineapple gazpacho.

She took Charles into the kitchen and settled him at the smallest island with a latte. Anastasia was on the phone, talking to Nanny about childcare. Her face moved through sunshine into rain as she listened. "I'm so sorry to hear that. Quite," she nodded. "Keep the fluids up."

Anastasia informed Kate that Nanny had a stomach upset. She would have liked to go into detail, as Nanny had done, but she had been trained too well.

"Which means I shall be happy to accompany you all to Buckingham Palace tonight to chaperone the children," she said, flatly. "Even Louis."

Kate nodded. She was distracted by George, who had crept silently into the kitchen. He sat at the table with his head in his hands. He had tried without success to deliver his speech flawlessly but something always seemed to get stuck in his throat.

"My father and David Attenborough have brought attention to the world's environmental emergencies," George said in a tremulous voice. "My father and I now wish to bring attention to what everyone – even L-l-louis, Charlotte and... and I – can do l-lo-l—locally," he said. Then, "I can't do it."

Kate glanced at the ceiling. "Remember what Pops says. Granny Diana is watching you and knows you can do it."

George sniffed. Where was Granny Diana when his throat constricted and the words felt like lumps of coal? When the sense that the future of the country lay on his chest like a bowling ball? He slid off the floor to join Orla, wrapping his arms around her curly mane and burying his head in her neck.

"Your allergies, George," Kate said vaguely.

George lifted his head. "Can I play Roblox?"

"May I."

"May I?"

Kate acquiesced. Charles nodded approvingly. "Jolly good. I like to see George taking an interest in highway architecture."

William walked into the kitchen holding the programme for The Briti-shot Awards. Orla skipped up with a ball and dropped it at William's feet, but he ignored her. He thrust the programme into Kate's hands. Charles put down his latte and moved to the leather sofa. He patted the seat next to him and Orla curled up with her head on his knee.

"Come on, then. We're all ears," Charles said.

"Ha, Pa," said William, irritably.

Kate invited William to sit down. William took a deep breath and said, "I simply can't be sure if we've made the right choice of winner."

He handed Kate a small piece of folded paper. She opened it, read the words written in William's strangely flat handwriting and raised her eyebrows. She passed it to the King, who squinted and then looked at William sagely.

WINNER: BIO BALLS

We are delighted to announce that the winner of the Briti-shot Awards is James Middleton, with his Bio Balls! James has worked tirelessly with his dogs to ensure that balls of the highest quality can bounce, roll and biodegrade, leaving you and your dog safe in the knowledge that playing with your dogs' balls won't harm the environment.

George looked up from his iPad. "May I see?"

Kate gave the piece of paper back to William who said, "What do you think?"

"I agree 100%. I think it's brilliant," said Kate. "James will be over the moon." She noticed Charles, whose knee was jiggling up and down.

"Do you think it might be seen as just a teeny bit nepotistic?" he asked.

"My feelings exactly," said William, unhappily.

"Which idea won?" said George, but no-one seemed to hear him.

"James won this on merit," said Kate, with feeling. "The judges picked him fair and square. He wasn't even the *under-dog*," she said, carefully, but William's face confirmed it was too early for gags.

"Interesting, this Briti-shot thing," said Camilla, who had returned from Kensington High Street laden with shopping bags.

"The word on the Street is that 'Scent to Heaven' should win. Glorious idea, taking that dreadful dead body aroma away from the get-go. I heard they use lavender from Lordington, too. The very best. Apart from the Duchy, of course. I've a body lotion and bath salts from there. Funnily enough, though they're designed to relax, they never fail to pep me up, don't they Charles? Might I be so bold," she asked, "as to enquire who the front-runner is?"

Kate remained tight-lipped. Why couldn't Camilla speak in plain sentences? Charles diverted his wife with a keen question about waffle throws.

Louis ran in, brandishing a tiny pitchfork. "The chick-chicks are gone," he said, happily.

George turned white. "Do you mean *my* chick-chicks, LouLou?"

Louis stuck his pitchfork into the arm of the leather sofa and nodded. "All gone."

George fled through the back door in the direction of the chicken run. Parth stepped aside to make room and then hung in the doorway like a bat.

"The Oates," your Highnesses" he muttered. "They've arrived at the Dorchester and are awaiting further instruction." He left the room, shutting the door behind him, a little too firmly.

Kate glanced at her hair in the copper cauldron swinging in the backdraft of Parth's exit and wondered if it was big enough to stick her head in. The thought of the handshaking that lay ahead that evening made her feel weak inside. George felt similarly, she was sure. Ever since his first Wimbledon final, he had been wary of offering his hand to anyone, for fear that they would engage him in light banter - which, of course, they always did. Whilst he could converse with the general public, she could feel the agonies George went through each time he met VIPs. She knew that deep down, George would prefer to spend time talking to his animals, rather than make small talk with a menagerie of humans. Her heart tightened. She counted to five.

Kate called Parth back and asked him to take George and Charlotte to The Dorchester to meet the Oates and get changed, with Anastasia in attendance. Anastasia sighed with relief and relaxed her shoulders. At least she wouldn't be in charge of Louis until the ceremony itself.

"We will meet you at Bucks P and I shall then pass Louis into your care, while I practise George's and my appearance with William," said Kate.

Anastasia hid around a pillar, reached into her shoulder bag for a small bottle, took a discreet swig and disappeared.

* * *

George banged on the door and let himself in. His eyes glittered with emotion.

"I found Margy," he said, levelly. "A cat got her in the rose garden." He sniffed. "For a Bantam she put up a great fight, but in the end she just couldn't..." His voice trembled. "Anyway, she's at peace now. The others are in shock. I'm going to find Louis." He looked at Kate for several long seconds, as if seeing her for the first time, then turned and started to walk away. Feathers drifted softly from his socks.

Kate shivered. She sensed something new in George. A change. A new aura.

"Channel that feeling, Georgie," she called after him. Where had she seen it before? Yes! In the late Queen Elizabeth II herself, during the pandemic. During those awful moments in Windsor Castle watching Her Majesty sitting alone, unable to offer comfort as she watched her husband's coffin during the funeral service. Georgie had the same resolute expression: loyal, resigned and stubborn. He'd behaved impeccably at the Queen's funeral. Perhaps it was going to be alright after all.

"William," she said, decisively. "James is a perfectly worthy winner. Now we must get going. I only have three hours to put up my hair."

The car slid out of the gates like a black seal. Louis played in his car seat with a cup-and-ball, the wooden 'plop... plop... plop' a chisel to Kate's brain. She leaned over and confiscated it, smelling something suspicious as she did so.

"Have you defecated, my darling?"

Louis nodded, pleased with his comprehension. Kate sighed. It was rare, now Louis was five, for accidents of this nature to happen, but not unheard of. She rummaged in the glove compartment for wipes, finding only a pair of Gucci sunglasses she thought were lost. William thumped the steering wheel, remembering too late what it would mean on social media, should he be papped. Kate placed a hand on his arm.

"What are you doing? Don't worry, babe - leave it! There are spare pants in Louis' room at Bucks P. Anastasia will take care of it."

"Anastasia hates us."

Kate was shocked.

"That's not true, darling. She made that nice speech at the Christmas meal, remember?"

He did. Anastasia, nicely lubricated, had said: "to their

Graces... and favours!" which had gone down an absolute storm with the household staff, as she'd held up party crackers containing bite size Royal family figurines made of fruit cake. There were six to collect, including Orla. William understood a full set to go in the four-figure region on those crazy American fan sites.

William let it drop. Next to him, Kate started humming; a low, melodious rendition of *Jerusalem.* They drove past Piccadilly and turned down Constitution Hill. Tourists milled like wasps around the Commonwealth Memorial Gates. *We are guardians of a precious flame,* thought Kate, recalling the infamous words spoken to the Commonwealth by Her Majesty Queen Elizabeth II. *Louis is my precious flame. Louis is my precious flame.*

"Why are you singing that, babe?" asked William, thinking back fondly of Westminster Abbey and Kate's wedding lingerie.

Kate was, again, shocked.

"It's Louis' favourite hymn! And Lottie's favourite rage tune!"

William glanced at his youngest in the rear view mirror. Louis' feet slowed their kicking until William's back-rocking stilled.

"He's asleep."

"Just as we get to Bucks P."

"Typical. Jinx!" they said together, smiled deep into each other's eyes.

"Let's do this," said Kate, forcing William's fingers into a high-five.

"Indeed," said William. "And when it's all over, let's sneak off to Super King."

"Deal," said Kate. She flicked her hair, gave Louis a shake

and exited the car to the waiting hordes.

14

CHAPTER THIRTEEN

Thursday 25 May 2023, Buckingham Palace, London.

Tess felt lost in a sea of luxurious pelts. The hotel lobby undulated in a tawny rainbow; expensively dressed women, milling around the check-in bureau like a bob of seals. Were there more furs than foreigners, or more foreigners than furs? Conversations in Japanese, American and Chinese drifted around her, words circulating silkily. The heirloom carpet exhaled small, triangular trodden breaths from pointy-toed shoes. Where were the loos, she wondered. The car journey had been long and cushioned. Her haemorrhoids were protesting.

"You take the children up," said Tess, and dived into the velvet stomach of the Dorchester.

Dan's tummy rumbled. Somebody somewhere knew how to cook steak. He herded the children into the lift; immediately, there were six of them.

"Look, six bogeys," said Jack, producing a fine specimen from his nose and holding it up for inspection.

Molly gagged.

"Stay away from the mirrors; they might crack," she said,

moving as far into the corner as she could. The doors opened. Jack and Mollie bolted like adolescent greyhounds down the corridor. Dan followed, trying to contain his excitement. The key card revealed more mirrors, milky light and a bed like a Christmas cake. The tang of leather was paired deliciously with the unctuous aroma of dark cocoa.

"Chocolate balls!" shouted Jack, grabbing two complimentary truffles from a gilt-edged plate and stuffing them into his mouth.

"Hey," said Mollie. "You're meant to share!"

There was a soft knock at the door. Parth cleared his throat: he wasn't used to being kept waiting by commoners.

"Come in, my man!" said Dan, delighted to have adult company. "Look at this!"

Parth eased through the door with arms full and leaned into the bathroom. Tess followed, and made a beeline for the window to stare out at the view over Park Lane.

"Marble! Bloody marble bloody everywhere!" Dan wrapped himself in a dressing gown, pulled the hood up and growled. His hand made the shape of a claw.

Parth smiled politely and cut to the chase.

"I've brought you some clothes," he said, dumping an enormous pile of plastic-covered garments onto the bed. The duvet rose, bubbled and settled around them like semi-whipped cream.

"It's an hour until your car arrives. There are three outfit choices each. Would you like to order room service? I would be happy to save you the trouble if it would be of help."

Dan stared at Parth. He'd already spotted labels from Yves Saint Laurent and Givenchy. He tried to contain his emotion, but it was too much. Water began to leak from the corners of his eyes, and he wiped his face with the dressing gown cord. Mollie was unmoved.

"What about the clothes we brought to wear?" she demanded. "The ones we brought all the way from Elderfield. And the *plastic* - what sort of message does that send about environmental concerns?" She rummaged in her backpack and produced a magazine. Tess stepped away from the window and focused on Mollie's latest reading matter.

"Did you know that the Natural History Museum - which, by the way," she said, pointedly, "is only a couple of miles away from here, so we could walk - says that plastic has been found 2,000m below the ocean's surface? Why aren't we there for this evening's awards if the focus is so firmly on our planet?" She placed her hands on her hips. She looks like a miniature Stonehenge, thought Tess, proudly.

"I believe these clothes need protection..." Parth began, finding that his tongue needed to work a bit harder than usual to get the words out.

Mollie snorted. Jack stopped lining up the snacks from the minibar and listened. Snorting meant Mollie meant business.

"*Clothes* don't need protection. *Animals* need protection. Earth needs protection!" she exclaimed. "George understands. Where is he, by the way?"

It was a good question, thought Parth. Where were Anastasia and the older children? He checked his phone: no messages.

Dan's eyes gleamed. He shed the dressing gown, took a deep breath and dove onto the bed, ripping open the sample garments. Parth clocked Dan's shaved chest. How did a middle-aged father of two get a six-pack like that? He tapped out a calendar entry into his phone for the following morning: *GYM - go hard.* Jack found the remote control and channel-surfed to a monster truck documentary. He settled down between pillows and applied pressure to the volume button.

Tess appeared in the doorway.

"I've just seen two security guards with Anastasia, George and Charlotte," she said, trying to make herself heard over the crunching of wheels on sand blaring out of the TV. "They're coming up to see us now."

Dan was standing on the bed, pulling on a pair of chocolate brown corduroy shorts. AC/DC thundered from the screen. The crotch was arguably the right height but the waist was nearing his armpits. He selected a burgundy belt for the hell of it.

"Back in the game!" he said, executing a hip-thrust.

"Dad, mind out of the way, they're about to crush those cars," said Jack, taking advantage of the booming soundtrack to disguise a fart into the duvet.

"What the hell are you doing? You can't be serious," cried Mollie.

"I think I look extremely dashing," said Dan, opening the wardrobe door and revolving on the spot to get the best angle.

"What is it about this family and mirrors?" said Mollie. "You might as well go and stand in the lift, Dad. You'll see your buttocks in 6-D."

"What a brilliant idea." Dan practically galloped away down the corridor, closely followed by Mollie and Jack.

Parth and Tess looked at each other and waited. It didn't take long.

"The Waleses are coming!" shouted Dan, as he catapulted into the bathroom. His muffled voice wafted through the door: "Oh Jesus. Why did you let me go out like this?"

Tess turned off Monster Trucks and hastily plumped the scatter cushions. She swept the remains of the chocolate balls under the coffee machine and sprayed a generous shower of sleep mist over Jack's duvet spot.

Anastasia knocked lightly on the door before entering. Charlotte and George hovered next to her, smirking into their sleeves.

"Once you're all changed, we can get moving," said Anastasia, briskly.

Mollie seized a cherry-red jumpsuit, ran to the bathroom and emerged seconds later with it on. George opened his mouth but Mollie got there first. "I look great, I know. C'mon, we need to practise." They disappeared together.

Anastasia left to find a quiet armchair in a corridor nook for thirty minutes. Jack put on a sailor's suit. He and Charlotte crawled under the bed where they used Charlotte's felt-tip pens to illustrate the bib with *Minecraft* blocks.

Tess surveyed the selection of dresses. What would work best on a pear-shaped, chubby-armed, perimenopausal woman, she wondered. She gave herself a little shake and reminded herself that this was a path well-trodden by many females: there was nothing special about her dilemma.

Floaty chiffon felt wrong. There was an elegant navy polka-dot high-necked dress but the waist looked dangerously restrictive. She took a gamble and reached for a sea-green cowl-neck corset top with matching skirt from Alexander McQueen. It hugged her curves. She felt slithery with sophistication. Shyly, she padded into the corridor in bare feet and coughed over Anastasia, who had fallen asleep near a house-keeping trolley.

"An excellent choice," Anastasia nodded sleepily, her hand creeping towards a packet of shortbread biscuits from a handy stack next to her on the trolley. She tore open the cellophane and manoeuvred two in her mouth. "In case I forget to eat later," she said, brushing crumbs off the brocade.

They left the building with the children. Dan was on cloud nine, having opted for a shiny mustard suit with a peony-pink tie. Tess audited their children. Charlotte was lecturing Jack on how being presented with opportunities should never be taken for granted. Jack remained silent throughout. When Charlotte finished speaking, Jack said:

"Did you hear me holding my breath? I've never held my breath that long before. Can you time me next time?"

Mollie cleared her throat and thought about the day Jack would have to fend for himself in front of Malcolm Swift at school without her. Shivering, she hugged her knees and asked the driver to shut the window.

Tess could imagine George's nerves, but his constant glancing at Mollie left her uneasy. He couldn't possibly become reliant on her daughter for support at public events; that way, madness lay. She had SATs next year, for goodness' sake. They drove down the mall. Flags waved, people stood three-deep along the sides of the roads and Tess felt as if she might as well be on the moon for all the grip on reality she had.

The car curled around the Queen Victoria Memorial and pushed on, past the main gates and around the back of Buckingham Palace to the South Gate. It glided through a gap in the iron railings and on through a courtyard, until they pulled to a stop in a nondescript area of tarmac.

"Is this the car park?" asked Jack. "Do we need to buy a sticker?"

They piled out. Mollie produced a lipstick from a pocket within her jumpsuit.

"It's cruelty-free," she said, filling her lips in.

"I wouldn't bet on that," said Tess, swiping the lipstick and rubbing Mollie's mouth with a tissue.

"Ow!"

"Told you. When you get to fourteen I'll consider allowing makeup," said Tess, hoping the shade would go with sea-green, for she had left her makeup bag on the floor of the Dorchester.

Jack's patent leather loafers reflected the towering white stone, like an iceberg. From over the walls came the sound of murmured shouts and cheers.

"All for me," said Dan in a daze to himself.

Mollie ran ahead with George. Inside, the building lowered temperatures and voices. Pale faces with luxuriant ringlets stared down with foreboding from the walls, and gold gleamed everywhere. Tess fumbled in her bag for sanitizer and doused Jack's hands with it.

"The great kings of the past look down on us from those stars, Simba," came a voice.

Tess turned. Louis was standing, eight feet up, on a vacant plinth.

"Get down!" hissed Anastasia. "What would Nanny say?"

Louis gave a roar, jumped off his platform and scampered around a corner.

"Mama and Pops organised for the cast of *The Lion King* to perform for my birthday," explained Charlotte. "Louis knows all the words."

William walked quickly up to Tess and Dan.

"Great to see you," he glanced down at Mollie and shook her by the hand. "We're almost there, though we've a small issue with the finalists," he said, chewing a fingernail. "They're all in the Green Room..."

"Appropriate name," said Mollie, with a nod.

"... except one. We're missing the Uniform Unicorn."

At precisely that moment came the sound of hooves on carpet. A low whinny emanated from a small white pony, which lifted its head and stared mournfully into the distance. Across its forehead protruded a horn, looped in silver tinsel and neon pink streamers. Across its shoulders stretched a school blazer and on its head, a baseball cap with a logo that looked suspiciously like two droopy breasts. A large man with a handlebar moustache slowed the pony to a halt.

"Pleased to be here. I'm Gerry. This is Pony Andrew. Sorry we're late," he said. "It took longer than planned to get dressed."

The pony stepped forward. It nudged William on the shoulder with its nose before burying its head in a large damask curtain and sucking a gold tassel into its mouth.

"This way, please," William windmilled with his arm. "Parth, would you take our guests to the Green... ah, does, um, Andrew need anything special?"

"He's fine," said Gerry, airily. "He went on the M25 and won't need another dump for a few hours."

Parth led them away, making a note in his calendar to let the Master of the Household know about the missing tassel and to put a veterinarian on high alert.

Through the corridors, they moved toward the Palace Gardens. Tess could feel the tension in her thorax. Or was it her larynx? A body part with an 'x' anyway. She looked at the screenshot schedule Anastasia had emailed. Any minute, according to the timings, Kate was due to appear for a rehearsed entrance and exit with George. Tess twisted her wedding ring. The last time she'd seen Kate they'd left each other inebriated;

how did one behave after such an occurrence? She thought how interactions with JoJo would go and gave a quiet chuckle. Imagine the response if she raised their drunken exploits as the first thing she said.

Kate walked like a regal giraffe towards Tess. Her arm was wrapped around William's waist. Heels like drawing pencils peeped out from beneath pale pink sequins. Bulgari jewellery dripped from her ears and wrists and a silver rope, clustered with pearls of decreasing size, tumbled into her décolletage. She said:

"Goodness, my head felt like the inside of a skip the morning after the last time I saw you!"

Tess felt instantaneously both seen and invisible.

"I love your necklace," she mumbled.

"It's Zara," said Kate, happily. "My high street piece - and the dress is recycled."

"She's worn it *twice* before," said William, proudly.

He led them into a room to the left of the enormous doors that led to the gardens. Assistants hovered with clipboards. Tess was offered cold drinks, hot drinks, sashimi and salami. George was whisked away to makeup. Tess took Mollie aside.

"Do you think he'll be ok?"

"We've practised a lot, Mum," Mollie looked at Tess steadily. "As long as he remembers the work we've done, he should hold it together."

"What sort of work might that be?"

"The usual," Mollie breezed. "I've tried to build his self-esteem through talk therapy and being interested in what he is interested in."

"Which is..?"

Mollie bent her hands into a bridge. Lines on her forehead

emerged, like a brass rubbing.

"Well, if you really want to know, he's quite interested in me," she said, blushing. "But that's just because he hasn't met anyone normal properly before and I'm no threat. He likes talking about our life, you know? Like taking Rowley to the vet and picking up his poo. He's never done either. F'rinstance, he's never had Shreddies. Or gone to McDonald's. He has to have poached eggs or kedgeree for breakfast. I just feel quite sorry for him."

"That's incredibly insightful of you," said Tess. "I'm sure George is very grateful for your help."

"I think so," Mollie looked pleased. "He offered me his maths tutor for a few sessions but she's helping out the Chancellor of the Exchequer this week."

George returned, swirls of bronzer barely disguising the pallor of his gills. Kate addressed the assembled Oates: "Those involved in the opening speeches, follow me."

The walk from the rehearsal room, through a gallery to the top of the Garden Steps made Tess gawp. More portraits, as well as innumerable priceless sculptures and artefacts, lined the entire room. There was barely a centimetre of wall to be seen. At the end, through floor-to-ceiling linen curtains, she glimpsed multi-coloured bodies, writhing like a pond of Koi carp.

"How many people are in the audience?" Tess found herself asking Kate.

"The same number that attends one of our intimate Garden Parties," said Kate. "Ten thousand or so."

As they came to a stop outside the French windows, Parth swooped in.

"Your Highness," he said, smiling thinly. "Your cue is the

words, 'unprecedented temperatures' in the David Attenborough montage. When you hear them, take your place behind the curtain with Her Royal Highness and George. It will lift as soon as the clip finishes."

William reached for George's hand. George shot Mollie a look that said, *help.*

Mollie clenched two fists and stuck out her chin. She mouthed, *you've got this.*

David Attenborough's booming voice intoned a final warning about what heat waves would do to the local British ecology, before rising to an optimistic conclusion.

"... plant bee-friendly flowers, such as lavender or sage. Consider digging a pond to provide damp, shady areas for frogs..."

"Let's dig a pond for Louis!" whispered Charlotte loudly, as she ran past Tess and Mollie, closely followed by Jack. "Come on, I know where the Head Gardener keeps the key to the main shed!"

"... so remember, whilst we may be seeing more and more of these unprecedented temperatures in this country, fortunately, you can help British wildlife with just a few simple actions."

As William, Kate and George stepped out onto the top of the steps, the crowd turned as one. A voice piped, "George, we love you!"

Tess and Mollie peered out through the glass. The lawn was fronted by television cameras and surrounding the bottom step was a tangle of cables and wires. Pull-up banners framed the stage, showing spherical Union Jacks being fired out of cannons. *Briti-SHOT!* read the slogans. Not a particularly eco-friendly visual representation, thought Tess. Still, at least there were no ballistic missiles. Mollie rubbed the side of her nose and scowled.

"They shouldn't make such a mess with the, er... equipment, George will find it distracting," she said.

"If he stares straight ahead, he should be ok," said Tess. As George turned with a worried look, she gave a thumbs-up, remembering her own jumpy breath as she had taken to the stage as a child, playing Oliver in *Oliver!*

At junior school, Tess had been cast in the lead role of the school play, based not on her acting talent but her diminutive size as a ten-year-old and ability to speak in a Cockney accent. Taking the part seriously, she had lapsed into Cockney during lessons, unnerving the teachers and, she was sure, contributing to lower coursework grades than she might otherwise have achieved. It wasn't her fault that, during her English oral exam - devising a television chat show interview between Macbeth and Lady Macbeth - she had slipped into rhyming slang part-way through.

"Come you fine and dandies, that tend on mor'al forts. Unsex me 'ere an' fill me from the crown to the ol' Marilyn Monroes."

The examiner, thinking Tess the most insolent child to cross his path in at least a term, had scribbled a firm 'D' in the margin of his notes. Tess had crumpled. She liked English but, since Mrs Pounds, her obese teacher, had actually wrung her hands in despair after 'oral-gate', she had felt a crushing sense of imposter syndrome on stage, or as a script-writer. Hence her pride in Mollie, who - as she watched George's performance - clearly had what it took when it came to a way with words.

Kate finished her thanks to the British public and her husband, and introduced George.

George stepped forward and said, "Thank you, Mama."

The crowd roared.

George cleared his throat. "My father and David Attenborough have brought attention to the world's environmental emergencies. My father and I now wish to shine a spotlight on what everyone, even children like me..." he glanced over his shoulder at Mollie.

"... even children like me can do, locally."

George paused. He stood on his toes and seemed to inflate by a couple of inches, blossoming like a sunflower before continuing with a flow of words that sounded like music. Cadences rang out like a sandpiper and not a stutter was uttered. Kate realised she was holding her breath. Beside her, Tess took her hand. Kate felt Princess Diana's ring press into her fingers. *Thank you*, she thought. *Your grandson is a credit to us both.*

When it was over, William took to the stage and gave George's hair a ruffle. He was beaming like a cod. He hadn't felt so elated since Kate had finally agreed to his vasectomy.

"As many of you will know, the finalists for the inaugural Briti-shot Awards gave us a tough few days of frantic tossing..."

Kate sniggered.

"Last night was a mutually enjoyable experience," she murmured to Tess.

"... but it is my great pleasure to now announce the winner."

William tore open a recycled envelope. Tess watched his Adam's apple bobbing like a cork.

"The winner of the Briti-shot Awards is... Bio Balls!"

From the giant speakers either side of the steps blasted the familiar Wimbledon theme tune. The crowd clutched their ears and handbags and watched, agog as four athletic Labradors, wearing printed Union Jack collars, bounded onto the top step, their jaws clamped around seaweed-green tennis balls. They sat in perfect unison for a few seconds, then dropped the balls, which rolled into the crowd. Simultaneously, two life size Briti-shot cannons - which Tess had taken for props - fired a barrage of identical green balls into high arcs. The Labradors leapt forwards, like high-divers, catching the balls in their mouths before landing gracefully in the middle of the mob. Four helpers scuttled towards the bottom step and placed water bowls in a row at strategic intervals and, at a command from a whistle pitched too high for the human ear, each dog took turns to canter to his bowl, deposit their balls and lie down on the bottom step, tail wagging.

The screens projected a close-up of the bowls. Fizzing like giant Alka Seltzer, the balls gradually shed layers of kelp. They became the size of tangerines. Then marbles. Then peas. Then the last morsel of organic matter vanished, leaving nothing in the bowls but vivid green soup.

"Let's welcome the founder of Bio Balls to the stage!" shouted William.

A tall man with a friendly expression bounded forward from the side of the stage. His beard quivered like a squirrel's tail and his eyes crinkled as he fronted the lectern. The crowd took a sharp intake of breath, then looked at each other in confusion.

"It's James Middleton," someone whispered. "Kate's brother."

"Wasn't Parth going to disguise him?" hissed William.

"He's too much of a free spirit," said Kate. "Parth tried to convince James to send a dog up in his place, with voiceover audio, but in the end, James thought it better to face the crowd himself. I've checked the small print with the lawyers: there's nothing actually in there that says family members can't win. Don't worry, it'll be fine."

"I am honoured to accept this award," said James. "Never in my life did I think my love of dogs would result in such a prestigious and humbling result. Dogs are the most commonly owned pet in UK households and for good reason. Yet dogs who love balls have a litter problem. We spend £7.5bn per year in this country on dog balls and treats. Many of those balls lie forgotten in fields, streams, ditches and parks, ruining our landscapes and the joy of men's and women's best friends."

He paused to check if the audience appreciated his nod to equality and if the general public was with him. Twenty thousand eyes confirmed it was.

"I have devoted the last few years to making the lives of our canine companions as enjoyable as possible, whilst caring for our increasingly fragile planet. Bio Balls are just the start of a beautiful relationship between dogs, humans ... and nature."

The crowd erupted. The Labradors performed a synchronised 'downward dog'. Kate joined William and George on stage and bear-hugged James.

Tess hurried into the depths of the Green Room, noticing Kate's wallpaper design for the first time. The pattern was mesmerising. Alpacas, dogs and unicorns romped across the walls in blazers and ties, playing 'catch' with tennis balls. Scattered at regular intervals within the pattern, a recumbent alpaca lay wrapped in a body bag with its eyes closed. Elsewhere a group of two unicorns ate toast with a light brown spread, while swatting at a fly with Union Jack flags. Tess gripped the arm of a Louis XVI chair and sat down.

97

Dan was nowhere to be seen. Hands shaking, Tess stabbed her phone and waited for him to answer.

"Did you see who won? I can't believe the nepotism at play!" she hissed.

Dan, who had been watching the ceremony on his phone said,

"I wouldn't worry about it." His voice sounded suspiciously far away. "He won the crowd over, and the Waleses can do no wrong in the eyes of the nation; James has saved a multitude of tennis balls from certain death. UK pet toy domination will be a walk in the park. With a dog," he added. "That's actually really good. Do you think I should use that at The Swan?"

"I hope you're right. There will be some people who are cross about it, I'm sure. Where *are* you?"

Dan weighed up telling the truth. The pro was that Tess might be able to help. The con was that he was quite fond of his own balls.

"I'm fine."

"That doesn't answer my question."

Dan glanced upwards through yellow-filtered light at a solid silver gardening fork and trowel, suspended from a hook in the ceiling. Dust motes danced in the updraft; the air was pleasantly warm and the scent of peat and petrichor permeated the gloom. To his right towered pyramids of porcelain potting trays. Seed packets, protected from damp by neoprene covers, lined the walls. Dan reached his hand out to squeeze a large polythene bag. *Duchy Dutch Mulch* read large red letters across a white background. Too many 'chs' thought Dan. *Tch.*

"I'm in a shed."

"Do you mean a dog house?"

"Aha ha ha. I was looking for George and Charlotte..."

"And?"

Dan said in a small voice: "They locked me in."

Tess was distracted by Anastasia running full pelt through the Green Room door. She careered through the dejected finalists, startling the Uniform Unicorn, which reared up, knocking over a tray of cacao brownies. The four Bio Ball Labradors appeared from nowhere; within seconds not a crumb remained. Anastasia clumsily hurdled the dogs, scooped up the tray and slowed to a halt in front of Tess.

"Have you seen Louis? I can't find him. I can't find him anywhere! I fell asleep..." she panted, the words tumbling out of her mouth like the marbles from Charlotte's favourite crystal jar.

"I've got to go, Dan. Stay where you are," Tess said needlessly, and hung up. "Where did you see him last?"

Anastasia listed the places she remembered. None of them sounded familiar to Tess.

"Would he go outside?"

"He knows he's not allowed. The climbing frame's being re-castellated."

The women shared a look and leapt to their feet. They scooted past a heap of fragrant body bags, lying like recumbent black panthers. They swerved a cage full of buzzing insects and a table laden with tubs of gleaming butter. *Bug Butter: Give Yourself a Buzz* read the packaging. Eventually, they reached the end of the Green Room. Beyond, lay a vast climbing frame, built to resemble Balmoral. It was deserted.

"Wait... where have the alpacas gone?" gasped Tess.

Next to the Uniform Unicorn's hay-strewn corner lay a pitiful sight. An abandoned exhibition stand, bearing high-resolution visuals of long-necked, smiling pseudoruminants, showed signs of recent occupation. Small pieces of carrot, broccoli and apple scattered the floor. Creased and torn leaflets advertising the first-ever swimming school for alpacas covered the carpet like bruised water lilies, as though dropped in a rush and trampled.

"The Spitting Water Swimming School for Alpacas," said Anastasia, "has left the building."

Jack and Charlotte rounded the corner.

"Have you seen Dad?" Jack smirked.

"I've heard him," said Tess. "He's perfectly safe, you naughty children. Have *you* seen Louis?"

"I saw him riding an alpaca in the corridor," said Jack. "He looked quite happy."

"But the alpacas are gone!"

Jack shrugged. He couldn't care less about alpacas; they didn't have engines.

"He must have gone too, then. Coming, Lottie?"

Charlotte considered her position. She knew full well her loyalties lay with her infant brother, who appeared to have vanished with a herd of domestic mammals somewhere away from Royal household premises. What would her parents say if they knew she had ignored Louis' plight and continued with a 'keeping the commoner hostage' game? How could she live with herself if something terrible happened?

"Yep, coming," she said. "Let us know if you find him. I'm doing LouLou's support reading tonight as Mama and Pops are having a late one."

"Don't you dare," Tess glared at them both. "You're staying right here, where we can see you. We are not adding a missing Princess to our problems."

Anastasia started to whimper.

Tess leaned over a table and picked up a leaflet.

"It says here, 'Spitting Water operates from a little-known destination in the North of England.' Sounds mysterious."

"Sounds suspicious," said Charlotte. She took Anastasia's hand, which was wobbling like a jellyfish. "I'm sure he hasn't gone far. Do you want me to tell Mama and Pops?"

"No," said Tess and Anastasia together. Jack and Mollie mouthed 'jinx'.

"We need to keep searching," said Tess, trying to keep her voice calm. "We'll tell Parth."

"Tell Parth what?" asked Parth, who had arrived on a hunch that something or someone might be in deep trouble, given it had been almost two hours since he was last called on by the Oates.

Tess explained.

"I'll get security on it," said Parth, and started stabbing his phone.

"I'll, ah, help clear up," whispered Anastasia, the guilt tugging on her chest like the water skiing harness Kate had made her wear in Norfolk last summer. She began sweeping leaflets into a pile. "Wait!" She held up a small, square envelope.

"What..?" said Tess.

On the front of the envelope was written, in a child's wonky script, OPEN ME.

"That's definitely Louis' writing," said Mollie. "I know from his reading record."

Tess ripped open the seal and pulled out what was inside.

15

CHAPTER FOURTEEN

"It's Louis' spellings," said Anastasia, and started to cry.

Tess held the list of words up.

"Red, bed, may, say, her, his, its, day."

"I can do all those," Jack said, proudly. "I bet Louis can't do suffixes."

"You're three years older than him. He wouldn't be expected to learn about root words yet," said Tess.

"Oh, he knows a few," sniffed Anastasia. "I hear him in the bath."

"Jack could be right; Louis probably should be learning more complex words if you take into consideration income equality," said Mollie. "Anyway, this isn't helping us find him."

Tess wished Dan were there. She thought of his broad-shouldered reassurance and felt sad she hadn't told him more explicitly how good he looked. He was the only one who could possibly shed humour on the gravity of the situation. He might be acutely annoying but his presence would neutralise Anastasia's misery. She instructed Jack and Charlotte to make speed to the shed and free him at once.

While Parth continued to bark instructions furtively into the phone, Anastasia held Tess's hand and asked her to pray for her. The life of a Lady-in-Waiting is hard, she said. There are things that can be forgiven but losing a child of the next King of England is not one of them.

William and Kate swept into the room to a reverent silence. Light from the sequins on Kate's dress danced on the table-cloths like fireflies. The more clued-up finalists and their teams wore wide smiles, dipping and curtsying like meerkats. Pony Andrew and Gerry, ambivalent now they had had a formal introduction, nuzzled and crooned at each other, while working their way through an asparagus quiche.

"Oh, what a night," breathed Kate. Her hair shone like ancient brass.

William said nothing; he rubbed his earlobe between his forefinger and thumb and started to hum Coldplay, softly. It had been tough but he had achieved his objective. Local environmental champions had been celebrated. He could fly to Mauritius on his private jet with a clear conscience.

Tess searched the room for something to focus on. The heavy, velvet curtains with gold brocade, the lush rugs underfoot, the never-ending trestle tables covered with white cloths, damp stains like Mollie's marbling. Dirty glasses, lying on their sides and discarded napkins with wedges of uneaten party food. A large pile of squeezed lemon quarters caught her eye before Kate's necklace hovered into Tess's peripheral vision. She found herself unable to look at it without being dazzled. She became aware of Kate's intense gaze and knew, instinctively, that her opinion was being sought on the wallpaper. She gave Kate a double thumbs-up and watched as Kate's cheeks bloomed.

"We should do the circuit," whispered William. "We need to commiserate with all the, um, non-winners."

"Of course. Let's do it with the children," beamed Kate, who had seen her brother off with a promise to have him over for Sunday lunch. She'd better ask the staff to get some vegetarian meatballs in, she thought. What could the dogs eat..? Venison was out of season and they had had that last time..."

"Where's Louis?" asked William.

The atmosphere froze. Looking around at the clutch of paralysed faces, like a cold water swimmer, Mollie dived in.

"He's disappeared for a bit. I think Spitting Water's to blame."

"Naughty boy; I've told him about doing that before," said William, crossly. "He learned it from Roger Federer at his last tennis lesson. He loves an audience. Was everyone watching? Has he gone to his Bucks P room to think about what he's done?"

"No," said George, simply. "Somehow, Louis has managed to sneak off without any of us knowing. We think he may be riding an alpaca. Possibly, it's an abduction." He stopped short of implicating Anastasia by name, though he knew the conclusion that would be reached. She often slipped George KitKats when she arrived at work; such a change from the stuffy Prestat chocolates that were his usual tea-time fare.

"*Anastasia?*" Kate turned to her Lady-in-Waiting with a look worn by female leads in films who say, "what do we do now?" Anastasia held her breath, waiting for the axe of blame to fall but instead, Kate took a deep breath and said: "OK. Let's fix this mess and find LouLou."

Anastasia smiled at Kate gratefully. Her employer had compassion, of course she did. Never mind that Kate had been known to go shooting and smear bee venom face cream on by the bucket load. She was sure they were sustainable bees.

"Of course, Ma'am," she said. "Might I suggest closing the gates?"

"On it," mouthed Parth from his phone.

"We must inform the Police," said William.

"On it."

"Watch the CCTV," said Tess.

"*On* it.".

"Check nearby hospitals, churches, homeless shelters and libraries," said Mollie, who had been Googling from Tess's phone.

Parth hung up and thought about his days at Number ten, where he had worked for a much more pliant crowd.

"I don't think we need to do that quite yet." Kate thought hard. What would Louis do, given the opportunity to ride an alpaca out of Buckingham Palace? Surely, he wouldn't leave without telling someone something? "Do we have any clues at all?"

"Just this." George flapped the list of spellings next to his face, forlornly.

Mollie grabbed it and held it up to the soft, glowing light of one of the chandeliers. She whispered something to George, who smiled slowly, then gave her a thumbs-up. "I knew it! Follow us!" she yelled, and ran towards the door.

Kate, William, Tess, Jack and Charlotte tore after them, George leading the way. Parth stopped the shocked onlookers from following by commanding a couple of security guards to man the entrance and read out privacy disclosure reminders.

Back through the corridors they ran, twisting and turning past busts of playwrights and scientists, philanthropists and mathematicians. Down a marble staircase, past rows of double doors leading to hidden wings and ballrooms, along another stretch of shadowy, carpeted opulence which gave way to a brighter, wooden-floored passageway. The cloying smell of chlorine hung in the air and aqua light bounced off the walls as they passed the indoor swimming pool.

"Keep going," puffed George. "We're nearly there."

Tess glanced at her phone, which had pinged with a message from Enid. "Not now," she muttered to herself, stashing it back into her evening bag. "I can only deal with one disaster at a time."

The group slowed outside a huge, white-painted door.

"The kitchens," said Kate, who had avoided breaking a sweat, thanks to daily aerial yoga. "What are we doing here?"

Mollie pushed the doors open to a smothering cloud of steam, as if stepping off a plane into a tropical climate. Inside, the air was replete with the sound of twenty three chefs whisking, chopping, pummelling and frying. Stainless steel kitchenware gleamed from every wall and copper cooking pots designed to feed hundreds swung like setting suns from the cavernous ceiling. Rich aromas of marinated meat, bubbling soup and red wine jus filled their nostrils. George, who hadn't been able to eat all day because of nerves, found his mouth watering.

Making a beeline for a pastry chef who had just pulled some meringues out of the oven, Mollie held the spelling list back up in front of the cooker display.

"If I'm right..." she said, squinting, "we'll soon find out where Louis is."

Without further hesitation, she grabbed a tea towel, pulled down the oven door and thrust the paper inside.

Kate gasped. William yelled, "I will not be sued for a burn

injury!"

Tess, who had realised what was happening, said: "You clever girl."

After a few seconds, Mollie retrieved the list and turned it over. On the back, in faint, brown letters was written:

mama and Pops I am with the alpaka man. going too hiz farm now. LouLou. PS poo poo Pops.

"How on earth..?" stuttered William.

"Invisible writing," shrugged Mollie. "I knew it as soon as I saw the pile of lemons."

William, who had actually meant how on earth did Louis nearly spell 'alpaca' correctly, nodded and smiled tightly. "What do we now?"

Tess, suddenly remembering Dan, said: "I think we'd better get out of your hair. I mean..." she faltered, glancing at William's shining head, "we'll leave you for the rest of the evening. If there's anything we can do, of course please let us know..."

"You will likely need to give a statement to the Police," said Parth, who had arrived from nowhere. "They're waiting in the burgundy drawing room to speak to us all."

Tess began to feel very tired. Her feet hurt and her brain, unused to so much splendour and mayhem, was buzzing. She missed Rowley's supper nudges; the slam of their neighbours' car doors and the flap of the letterbox in Elderfield.

"I need to find Dan," she explained. "And get back to the dog sitter."

Kate said benevolently: "You must go. Now we know where Louis is, the Police will have him back with us in no time. It might be best not to embroil you all in this. After all," she said, seriously, "it doesn't look good for our security measures to have to involve an - er - ordinary family involved in our affairs."

Tess felt as if she had been slapped in the face. What had happened to the bond they'd formed over chopper talk? She was about to say something but felt a pang of guilt. How ungrateful it would seem to complain now, after all the hospitality and opportunity that had come their way in the last couple of weeks.

"How can you be so calm?" Will thundered at Kate. "We don't know what this Spitting Water chap will try, or want in return."

He thought back with a shiver to the story his father had told him of the attempted kidnapping of his aunt, Princess Anne. In 1974, a 'victim of mental illness' had rented a car and tried to abduct the then-23-year-old Anne after her nuptials to Mark Phillips, a commoner. Charles had warned that this might happen to William himself on marriage to Kate.

"There's nothing anti-Royalist commoners hate more than seeing us fraternising with their own," he had said. "We are, after all, celebrities in their eyes and it's astounding the tricks some people try to pull to make a fast buck."

"Pound," William had said, piously. He fundamentally disagreed, being of the mind that should one encounter a kidnapper, it would be Kate whose graceful, heavily moisturised neck would be on the line - but he had, nonetheless, consulted his wife on seating plans for Ladies-in-Waiting and aides in the family's vehicles. The family were well-practised in 'ducking and covering' drills with the children in the car and George, Charlotte and Louis all knew where the cans of mace were stored and how to use a window punch tool.

Tess seized the opportunity and fled with Mollie and Jack.

They pushed past men with walkie-talkies, neon tabarded personnel hurrying purposefully in the direction of the gardens. Jack produced a key and ran ahead with Mollie.

"Wait here, Mum," he said. Minutes later, they reappeared with Dan, looking sheepish. Sweat stains bloomed on his mustard suit like a shadowed Sahara. A cobweb hung off one shoulder and his right knee was covered in dirt.

"Have a nice rest?" Tess reached out and took his hand. "You've missed all the action."

"Can we go home now?" asked Dan. "I think I've had enough."

They found their way back to the car park, where Parth had arranged a car to meet them. As they clambered in, Tess remembered the message from Enid. Once seat belts were fastened, she steeled herself to look.

I know about the Oscar's situation and I am disappointed you did not feel able to come to me prior to seeking alternative employment. I assume that you are dissatisfied with your current role and so I am willing to revisit the scope of your work. I look forward to discussing further on Monday.

Tess's heart sank into the floor. She felt it burrow beneath the car and drop onto the tarmac of the Mall below where it was squeezed under tyres, before careering to the side of the road and ending up at rest just far enough from the tranquility of Green Park to allow tourists to trample it into oblivion. She knew full well the meaning behind the text. Enid would take this opportunity and shake it like Rowley with a sock, using Tess's disloyalty until she had manipulated her position into whatever shape or form took her fancy.

As the car wheeled around Trafalgar Square towards Waterloo Station, their cases already safely stowed in the boot, Dan said softly, "I think that went well."

Tess looked at him sorrowfully. "Prince Louis is missing and we're accomplices, wearing clothes costing more than six months' mortgage payments." Anger made her voice rise. "What exactly, out of the evening we've just had, do you think went well?"

"George made his speech," said Mollie, quietly. "And Louis wrote a full sentence."

True, thought Tess. True. Take joy where you can find it, she reminded herself, and closed her eyes against the London night.

CHAPTER FIFTEEN

The car had turned right, to begin its journey across Waterloo Bridge when Tess's phone rang.

"We need you to come back, urgently," hissed Parth. "There's been a development. Tell the driver to turn around, please. We need you here *now.*"

Desperation from Parth sounded wrong: like a dog miaowing, or a lawn mower on a snowy day. Tess felt unease and intrigue bubbling in her stomach like the bicarbonate of soda in one of Jack's science kit experiments. It must be something very serious for Parth to sound so distressed.

Mollie and Jack, dozing in the back of the car either side of her, stirred, yawned and shut their eyes again. Despite her exhaustion and the imminent departure of the 11:37pm train (the last to Elderfield), Tess knew arguing was futile. Peering out at the lights on the South Bank, she wondered about Anastasia, who had been conspicuous in her absence from the scene for the last thirty minutes or so. Would she get the sack? Or, worse, be implicated in Louis's disappearance?

Tess relayed the instruction to the driver. From the front

seat, Dan turned and looked steadily at Tess. He mouthed something that might have been, 'I love you,' but was more likely, 'olive hue,' given that he was grinning delightedly and pointing to the lining of his jacket. Tess focused on the IMAX cinema, looming ahead of them like an alien planet. She remembered the glee at buying ice-cream with Dan as they waited to see a Bond film there, pre-children. She'd had mint choc-chip. Simpler times.

As they approached Buckingham Palace again, blue flashing lights lit up the trees and muted sirens wailed. Confusion reigned. Negotiating the approach was challenging: the car crawled through the crowds of onlookers until it arrived at a police cordon. A large, uniformed body loomed through the window. His head bobbed down and took identification. When he realised who the passengers were, his face softened.

"You're expected in the burgundy drawing room. Keep your heads low, please. These paps are like piranhas."

Tess took one look at Kate, reclining without bothering to lean her legs, tear-stained and mottled on the sofa, and knew things were not going to plan. Her hair had come out of its chignon and curled limply around her elbows, like the tentacles of a dead octopus. Her manicured toes flexed furiously and the Zara necklace twisted in her fingers as she rolled the pearls back and forth. William sat next to her, smoothing her knee.

On a love seat in the corner, King Charles and Queen Camilla sat, looking stunned. Camilla held a copy of *The Tiger Who Came to Tea* in her lap, drizzling its cover with fat tears. Across the tiger's face, Louis had scrawled his name with red crayon. George, Charlotte and Anastasia were nowhere to be seen.

Parth hovered near a drinks trolley, his fingers twitching. Kate let out a sob. William holding her hand, gulped two mouthfuls of water directly from a jug in front of him and stood up.

"I'm sorry we had to bring you back here," his voice trembled. "Word has spread about the – ah – incident somehow. And we've had a terrible – um, er... that is to say," he glanced around to check all the doors were shut. "We've just had contact with Louis's kidnapper."

Mollie brightened. "So you know he's safe?"

The look on Parth's face was the definition of inscrutable, thought Mollie, thinking Pearl would give her a gold star for correct word usage.

"We don't know he's *not* safe," said Parth, carefully. "We've heard his voice from an anonymous phone line. He said he had a wobbly tooth, but we're assuming that's a natural state of affairs rather than assault."

Kate gave a low moan. "He's only just turned five. It'll be his first missing baby one!" She couldn't bear the thought of not being there to photograph it. Already, she'd drawn sketches of a potential wallpaper with George, Charlotte and Louis' discarded dentals. Working title: 'Crownstooth'.

Tess looked impatiently at Parth. "I don't understand why we needed to be brought back? What do we have to do with any of this? Do we need to give a statement?"

Parth shifted slightly on his feet. "You need to tell me everything," he said. "Then I will relay it to the Police, who will also want to question you directly."

Dan came to life. "The Parth of least resistance!"

Tess looked at him coldly.

"Well, that's quite ridiculous," said Mollie. "If we're going to do this properly, and Louis is to be returned safely, surely the most obvious thing is to go straight to the Police."

Parth crossed the carpet and knelt down. A grown man, he thought, begging a nine-year-old girl to give him the benefit of the doubt. How could his career have sunk so low? He cast his mind back to the parties at Downing Street during lockdown, and their associated questionable morals. So much less complicated than this. But needs must.

"Mollie..." he began.

"Tell them, Parth," choked Kate.

"Tell us what?" Tess looked worried.

"Trevor has a condition," said Parth. "He has requests related to Louis's return."

"Trevor being..?"

"Spitting Water's CEO."

Mollie snorted. "What a bully. What a cheek! So he's got sour grapes about not winning, has he? Do his alpacas need armbands? Swimming caps? Does he need help with husbandry? He's not worth the time of day. Give the man what he wants, for goodness sake, so we can all go home and Louis can put his tooth under his pillow."

"No," said Dan, quietly. "Bullies need facing. Whatever this Trevor wants, we listen but he must meet our - I mean, your - terms."

Wisely said, thought Parth. He began to explain Spitting Water's demands to a rapt audience.

CHAPTER SIXTEEN

Thursday 25 May 2023, Elderfield, West Sussex.

Enid lay motionless in a hammock imagining clean, white skulls circling overhead. Moonlight glowed beneath her eyelids as apple tree boughs stirred in the fragrant breeze. If she strained her ears, the roar of the motorway intruded on her thoughts but she channelled the distraction: motorways were good for roadkill; good for collateral. The temperature was pleasant for May and, at nearly midnight, the air still held a mildness that warmed Enid's frosty heart. She trailed her fingertips across the recently laid composite decking. Neat furrows bumped under her short nails, like the ridges on a young fox's jaw bone.

Tess's betrayal smarted like a snowball between the eyes. Never in the last five years would she have imagined her line report to have contemplated changing jobs. The stability of her position and the direction and example Tess had in Enid as a manager was, surely, something to be cherished and revered.

No-one understood the theory of school communications like Enid. She read the Ofsted school inspection handbook every three months, to ensure she kept up with any changes and knew what the CEO of the Trust's objectives would be before he had settled them himself. She understood what it took for a re-brand of a school to pass muster with every stakeholder audience. She could organise a raft of photography shoots in a heartbeat. But Tess – Tess was the one who really understood how to communicate the culture and heart of the schools in the trust with empathy, flair and economy.

Enid grimaced as she recalled the cheerful 'welcome back' public relations campaign Tess had run following the end of the last coronavirus lockdown. Despite schools remaining open throughout the pandemic, to under-served children and those of key workers, the return of all children to school had been a joyous occasion that, for The Wenceslas Academy Trust (TWAT), had resulted in huge amounts of local press coverage and an interview with the CEO on BBC's Today programme. All thanks to Tess and her foresight: she had worked hard to provide schools with packs of branded balloons, b-roll, press release templates and prearranged media slots. Tess had been rightly praised for her initiative by Head Teachers and governors, and the reputation of one of the trust's more challenging schools had soared when parents saw the effort put into welcoming students back. Enid had been somewhat puzzled. She hadn't thought to make any ceremony around the fact that children were returning to school. The truth was, when it came to young people, Enid was entirely ambivalent.

Marilyn, Enid's wife of four years, ventured into the gloom. Her bushy eyebrows loomed over the hammock and her tall frame blinded the moon.

"Are you planning to lie out here all night?"

"I might."

"Bambi's ready for her examination."

Enid flashed a smile, which was lost in the dark, and pushed herself up. She followed Marilyn's sturdy back into the kitchen of their gorgeous, new-build barn and shaded her eyes from the spotlights' glare.

Donning protective goggles and peering into a bucket of bleach filled her with joy. Having scraped out the flesh, blood and brain matter from inside a young deer's skull and removed the fine bone structure from inside its nose, it had remained in a bucket of water for two days before being gently boiled and cooled. Finally, Enid had placed the skull carefully in a hydrogen peroxide mix for 24hrs. Now, as she reached in with gloved hands and slowly drew it out, she saw with satisfaction that the skull was in exquisite condition.

Moving to the sink, Enid rinsed the skull under running water and held it aloft. There was a small crack in the right mandible, now that she looked at it from a side angle, but that could be fixed with glue.

"Another one for the wall?"

Enid nodded. Rabbit, squirrel, badger, fox, deer, even cat and dog skulls adorned the left hand side of the kitchen, above the granite dining table. Marilyn's veterinarian practice was a treasure trove of animal corpses and Enid made full use of the perk, devoting a chunk of her weekends to skull rejuvenation. It was the perfect relaxation activity, she would enthuse at the monthly dinner parties she and Marilyn held, with the beautiful and important people from the upper echelons of the parish council, not to mention a nice little earner.

"You'd be amazed at the prices some people pay for an impeccable stag skull," she disclosed one night a couple of years ago, to TWAT's Chief Executive Officer.

"I might be interested in a discount," the CEO had said. "I know a couple of DfE contacts who would be very interested in these for, ah, personal use."

Thus, the furtive and unconventional deal had been struck. Enid kept the CEO in a healthy supply of small craniums for his lobbying purposes and he chose to believe her when she explained the success of and took the credit for, Tess's campaigns - even though the truth was obvious to the full staff body.

Tess's departure would be a disaster, both for TWAT and for Enid. There were no two ways about it. Enid's jealousy of Tess's creativity burned her temples like 10% peroxide. Try as she might, she could not write articles about compelling Duke of Edinburgh volunteering milestones, nor create engaging Instagram ads about summer productions to save her life. She simply didn't care about children's achievements enough.

"What's on your mind, 'nid?" asked Marilyn.

Enid winced. 'Nid' had not been agreed upon as an acceptable nickname, but battles must be picked.

"Just work."

"Anything I can do? I'd like to help but it's really late. I've got two canine ACL repairs and a tortoise that needs stomach surgery tomorrow."

"Can you persuade my assistant to stay in her job?"

Marilyn's eyes narrowed. "You mean Tess? She's not your assistant, she's a manager."

"Sort of." Enid scowled.

"Have you talked to her about it?"

"I will. It's half-term next week so I'll leave it a week for her to squirm and talk to her when we get back."

"Go easy on her. I'm sure she was planning to tell you she

was looking around. She'll have her reasons." Marilyn liked Tess; admired the way she juggled family life with a relatively stressful job. She didn't know her well, of course; Enid always seemed to avoid the suggestion of socialising with her, saying they spent enough time at work together. "Remember when you were the little fish in the big pond?"

"Hmm. Not really. I've always felt like a shark in a puddle."

Marilyn looked at her lover affectionately. "A fish out of water, then? Sharks are generally highly misunderstood and hardly ever pose a danger to humans."

Enid hung the skull from the sink tap to dry overnight. Sensing bedtime was close, Marilyn weighed up whether to broach another tricky subject. She cleared her throat.

"There's something I forgot to tell you," she said. "Rachel's left us again."

Enid paused her staircase ascent and sighed with annoyance. "What is it this time?"

"The usual." Marilyn took Enid's hand and held it against her cheek. "Problems with Malcolm, and she thinks she can get more money elsewhere."

"Ah."

"Which, of course, she can't."

"No."

Enid felt only a soupçon of guilt. Her main sense was one of frustration. Rachel Swift was a superb and near-silent cleaner and the only person they had found for years who didn't balk at brushing the teeth of their skeletons. She was paid the going rate by Marilyn and Enid, but periodically left notes on the mantelpiece announcing her resignation (with no notice given) unless her pay increased.

"She's got us over a barrel, though. And it can't be easy

single-parenting that awful Malcolm. I saw him communing with nature on the village hall gatepost yesterday. I'm sure the hollyhocks will suffer as a result."

"I'll talk to her on Monday."

"If she turns up."

"She will." Marilyn smiled. "You do the tough conversation with Tess and let me handle Rachel. It will all be fine. Now, do come to bed. I've got some flesh and bones that need some tickling."

18

CHAPTER SEVENTEEN

Thursday 25 May 2023, Buckingham Palace, London.

"You must be bloody joking! What a bloody cheek!"

King Charles stood up and checked his cuffs and hand-kerchief. This always grounded him, he found, even when they were hidden beneath threadbare tweeds as he lay hedges at Sandringham. Finding both intact, he settled into quiet seething.

"Could you play it again, Parth?" said Kate, weakly.

Parth reached forward and pressed 'play' on his phone for the second time. After a short pause, a male voice with a faint northern lilt started to speak.

"Ye majesties. I've yer boy Louis with me. Don't worry. He be safe. The name's Trevor. Trevor Malpas. I run Spitting Water - the world leader in alpaca swimming lessons, operating right here in the UK. But ye'll know that already from me shortlisting for the Briti-shots." The voice turned gritty with resentment. "Which was a complete and utter disgrace. A fix."

William turned a worried look towards Kate. "I told you

picking James was a mistake."

Kate held a finger up to silence him. They both knew the worst was yet to come.

"It is clear to me," continued Trevor, "that the modern monarchy, whilst in some respects living in the modern world and, admittedly more on point and current than previous generations, obviously has huge problems – one being that it still has no real concept of living a 'real' life. Were I to ask you what the current Bank of England interest rate is, would any one of you really know?"

"It's about sixty five percent," said William, confidently. A ghost of smugness skittered across his lips. He knew people were still interested in banks but he was sure their popularity had waned slightly. Since he'd picked up a copy of the *Windsor Times* last week from Parth's study, he had seen that another high street branch was shutting. So they couldn't be that popular. Sixty five percent seemed a reasonable guess.

"It's heading towards 4 percent and inflation is climbing to 15 percent. I've started to make my own wine with a kit from Boots," said Anastasia, who had returned from putting George and Charlotte to bed and thought about her own bank balance every ten seconds. She took in the Oates' presence, the shattered faces of Kate and William and collected herself. Parth looked anxious and, seeing his finger quivering like a moth over a flame, she walked sedately to a Dunelm chair - which, Kate assured her, was beloved of Queen Elizabeth II - and settled down to listen to the rest of the recording.

"It falls to me, therefore, not only to save the world by teaching alpacas to swim so they can help non-swimmers in Asia with their kelp farms, but to bring the British monarchy back down to earth. I will return Louis in one piece within six weeks if - IF ye ken prove to me ye understand what life is like in the real world for real people. There will be a test, and if I decide ye have not passed it, I will take Louis as my apprentice and go to live in South Korea. Details of the test will be sent first thing in the morning via an encrypted link to the gentleman Parth's email address. The subject heading will read: Half-term homework for Louis." Trevor laughed; a raspy, hollow sound. "Get it? It's actually *work* for *you* to do to get *Louis home* safely."

"Not funny," said Kate and Mollie together.

"Jinx," said Jack and Charlotte.

The recording went quiet for a few seconds, then Louis's voice piped: "Hello Mama and Pops. My alpaca is called Orange. I love him. I rode him into a lorry and when I came out it was raining and a man gave me somefin' called parkin. I will come home soon but I have to help teach Orange how to swim first, so that he can teach people in Souf Career because they can't swim so they drown when they try to grow seaweed. PS my tooth fell out. I hope Morwenna can find it."

"Who's Morwenna?" asked Trevor.

"My tooth fairy."

Trevor grunted: "You won't find no fairies here, son." The recording finished.

Silence fell. Kate gave a hiccough and murmured, "... knew it. Morwenna's never gone further north than Norfolk."

Mollie said: "He did use a double negative, though."

Parth looked out towards the sheltered palace gardens where night bloomed thickly. Torches shone as the final Briti-shot paraphernalia was packed away. All knew that on the other side of Bucks P, hive-like activity and Morwenna's certain no-show meant that sleep would be as elusive as a unicorn in uniform.

CHAPTER EIGHTEEN

Friday 26 May 2023, Elderfield, West Sussex.

Thank God it was almost half-term, thought Tess as she waited for her PG Tips to stew. To make the most of the time before the family would wake, she started loading the washing machine with four sets of home clothes, a Primark strapless bra and her Alexander McQueen corset, which floated like a butterfly on top of the mound of faded t-shirts and pants. A car had taken them all the way from Buckingham Palace back to Elderfield at two o'clock in the morning and now, as the church bell signalled seven, Tess felt the house softly inhale and exhale as the rest of the family slept. She was running on empty, but what was new? Rowley stared at her between sections of fringe, a tennis ball ensnared between his paws. The oven hummed, its innards stuffed with gently warming croissants from Lidl. Chocolate and hazelnut spread stood in the middle of the table, surrounded by a clutch of cutlery. Boiled eggs simmered on the hob. A family breakfast well-earned. Tess dropped her tea bag into the bin and switched on the radio.

"... rumour has it that his whereabouts are unknown," said the new BBC news presenter, chirpily. "Can you confirm or deny this?"

Tess put the top back on the milk and listened hard.

"We can confirm that Prince Louis is safe and well. His whereabouts are known and there is no cause for concern," said Parth. Tess was impressed with how bright he sounded, given he must have had close to no sleep.

"It is common for children of the Royal Family to undergo - ah - private tuition for certain skills and this situation is no different. Following last night's exceptionally successful Britishot Awards, Prince Louis who is - as I think has been proven - a very independently minded five-year-old, has chosen to improve his understanding of the animal kingdom, and is taking a little break over half-term to become more familiar with the, er, opportunities the natural world can afford us.

"Ah, but therein lies the question," said the presenter. "The natural world may afford the likes of Prince Louis an education, but can *we* afford it? The taxpayer, I mean. The cost of the Royal Family has gone up 17 percent from last year. Isn't it time the monarchy realised its time is up? The Sovereign Grant can't just be spent on mending the drains. What's Prince Louis's half-term holiday costing *us*?"

The seconds ticked by. Parth said nothing. Tess screamed silently, "Bridge! Bridge!" *Who* was responsible for Parth's media training? Anyone could hear that this was a classic example of where an interviewee should address the question and move swiftly onto their intended messaging. Yet, instead of communicating the importance of Louis providing a role model to other children in his strong bond with the environment, Parth said meekly: "I'm afraid I shall have to get back to you on that."

Tess banged her cup of tea down onto her rubber chopping board. Speedily, she typed out a WhatsApp message to Parth: *Bad luck with the BBC. Next time, let me handle the media relations. I can teach you a few things!*

She read it through as good practice dictated, added a smiley emoji, deleted it again as well as the exclamation mark and pressed 'send'.

Turning her attention back to the kitchen, she spoke tenderly to Rowley.

"I'm sorry, Row. I've neglected you recently. How about a good old walk and a swim before breakfast and waking the troops, hey?"

Rowley yawned and thumped his tail. If they went towards the stream, it was possible that Kayoss would be waiting on the banks with her owner; she had woofed an invitation yesterday when the dog walker had taken him there for a cooling swim. They'd caught each other's eye by the upside-down pram near the bridge and briefly enjoyed a tug of war with the same stick. Any time in the afternoon would do. Even if she wasn't there, the scent of her would keep him happy for the rest of the day. Balls and Kayoss. Kayoss and balls. Life was good.

Tess ran upstairs on tiptoes to assess the levels of slumber. There was no sign of movement, even from Jack. She came back down, turned the croissants off, drained the boiled eggs and removed Rowley's lead from its hook. As she was tying her trainers, she was interrupted by a faint knocking.

Tess opened the front door a crack, conscious she was wearing one of Dan's t-shirts with pyjama bottoms and her hair, still stiff at the sides from last night's fixative spray, was in a less than competent 'mum bun'.

On the doorstep, at six minutes past seven on a Friday in late May, stood the Princess of Wales.

Tess could only tell it was Kate from the sublime cut of her trench coat, the sleek lock of chestnut hair escaping from beneath a peroxide wig and the fact that she had to look up slightly to look at her face. When she did, she gasped. The desolation was plain. If it weren't for her cheekbones, Tess thought Kate's eyes might sink without trace into the tender, puffy skin. There were no tears left; Kate's face was a case study in desertification.

"I had to see you. I didn't know what else to do. Anastasia drove me. She's taking the Merc for a spin while she waits, but I only have an hour." The huskiness in Kate's voice propelled Tess to take her hand and usher her into the kitchen. She handed her the cup of tea she had just made. She took a breath, ready to apologise for the hand-painted mug with 'Happy Mother's Day' written in Jack's thumbprints, half-empty laundry basket and the general mess, then stopped. This was her domain. Her laundry. Kate could take it or leave it.

"Croissant?"

Kate asked weepily: "Is it Laurent Duchêne?"

"Lidl."

Strange, thought Kate. An area of Paris she hadn't heard of. "I haven't done my yoga yet and I usually stick to protein before noon, but yes, please."

Tess put a croissant on a plate and passed Kate a teaspoon. "I think you could make an exception today. Chocolate spread is best just dolloped on. And the eggs are ready."

Kate ate with voracity. Through choked sobs and tangled blonde nylon, she slugged tea and gulped down lumps of Lidl's all-butter with the speed of a baby starling. Rowley looked on, whining with jealous awe. When only the last smears of spread remained, Tess passed her a boiled egg, a beaker of water and a sheet of kitchen towel.

"How can I help?"

Kate tapped the shell experimentally and rolled a piece between her thumb and forefinger. "Do you have any soldiers?"

"No, that's your prerogative."

Kate gave Tess a watery smile. Tess turned away to put two slices of white bread into the toaster and said: "I mean, how can I help you with Louis? Has the email arrived? What test do you have to take? And... well, um... what are you doing here?"

There was a creak from above, followed by a muffled thud; seconds later, Mollie appeared, dressed and blinking.

"Oh, hi," she said to Kate, without giving her a second glance. She pulled a carton of apple juice from the fridge. "Thanks again for the jumpsuit, by the way. Any news on Louis? Do you have to take an exam?"

"Well, yes, actually." Kate cast a nervous look around the kitchen. "As you know, Trevor's demands are somewhat... challenging. Are we safe from bugs in this room?"

"Not really," said Tess. There's a wasp's nest in the right-hand corner but Arran's coming to blast it with a fumigator this week."

"They're everywhere," whispered Kate. "I had to lie to Parth about coming here this morning and William was very disapproving. He only let me go because I told him this is our only chance."

"What is?"

Kate took a deep breath and shut her eyes. Her lips wobbled, parted and words erupted from her mouth like lava. "To get

Louis back, we will need to..." she swallowed. "Move in with you for a short while."

Tess dropped the slices of toast. Rowley uncoiled from his bed like a hairy slow worm, wolfed, gagged and disappeared back to his bed again. "I'm sorry, I... *what?*"

"Is it because you can't get your team of experts to help you out?" said Mollie, steadily. "Does our family really have to get you out of *another* hole?"

Kate shifted in her seat. From deep within the folds of her trench coat, a mobile phone trilled. She looked at it for a second or two, then put it away. "It's William. He'll be calling to see how I'm getting on."

"How *are* you getting on?" Mollie asked with a trace of contempt. Tess noted the rising inflection with a degree of nervousness. It was the same note Mollie reserved for Jack when she discovered her binoculars or nail varnish were missing. It rarely left the recipient on high ground at the end of the conversation.

"I mean. You kindly invited us to your house - but only because you wanted something from me for George. You then *kindly* invited us to your Briti-shots - but only because you wanted something from me for George. Now you want to *kindly* invite yourselves to our house - but only because you want something from us for Louis. The hundred million or so people like my mum and dad have paid your family over the last year should mean we're worth more than a couple of designer outfits and a few glasses of wine at yours."

"Very nice wine," said Tess, quietly. She looked at her daughter with admiration and awe. She couldn't have put it better herself. However, she was genuinely curious about the request.

"I'm sorry, I don't follow," Tess said. "You'd never fit into this place, I'm afraid. It's 1,000 square feet and that includes the bird table. There are two bedrooms and a box room, and our washing machine has no chiffon or crepe settings. I mean, it's not that we don't want you here. Just that it would be a bit of a squeeze."

"Of course," said Kate, dabbing her nose delicately with a silk handkerchief. "Silly of me to ask. It's just that the demands being as they are, I thought it might be the most expedient means of rescuing Louis. It was unthinking. Of course, you will have half-term plans of your own."

"Yes. We're going to Paultons Park," said Mollie, staunchly. "I suppose you could stay here that day and dog-sit Rowley."

Kate focused on the motes of dust, dancing in the lemony light from the window above the sink. Dog hair piled in spiky drifts against the skirting boards. She absorbed the collage of family information taped to the fridge: Head Teachers' awards, a dog vaccination reminder and an invitation to Jack for a birthday party at Play Planet. A dripping tap soaked a trailing shirt sleeve from a pile of unwashed laundry on the counter.

She eased her buttocks on the creaky wooden stool and battened down the hatches against the swell of despair that rose again. She thought hard. Trevor's list of demands had been succinct, if baffling. It reminded her of the game played by the hopefuls on TV's *The Apprentice* when groups of ambitious 20-somethings scoured London for objects they had never heard of. Another reality show she'd watched with Harry, before he'd moved abroad. Oh, H, thought Kate. Where did everything go so terribly wrong? Let's forget the bridesmaid dresses texts. Come back for a visit. William misses drinking whiskey sours and I miss throwing wellies with you.

"Are we allowed to see the email? Could you read it out?" asked Tess.

"No one but William and I have been permitted to see it - and Parth, of course," said Kate. Parth had looked stern and said: "We don't want a screenshot circling." So Kate had memorised the words until they were imprinted on the inside of her eyelids. She closed her eyes, opened her mouth and intoned, as if reading an obituary:

"For centuries, the Royal Family has lived a life of immense financial privilege at the expense of the taxpayer. Worse, it has lived and continues to flaunt a life of environmental hypocrisy, championing rural enterprise and conservation whilst spending hundreds of thousands of pounds on private travel and personal grooming. Climate change is not helped by the private jets and air conditioning that are apparently so necessary for Royal Tours. Millions of pounds worth of home renovations could be spent on solar panels and wind farms for under-served communities but what do we see instead? Fourteen-bed mansions with tennis courts and swimming pools.

Enough is enough. If the monarchy is to become truly modern, it is going to need to prove itself in the real world. I have taken Louis as insurance. I will teach him, in the next six weeks, how important environmental enterprise really is. Meanwhile, the rest of the Wales family is encouraged to study modern life in the UK, and study it hard. The test at the end of these six weeks will evaluate whether the Wales family can:

Find and live in a house no larger than 1,000 square feet, with no staff.

(Both parents) find and remain in paid employment for at least four weeks.

(Both children) attend a state primary school for at least four weeks.

Complete a weekly family food shop with a budget of no more £70.

Take a day trip to Paultons Park in a 2007 Volkswagen Passat.

Raise at least £100 for the local community.

Take the family dog to the vet for its vaccinations.

Manage on a budget of £10 per month for skin and haircare.

In the last few words, Kate's voice caught and cracked. She stared into her tea mug at the milky brown liquid and shook the last drops into her mouth. What was this cut with? Brick dust? Rooibos premium loose leaf tea blend seemed a million miles away.

Mollie narrowed her eyes. "So you thought you'd take the easy route and move in with us, rather than actually house hunting?"

"No, no, I..."

"It really is out of the question. I'm so sorry." said Tess.

Jack came into the kitchen, naked apart from a pair of socks. He collected a plate, spoon and croissant and stood in front of Tess, ignoring Kate.

"If someone gave you a diamond, would you make them a time machine?" he asked.

"Yes," said Tess.

"What if the diamond was fake?"

Tess thought for a minute. "I don't know," she said. "What would you do?"

"Kill them," said Jack, and headed towards the table to sit down.

"I know it's out of the question," said Kate. "I just thought...

"

"Blimey," said Dan, walking into the kitchen. He looked well rested after his shed incarceration, but his hair flopped over his brow, as if it had run a marathon and still needed a shower. "Hello," he nodded at Kate. "Any news about the boy?"

"Well, yes, actually..."

"Good stuff. The police seemed to know what they're doing." He stuffed a croissant in his mouth, kissed Tess on the top of her head and said: "Sorry I can't help with school this morning. I'm off to Pearl's place to rehearse for the gig. No offence," he said, looking at Kate, "but I'll get a bit more peace there."

"Fine," said Tess, knowing Pearl had only agreed to Dan's occupation after Tess pleaded with her for a morning off from his practice gags. For some reason, JoJo had raised her barre again. "Wait! Does Pearl have any bookings over half-term?"

Dan screwed his eyes. "I don't *think* so."

Tess looked at Kate, a thought taking root in her mind. "I think I might have a solution," she said. She dialled Pearl's number and put her on speaker phone.

"Hello, love?"

Tess said, more confidently than she felt, "My lovely. I've got a query booking for your AirBnB. It's a nice family of five... four. Yes, *that* family. I'll fill you in as soon as I can. Yes, the children can share a bedroom... and there's a dog. They'd need it for half-term and possibly up to the end of the summer term, too. Six weeks in total."

Pearl considered. "Do they know it's £25 extra for the dog?"

Tess looked at Kate, who nodded and mouthed, "that's fine."

"Yes. They'll take it," said Tess. "Thank you. Dan's on his way over." She hung up and smiled triumphantly at Kate. "You can move in tomorrow, as soon as the security deposit has been paid."

Kate attempted a smile. She could use her secret credit card to pay the deposit. It only had wallpaper-related transactions: printing and manufacture of 'Safety - in numbers' and an Etsy marketplace payment. Plus, it was in her middle and maiden names: Elizabeth Middleton.

As if reading her mind, Tess said: "You'll all need pseudonyms, won't you? And disguises. You can't very well turn up in Elderfield looking like, well, the Royal Family."

"What will happen to the Emilia Wicksteads, Jenny Packhams and Vampires Wives?" Kate had asked Parth when the gravity of the situation and the realisation that designer clothes were not part of the equation had sunk in last night. Parth had looked briefly floored before Anastasia had whispered, "red carpet togs," and it had dawned that Kate meant her nicest dresses.

"They will be kept in storage, as usual, Ma'am," Parth had lied, knowing full well he would be shuttling a couple back to try on in the bedroom as he was wont to do when the opportunity arose.

Kate took stock. Things were brightening on the horizon. She just needed to break the news to William that life for the next six weeks would be slightly different from the normal state of affairs. She would sell it to him as an adventure. He would do it for Louis, of course he would. And George and Lottie might enjoy a few weeks without Nanny, even if the thought of it felt like the time she stared over the edge of that holy place in Machu Picchu. They had always tried to model themselves on Diana's style of parenting, anyway: William still spoke fondly of queuing at Thorpe Park. Paultons Park had wonderful reviews and would be great fun, surely. What could possibly go more wrong than it already had?

20

CHAPTER NINETEEN

Saturday 27 May 2023, Elderfield, West Sussex.

Mollie stood in the middle of the pavement outside her house in the shade of the spindly plane tree and checked the church clock again. It was the first Saturday of half-term: ordinarily, she would be having a lie-in but today was no ordinary day. Five to nine. If all had gone according to plan, the taxi should be rounding... She craned her neck. Was it? Yes, there it was. A shabby looking Citroen Berlingo Multispace with a splintered sign on top reading 'A to Z Cabs' came into view. As it approached, Mollie could make out a tall figure in the passenger seat. Behind him, a familiar profile with the same bleach-blonde wig was turned towards two young children in baseball caps, who were gazing out of the window, entranced at their surroundings. On seeing Mollie, both smiled and raised their arms, waving shyly before the lady next to them pushed their hands down with a practised swoop.

In the back seat, two more people sat furtively, their heads bowed together as if in prayer. Both wore baseball caps with pristine peaks.

"Mum, is that..?" asked Mollie. "I didn't know they were coming, too."

Tess, who had come out of the house with Rowley, peered and said, "Hard to tell but - yes - I think it's the King and Queen Consort."

The taxi slowed to a halt. From under cover of a hedge, keeping a careful distance from Rowley, Billy the tailless cat looked on with disinterest at the new arrivals. The driver, a conscientious, monosyllabic man with raven curls, got out of the car and lifted four smart canvas holdalls out of the boot while William bent over his own lap. The driver hovered next to the passenger door for several minutes before William straightened and handed over a fistful of money. There was an awkward pause while the paper and coins was counted, then he handed a fifty pound note back to William, before opening the back doors so that Kate, George and Charlotte could get out.

"Thank you so much," said Kate, removing blonde hair from in front of her shoulders with a practised flick and risking an ivory smile. She was used to drivers being available twenty-four hours a day but out of choice, William would drive her or she drove herself. It was a novelty to have someone unfamiliar who needed paying. It took her back to wild nights in Chelsea pre-Princess, where there were two paps around at most, and she couldn't deny the thrill of knowing that they seemed to have got away without this driver suspecting who they were.

"He was brilliant. Did Parth book him?" she whispered to William as they watched him drive away.

William nodded, remembering again with a shudder that it had been the last act of direct support they would be allowed to accept from Parth for the next six weeks. From this moment on, they were on their own in Elderfield. Deep in his trouser pocket, he clutched his lucky gold DofE badge and squeezed hard.

"Pops, you'll almost certainly say no, but..." piped Charlotte.

William said nothing, rearing his neck like an ostrich to identify which of the people walking along the opposite pavement were coming to help him with the bags.

"May I play Roblox with Jack? I did my gymnastics practice before we left."

"No," snapped William. He raised an arm tentatively in the air. Why was nobody stopping? Seeing his furrowed brow, Kate nudged him gently.

"Babe, we have to, um, do this ourselves." She stood with her feet hip-distance apart, as if preparing for a goddess yoga pose, bent at the knees and lifted two holdalls onto her shoulders without straining her back. Thank goodness for Pilates and a granite-like core.

Camilla joined in, leaning down and raising the remaining two holdalls with ease.

"Compost," she said, in reply to William's raised eyebrows. "Weighs a ton but does wonders for one's bum."

"I should say," said Charles.

It had been twenty four hours since breakfast at the Oates' kitchen table and in that time, purpose had gripped and shaken Kate like Tabitha attacking a tenderloin. Upon return to Buckingham Palace, she had filled William in on the plan and had been quick to point out that their disappearance from public life for six weeks would not go unnoticed.

"Oscar's will want answers for a start, even from us. I don't think you're allowed to take your children out of school during term-time without the Head Teacher's permission. It's frowned upon hugely," said Kate, who had not been frowned upon at school since she packed away a teacher's pencil case in her satchel by mistake, aged ten. She shivered; the guilt still festered.

"We'll say we've gone to a secret location to prepare the children for their futures," was William's response. "It's the truth. And never in a million years will they think to look in," he coughed. "Elderfield. The most likely thing is that the press will think we're in Bucklebury with your parents. Or, as Pa and Camilla are involved, Balmoral. And they won't try too hard to get to Scotland; the midges are awful after May."

After consultation with Charles, and an agreement that for moral support and extra childcare, the King and Camilla should be involved, the wheels were set in motion. A trusted group was formed: Parth, Anastasia, Charles, Camilla, as well as James Middleton and the Wales's gathered in the disabled toilet off the Royal Library. It was bug-free and even with the drum kit, which Charlotte insisted on bringing to remind her of Louis, there was plenty of room. Parth laid out on the carpet a six-sided document he had put together with Tess and Mollie's help that morning after an encrypted video conference call. He turned to the property details of Pearl's AirBnB.

A beautifully renovated 1000 square foot annexe, perfect for couples, friends or families, nestled at the heart of Elderfield, 20 mins from Portsmouth and 75 mins from Waterloo.

Your host Pearl Whitehead welcomes you to The Nook, a first-floor annexe attached to The Schoolhouse, lovingly renovated for those who wish to spend time on the nearby picturesque south coast or enjoy all that Elderfield has to offer.

The Nook is an open plan, airy flat. Perfectly restricted to one floor, you will find a lounge space, dining table, kitchen (with fridge freezer, microwave, induction hob, slow cooker (upon request), kettle and toaster, shower and w/c with wash basin. Please note that the shower area is separated by a wall but no door, so you will need to know each other well! The sleeping space is further divided into three distinct areas by wooden beams. Area one features a double bed. Area two features a single sofa bed, chest of drawers and clothes rail. Area three features two refurbished IKEA single beds (perfect for children or adults). Area three can be closed off by a curtain. Note: we refer to three bedrooms but please understand these are not separated by walls. All bed linen and towels are provided.

The walls are adorned with artwork by local artists. This art is available to buy and changes regularly. The Nook has its own private garden area, complete with outdoor table and chairs and BBQ. This garden is fenced off from next door, offering complete privacy.

Where you'll sleep
Bedroom 1
1 x double bed
Bedroom 2
2 x single beds
Bedroom 3
1 x sofa bed
What this place offers:
Kitchen
WiFi
Garden
Children's books and toys
Hair dryer
Lockbox
Not included:

TV
Security cameras
Washing machine
Air conditioning

At least it has a hair dryer, said William, looking at Kate anxiously. How would she cope without a personal stylist and a weekly trim? He squeezed his DofE badge. If the worst came to the worst, could he wield a pair of nail scissors? Would Kate let him?

"No TV's fine," said George, calmly. "I'll take my iPad and use WiFi."

"I bag the sofa bed," said Charlotte. "I need to practise my backwards walkovers."

"You'll both share the twin room," said Kate, sternly. "We'll need the sofa bed for Tabitha."

"Ah," said Parth. "Actually, ah, Pearl's had second thoughts. She says that dogs aren't allowed."

Kate looked at him, stunned. "We can't possibly leave Tab. We paid a £25k deposit!"

Parth looked at her, stunned.

Tess said: "It was twenty five pounds. But Kate's right."

Sensing progress stalling, Parth also promised to see what he could do and moved on. "You'll note there is little to no storage. For this reason, as well as security purposes, you will be restricted to a bag each, plus a luxury item and a book."

"Like Desert Island Discs?" asked James, who prided himself on understanding pop culture. He was thrilled to have been invited to this convention. James felt mildly guilty about his role in his nephew's disappearance, but then again, perhaps it was about time his sister and her family saw how the other half lived. Poor Louis. Things were looking up for him, personally though. First the Briti-shots win, now a real meeting with real people, not dogs. His wife would be thrilled, too. She was always telling him to get involved with something serious.

"Not really," said Parth.

It was Charles and Camilla's accommodation he was most concerned about. The problem of how to explain their disappearance from public life and conceal their whereabouts had been eased by the fact they were due a period of privacy after a marathon run of appearances and the revelation that Pearl had recently acquired a Shepherd's Hut and had been planning to renovate it ready for the summer holiday season. The problem was, it had no running water or electricity.

"It's not quite there yet," Pearl had told Tess. "But if they don't mind showering and bunking down with the family if they want a natter when it gets dark, it's really quite a romantic space."

And now here they all were. Following the Oates down the short, bumpy front path to the shelter of their porch, Dan fist-bumped William awkwardly before heading back upstairs to work and Tess pulled Kate into a hug. Kate said nothing but her lips trembled and her eyes felt itchy. Why were they here? She had done everything she could to make Louis's life full and keep him safe. Motherhood was not easy. She had put up with well-meaning advice from strangers in every country from Australia to India about appropriate ways to handle tantrums and how many climbing walls per residence were needed for growing offspring. She had modelled the children's upbringing on her own, making sure she was heavily involved in running down hills and crawling through playground tunnels. Now, in Windsor, with the children's school only a fifteen-minute drive away, she made sure to check the uniform layouts had been executed by Nanny and check the homework had been done and overseen by Nanny every evening before she indulged in a G&T with Slimline tonic. Hands-on was the word, or words. But now she would have nothing to oversee and everything to execute. She would have to dress up every day, yet have nothing to dress up for. Her hair was due a trim *and* colour next week. And if they didn't achieve their objective of reclaiming Louis, Mauritius was looking very shaky indeed.

"Let's get this show on the road." William struck out from the porch, turned onto the pavement and strode determinedly to the right, before realising he had no idea where the AirBnB was. Kate looked after him fondly, recognising the trait he inherited from Charles. Questionable direction but plenty of purpose.

"We have to get the children ready first," she called, venturing out onto the path and touching William on the arm. William gave her a crestfallen look but followed her into the Oates' house. There hadn't been time to disguise the children fully before the journey to Elderfield and so they had made do with baseball caps given to them by Justin Trudeau. But preparations for full facial makeup had been set up in Elderfield. Tess had cleaned the kitchen and prepared a table full of Superdrug's own brand cosmetics; Pearl and Tess assumed positions on one side and indicated that William, Kate, Charles, Camilla, George and Charlotte should line up on the other.

"I printed off the pictures Parth sent," said Mollie. "He seemed to know what would suit you all, so this shouldn't be too difficult."

"Did you speak to Nanny?" said Kate.

"She was very helpful, too. Both seem to know your children extraordinarily well," said Mollie, giving Kate a look of such undisguised contempt that Kate took herself off to the corner near the cutlery drawer, lodged herself tightly next to the toaster and twisted strands of blonde hair around her fingers as she watched the transformations take place.

First, Pearl smoothed hair away from faces. "Have y'acted in many school productions?" she asked Charlotte, concentrating on the magazine cut-out in front of her. "*Blood Brothers? Robin Hood? Joseph?*" Parth had chosen a picture of Annie from *Annie*. It was simple, yet dramatic. She selected a hair dye named 'Chilli' from an old ice-cream box of colours and a brown eyebrow pencil and started to sprinkle freckles across Charlotte's nose with abandon.

"Our drama teacher prefers female protagonists. I was Medea in *Medea* in year two," said Charlotte. "She kills her own children."

"Well, Annie is very spirited," said Kate. "I think she's a fine role model."

An aeroplane droned overhead. Charles pushed his chair aside and stood by the window, looking up.

"I say, are you directly below a flight path?"

"Aren't we lucky?" said Mollie. "You're not the only ones who get to watch shiny, million-pound vehicles pollute the environment daily."

Charles noticed the shatter-proof crockery for the first time and felt a pang of nostalgia for his own childhood. Perhaps this sojourn would provide an opportunity for 'back to basics' bonding with two of his grandchildren. Kingship had proved slightly more time-consuming than he'd thought and he could do with a break.

George was next. Pearl checked her makeup bag - yes, she'd remembered her purple eyeshadow. Carefully, she applied talcum powder to George's face, then smoothed a fine indigo dust under his lower lashes. She used a large blusher brush to apply touches of dark bronzer around the juvenile hairline and jaw. Finally, she shook a conker brown pigment into his sharp blonde mop and muddled his hair until his parting was a distant memory.

"There. Oliver Twist, if I am not very much mistaken," she said.

George peered into Pearl's compact mirror. "I look - like a normal boy," he breathed. Light shone from his eyes and he looked rapturously at Mollie. "What do you think?"

"Get mum to teach you some cockney rhyming slang and you'll be all set," said Mollie. "You look great - like a proper year five."

Pearl worked her magic on William next, whose defined arms and bald head lent themselves well to a rugged Bruce Willis. A sleeveless vest and jeans were acquired; Kate drooled. Charles was given a false beard and glasses and became instantly anonymous - from King to kindly professor. Camilla was persuaded by Mollie to don a sharp, black wig and grey pencil skirt, giving her the air of a police superintendent. Kate was last. Desperate to surrender her blonde tresses, which were beginning to mess with the overnight hair mask she had applied underneath, she begged for a fringe and to be made over like Audrey Hepburn but Pearl was firm. "You're simply too beautiful already," she said, sorrowfully. "The best thing for it is this."

She produced a warty, angular prosthetic nose. "Left over from last year's *Wicked!* I was thinking it might come in handy for Christmas, as the children are tired of identifying the caretaker as Santa year after year, and this is a much more worthwhile cause."

Kate took the nose and weighed it in her hand. She frowned. "How does it stay on?"

"We'll need ample amounts of medical grade glue on both the nose and the face," said Pearl.

"What if it reacts with my Creme de la Mer?"

"You won't be using that for a while, remember? And a breakout of acne might help your disguise even further, given your usual flawless finish," suggested William, flexing his triceps. "Don't worry, babe. I still would."

Pearl affixed the nose with studied concentration. She added blue eyeshadow and a slick of lipstick from a tube named, 'Candyfloss Shimmer' and held up a small, magnified mirror. The room held its breath.

"Goodness. I look like an eighties film star," Kate smiled. "Jane Fonda, or the lady from Dirty Dancing. Yes. Yes, I like it."

"You look pretty, Mama," said Charlotte. "A bit like Granny Diana."

"So do you, Lottie, in her early nannying days." Kate beamed, admiring her profile. It really wasn't bad at all. In fact, if anything, the proboscis complimented her racehorse sleek. "But remember, beauty is in the breeding."

Satisfied, Pearl packed the makeup away. Tess and Mollie stood up.

Mollie said: "Mum and I have some instructions to read out now. Please may you listen."

George perched on the edge of a stool and gazed at her. His heartbeat quickened. He'd learned so much from this girl. He trusted her implicitly. She was a born leader. He didn't know what was going to happen about Louis, but with Mollie at the helm he suspected it would be an eventful ride. It would be nice if she stopped being so horrid to Mama, though.

Tess stood. The kitchen simply wasn't big enough for eleven people and she squeezed past Charles and Camilla to stand near the door. Charlotte and George joined Jack to sit cross-legged on the floor. Tess cleared her throat.

"We will now walk in convoy, in pairs, to Pearl's annexe. If we meet anyone known to us, I'll introduce Kate and William as 'old family friends' who went to school with Dan and are visiting from somewhere up east."

William frowned. "But Dan wears tracksuit bottoms."

Pearl threw him a pair of nylon joggers. "So do you, now."

Tess said: "You all look... a little different now, which is half the battle, but you will also need aliases. I would suggest that first names remain the same, though with tweaks."

As Tess spoke, Mollie passed around a roll of self-adhesive address stickers and six felt pens.

"Please write the following on your label, then stick it to your chest. Charles will be Carl. Camilla will be Mills. William, Liam. Kate, you can be Lizzie - you'll see why 'Catherine' doesn't work shortly. George, we're suggesting 'Gee'. Charlotte, I know you go by 'Lottie' but I think 'Tilly' is best."

The group bent dutifully towards their laps to scribe, apart from Charles, who leaned on William's back and said: "Liam and Carl. Sounds like a real pair of toerags, eh?"

"Your surname is a tricky one," continued Tess. "We need something that identifies you all as being from the same family but is common, not regal and easy to remember. Something inconsequential, discreet."

"Battersby-Jones?" said George. "They're everywhere at Oscar's."

"Nothing double-barrelled - and Gee Jones won't work," said Pearl, firmly. "It will bring more attention your way, not less."

"It should be something that honours Mummy's name," said Charles. "And Daddy's."

"Funny you should say that," said Tess. "Parth and I have come up with an idea we think you might like. Mousor: a combination of Mountbatten and Windsor."

"Cat Mousor," said Kate, pulling a face. "I see what you mean now."

William lifted himself up using the windowsill and took the opportunity to do a couple of low pull-ups. "I like it. Simple but memorable."

Pearl took over. "Glad that's decided. Now, we'd like you to undertake a little exercise. We've provided a potted history on a sheet of rice paper for you to memorise. When you've done this, please pass them back to Rowley to destroy them. Next, pretend you are meeting each other for the first time: how do you introduce yourself? What is your background story? Try to keep the information short, succinct and pleasant. Remember to smile and nod: imagine you are on a tour of Jamaica or at a society wedding. It is virtually the same small talk, only you will be required to speak about yourself a little more than usual."

"Righto," said Charles. "Here I go. The name's Carl. Carl Mousor. Probably the best name in the world."

"Wait," said Mollie, and sorted them into pairs.

William, who had Camilla as a partner, said: "Ah, um, hello. My name is Liam. I am holidaying here in Elderfield with my family." He checked his rice paper. "I am currently between jobs, as my brother and I started to work in the family business together, but things didn't work out..." He broke off. "I say, isn't that rather close to the bone?"

Rowley raised his head at the mention of 'bone' and snapped vaguely at William's hand. To his surprise, his mouth came away with a crackly piece of something edible. Lovely, he thought. These people can stay, even if they do speak nonsense.

After half an hour, the practice introductions were complete. Tess led the charge, including Dan who declared he needed a work break, out of the front door and along the pavement towards The Nook. Kate found herself craving a pair of sturdy Berghaus walking shoes or, at the very least, a box-fresh pair of Vega trainers. Instead, Pearl had furnished her with a chunky pair of plastic shoes from what looked like a fancy dress shop.

"Do you like the Crocs?" Pearl's eyes twinkled at Kate. "They're waterproof and genuine - vintage, if you like. I thought they would go wit' yo' flares."

"Yes, fantastic. I'm sure I can make it work." Kate smiled bravely. Who was this woman? She'd encountered similar personalities before; women and men who were overflowing with positivity and eccentric style, but only backstage at the BAFTAs.

Headway was glacial, as Mollie stopped at intervals, providing a running commentary on local landmarks.

"That's the corner shop, where they have cameras, so make sure your disguises are immaculate if you go in."

"Can one buy magazines? I shall miss my *Country Life*," said Camilla, smoothing her bob.

"There's plenty of nice walks around Elderfield," said Dan, hoping the joke would land, but Camilla remained pensive. As the group reached the corner of the pavement before The Nook, Charlotte stubbed her toe on the curb and yelled: "Ouch, Mama!"

"Did we pack the magic spider blanket?" asked Kate.

"No," William grimaced. "There wasn't room in the holdall. Never mind. I'm sure there are plenty of spiders around here. Nanny can find some and make another... " he faltered, remembering that, having been given six weeks off, Nanny was in the air on her way to see family in Spain.

Kate gritted her teeth. Perhaps it was time, now, for Lottie to face up to the challenges of daily life without the intervention afforded to her by privilege.

"Don' worry, I' got plasters an' Germolene at The Nook," said Pearl. "We nearly there."

William gave Charlotte a piggy-back, trying to ignore the trickle of blood that flowed from her foot, smearing his sweat-pants. It reminded him of the days flying the air ambulance. There were a few casualties to witness back then: a spot of his daughter's blood shouldn't faze him. And yet...

"Man down!" shouted Charles, as William hit the pavement.

Mollie was first to his side, with Kate taking William's wrist and holding it to her ear.

"There's a pulse," said Kate, with relief.

"Of course there's a pulse, he's only fainted," said Pearl, over Charlotte's cries. The noise prompted doors to open and, from number nine, JoJo Bindman came hurrying out, wiping her hands on a tea towel.

"Tess! Dan! Is everything ok? I was just recording one of my online exercise classes and I heard a scream... " JoJo took in the scene: a tall man lying sprawled on the pavement with a crying young girl, surrounded by a group of people looking sheepish. Charlotte, who had met concrete tailbone-first, continued to wail softly.

"Everything's fine," said Pearl, with enviable poise. "This is a friend of the Oates' - Liam - down for a few weeks visiting. He doesn't like the sight of blood. It's perfectly alright; it happens all the time at school, doesn't it Jack?"

Jack nodded, the memory of waking up face-down in the sandpit after scratching an elbow scab still front of mind.

"Would a glass of water help?" JoJo asked.

"That's so kind of you. I am a little parched," said Charles. Who was this vision in Lycra leggings and a crop top? He felt like taking a little walk with her around the block. "Perhaps you could show me around your neighbourhood while - ah - Liam is seen to?"

Tess felt duty-bound to intervene. "JoJo - thank you so much, but I think we have all this in hand." She took a deep breath. This was it: there was no going back now.

"These are Dan's old friends, the Mousors. They're down from, ah..." her mind blanked. What was in the West? " ... Wales." She kicked herself and felt Mollie's hand-squeeze, but it was too late to retract. "They'll be staying in The Nook for a few weeks." She introduced them one by one. Thankfully, only George's poker face wobbled, when Mollie snorted at Tess saying, "Gee."

"Pleased to meet you," said JoJo. "I'm happy to help with anything required. If you fancy joining me for some exercise while you're here, just let me know."

Camilla took Charles' arm before he could reply. Kate and Dan stood either side of William and took an arm each. Mollie took George's arm and Tess stood at the back of the group with Rowley, thinking: *What the hell have we done?*

Kate saw The Nook first. She had been keeping her eyes peeled for a quaint, slate-grey or olive-green painted front door, with perhaps a bay tree either side and a cedar slatted front. Rather like Nanny's annex at Anmer. If they were lucky, there might be fresh orange juice in glass bottles, jute flooring and a rope swing with a wooden seat in the back garden for the children to play on. She swallowed the hard lump in her throat. Louis loved swinging. At Anmer, and now in Windsor, he would shimmy up tree trunks in seconds with a length of hemp between his teeth, tie it tightly around a branch with a knot taught to him by sailing legend Ben Ainslie and create a rope ladder for his siblings to enjoy.

"Here we are," said Pearl, stopping in front of a garage.

"Are we getting in another car?" asked Kate.

"No - this is The Nook." Pearl produced a bunch of keys and opened a small door on the right. A flight of steps leading took the group immediately up to the accommodation level.

William gave a low whistle as he surveyed the room. The wooden floor was patterned with dark red paint splatters, criss-crossed here and there with deep gouges. The double bed, just visible through a large, white painted beam, was covered in a clean patchwork quilt, the material a bright mix of polka dots and stripes. On the left wall stood a miniscule table with a toaster, kettle and IKEA grey mugs. A small hob, microwave and fridge clustered together near the sink. The scent of honeysuckle and roses drifted in through the open window over the loo, which was cordoned off by a low, plaster wall. Taking three steps forwards revealed two single beds and a sofa bed at the end of the room. On the sofa bed sat Tabitha, gnawing on a shoe-shaped chew.

"Tab!!" George hurled himself onto the bed. Tabitha let out a bark and ran to Kate for reassurance.

Kate felt water prickling her eyes for the second time that morning. "My fur baby." She knelt and gathered Tabitha in her arms, untangling a blonde nylon tendril gently from her collar. Catching Pearl's eye, she said: "Thank you."

"As long as she don't do her business inside and you clear up before you go," said Pearl.

"Of course," said Kate. "Anastasia can find a vacuum cleaner and... oh." She stopped, remembering this duty was no longer outsourceable and Anastasia was not there. "Of course. We'll manage."

Tess wondered how long she might reasonably stay before she could make a polite departure. She wondered, too, about Anastasia. What had happened to her? She felt exhausted. It was almost lunch time on the first day of half-term and she hadn't even thought about a food shop. She began to make her excuses but William stopped her.

"Could I come with you to the supermarket? We have a weekly food budget to stick to and I could, ah, use your help to make sure we get, ah, value for money."

Tess cringed but relented. Kate added, "*Liam*, darling, why don't I go? You're probably still feeling light-headed. I'm sure I can blend in - and besides, I need to give walking in these, er, Crocs a little more practice."

"I'll come, too," said Camilla. "It'll be a jolly good laugh."

That settled, Tess led the women back to her house to collect some bags for life.

21

CHAPTER TWENTY

Sunday 28 May 2023, Spitting Water alpaca swimming school – location classified.

Louis was surrounded. He picked up a stick from the ground and thrust it into a large, muddy puddle, then crouched down, studying the water without moving a muscle. Seven long necks bent forward. Suddenly, Louis brought the stick out with a flourish, waved it at the soft, inquisitive noses and yelled: "Go away from me, poos!" He turned and ran up the hill, delightedly, chased by seven delighted alpacas, all enjoying the novelty of an afternoon game.

As he neared the top, Louis's pace slowed. Looking back, he could see a winding country road, lined with terraced houses and cars parked like Lego bricks. The gate at the bottom of the field was padlocked, with barbed wire running along either side and above. Louis tried not to look at this; tried not to think of the night he had arrived with Trevor and Orange, in the pitch black with owls hooting overhead. As they had driven through the gate, he had told Trevor the joke his mother loved:

"What does a clever owl say? To whom!"

Trevor hadn't laughed, just asked Louis to explain it, which he had been unable to do. Orange had made things better, by licking Louis on the face as he slept in the passenger seat of the pick-up truck. Louis had drifted off, listening to the sounds of the wheels moving slowly uphill and seven alpacas urinating, and woken to find himself wet.

There was little sympathy to be had from Trevor, who had stood Louis under a cold tap outside, passed him a bar of soap and a crusty towel and showed him into a downstairs room of a small, cold farm house, with a single bed and a table with a bowl.

"This'll be your 'ole for the next few weeks," he barked.

Louis wished he had said more in his secret note to the family. He had no doubt Charlotte and George would work out the lemon juice trick, read it and come and find him soon. But still, he wished he had made it sound as if he was having just an average time, instead of a lovely one. He should have put, 'P.S my cold is worse' or something similar, to convey the message of discomfort. Oh well, he thought. I'll tell them when I see them. He sat down on the warm grass and hugged his knees to his chest with anticipation: Trevor had told him that tonight would be the night he could contact Mama and Pops.

Orange lumbered up, her eyes fringed with lashes like spiders' legs. Louis reached up to stroke her bristly flank.

"Hello, Orange. Would you like to come home and meet my family? We've got a dog called Tabitha but she's not bitey. We used to have chickens but I let them all out and one got ..." his voice died. "I was a naughty boy. Mama and Pops won't buy George another Bantam, and I thought by coming with you and Trevor to your farm, I could get one. But you don't have chickens here."

Plops of water started to fall on Louis's Amaia Kids shorts, which he had worn solidly for two days. Looking up, raindrops fell into his eyes, mingling with tears. He felt the rasp of Orange's tongue across his forehead and cheered up slightly.

"Decent weather for swimming!" came a loud voice from behind him.

Trevor Malpas marched towards Louis, who scrambled to his feet. A leather gilet hung loosely about his shoulders and his wild, white hair blew like dandelion seeds in the wind around his head. He walked with purpose and direction.

"Are you ready for your first lesson?" he boomed.

"B... but it's nearly time for FaceTime. You promised!" said Louis.

"Ah, yes. I know I said we'd see your family on video tonight but when you're dealing with nature, you have to seize the day. I will give you some paper and a pen and you can write them a little note tonight."

Rage stirred within Louis's rib cage. He gripped his stick firmly, then thrust it forwards, into Trevor's face. It stopped, inches away from Trevor's upper lip: Orange gazed serenely ahead, tail flicking, the stick at her feet.

"They don't usually do that," said Trevor, with a nod of approval. "She must like you a lot to take a stick from your hands. That'll be useful, that will, when the swimming lessons start. Come on," he handed Louis a pair of small, shiny briefs, "I picked these up this morning. No time like the present."

Together, they made their way down the other side of the hill, followed by a troupe of alpacas, marching like storm troopers behind them. Louis had seen the long, low, wooden hut from the farmhouse window the previous night and wondered what it was. Now, as they approached, the wet-dog smell of stagnant water grew closer. Louis thought about the swimming pools he had known: like George and Charlotte, he had learned to swim in Bucks P's pool - a blissful experience with a near-amniotic ambience. The pool at Anmer was great fun, of course, as was the one at Windsor, and he had visited the oases of friends frequently enough for some of them to keep spare pairs of his favourite elephant trunks to hand. He stopped daydreaming as he realised Trevor was talking.

"... so you see, they really need our help."

"Who do?"

Trevor snarled. "Have you been listening to a word I've said?"

"Not really."

Trevor stopped. "Then listen now, and listen well. Climate change: it's real. Your Da thinks he's changing the world with speeches and sustainability units and Briti-shot awards and that. He's not looking at the big picture in a modern way. The future, as anyone with their eyes open can see, is seaweed farming."

Louis's eyes widened. "Seaweed doesn't grow on farms."

"Oh, yes it does. Seaweed is healthy and nutritious and, above all, the untapped resource the Earth needs as it warms up," said Trevor, narrowing his eyes as the alpacas closed in, forming a ring around them both. They were outside the front door of the wooden hut now and Louis could practically taste the metallic tang of the water that lay within.

"In Asia and other places, for example, Zanzibar, Africa, seaweed farming is a lifeline for the poor. Its popularity in the UK is rising rapidly, too. But seaweed farming, which has traditionally taken place in shallow waters, is quickly declining owing to climate change, over-utilisation of shallow water,

Covid-19 and price. Deep water farming is viable, but this silver lining dulls when you consider the huge problem that is that the farmers are unable to swim. In African regions, it tends to be women who cannot swim, nor own boats. This is a tragedy!" Trevor hit the ground with Louis' stick, scattering the alpacas. "But, luckily, we have the means to help."

"With alpacas?"

Trevor nodded, opened the door to the hut and pushed Louis under his arm, towards another door which led to a large, deep pool. The alpacas lined up and passed through after him.

Louis dipped a finger in the water and sucked, just like Nanny told him not to. "Isn't this freshwater?"

"Clever boy. It is. We're a little too far from the sea to practise off the beach but my plan is to take the herd there for a test run, once they've learned the basics."

"Why alpacas?"

"They're very at home in hostile environments and they look sweet."

"Why do you need me?" sniffed Louis.

"Same reasons."

Louis's chin wobbled.

"Seriously. That's the genius of it. You'll be the face of Spitting Water. A cheeky, adorable prince, loved by the world and its cousin. We'll start in Asia, then wheel it out in other countries, ending with the UK. You can swim, can't you?"

"I just passed stage three."

"Of course you did," smiled Trevor, thinly. "I could have guessed. Now, go in there," he nodded towards a wooden cubicle door, "and get changed. I'll meet you here in two minutes."

Louis did as he was told. Climbing down the steps into the

lukewarm, green water felt soothing, like being tucked into bed by Mama. He surrendered to the silky embrace and doggy paddled a few strokes to the sloped shallow end.

The alpacas took tentative steps into the first few centimetres of water. A couple of them lay back on their hind legs before tipping over onto their knees, bowing and cracking like rusty see-saws.

"Take one by the lead," urged Trevor, and Louis reached out to grab a black strap dangling from Orange's throat. "Steer it into the deeper water."

Louis walked slowly into the middle of the pool, followed by Orange. "There's a good girl," he crooned. "Just a little bit further."

When the water was up to Orange's chest, Louis began to swim. To his amazement, the alpaca lifted its own breast and paddled alongside him, eyes bulging placidly, head bobbing like a tortoise.

"This is like swimming with dolphins from Grandpa Wales's islands!" yelled Louis. "I love it!"

"I'm glad you're having fun," beamed Trevor from his side of the pool. "We've only just started, though. Next: the dive."

22

CHAPTER TWENTY-ONE

Sunday 28 May 2023, Elderfield, West Sussex.

William was eyeing the pedal bin in the kitchen area when Kate's phone rang. The contents of the bin were already overflowing after a visit to Tesco and a lunch call to 'Just Eat', despite the family spending less than a day at The Nook. But how did one empty it? Tapping the question into Google, Kate's phone ringing faded into the background as he read an article in *Good Housekeeping* titled: *How to clean your bin.* He pored over the tips: line the caddy with newspaper; don't over-fill the bin bag or it will split and make the job twice as messy. His blood tingled. Of course: he could see the logic of both pieces of advice, as clear as day. This was better than a boogie to Faithless, he thought. This information was gold dust!

Bed springs creaked from the main sleeping area and Kate came into the kitchen after an afternoon nap, accompanied by George and Charlotte, rubbing their eyes. She looked at the bin and thought, *my God, that bag is hideously full*, then answered the phone.

"Tess, hello. Tonight? Oh, I'm not sure we can. What if Trevor calls? … Oh, really?"

"What?" mouthed William.

"Thanks, Tess. Six-thirty, then. We… we'll see you there." said Kate and hung up.

"The Oates have invited us to the pub up the road. It's an early nineties disco night. Apparently, it's a regular Sunday affair and Dan is doing stand-up comedy, too. I've nothing to wear, of course, but it might be fun to get out and have a change of scenery."

William had once enjoyed a whole weekend of fame at Eton when he had suggested, in an address to the elite group of prefects, that a small fine be introduced for boys who refused to dance to Spiller's *Groovejet*; possibly the greatest UK clubbing hit of all time. His heart beat faster as he remembered having the opportunity to demonstrate the right way to nod one's head along to the classic.

"Absolutely. What time are we being picked up?"

"We can walk it," said Kate, who had no idea exactly how far it was. "They do the open mic first, and Tess says that if we like, we can buy some…" she whispered, "chips."

The Swan had a mixed reputation. It stood at the end of Love Lane, a lone, detached, dirty white building, looming over the terraced houses like a battered moth among caterpillars. Popular with an older crowd, the pub provided a haven from domestic life; somewhere to kill an hour or two in the week, while someone else did supper, bath and bedtime. The bar staff were teenage, the beer was cheap, the gin choice was limited. It had a regular open mic night. Tess gave it a five out of ten. Dan gave it eleven.

Knuckles rapped at the door and William gasped.

"Did we leave the bottom door unlocked?"

Kate looked blank. She hadn't locked her own door for over a decade. Camilla and Charles came into the kitchen area. Camilla took off her coat and lay it carelessly on the countertop, revealing a black apron with 'Old Lives Matter' emblazoned across the chest.

"I've come to help with the children this evening," she announced. "I'm sure they would like some time with me, wouldn't you, lovelies? I could make you some supper. Read you a story?"

"Can it be, *Treasure Island?*" asked Charlotte. "By Robert Louis Stevenson?"

"How's the Shepherd's Hut?" asked Kate hurriedly, before the tears started to escape again at the mention of Louis. Parth had texted her to say they were tracking Trevor's movements carefully, using drones and long-distance thermography, but Louis's thermal image seemed to be doing lengths of a swimming pool and so it was unlikely there would be a call this evening.

Charles looked out of the window and saw the hunched, wooden structure. It was painted sky blue, with steep, wooden steps and looked consummately charming from the outside. Inside, it rattled and rocked and had little fluffy squirrels hanging from the ceiling. He hated it.

"It's fine," said Camilla. "The curtains have seen better days and I'm going to re-do the seat padding and take out the side units to make more storage space with shelving, but the period features are stunning. I feel quite at home."

"Have you checked with Pearl that it's ok to make changes?" asked Kate.

"Oh, yes. She and I are getting along famously," said Camilla.

Charles looked as if he was about to say something, but George interrupted: "Mama and Pops are going to the pub."

"Well, ah, only if it's ok with you," William said.

"Yes, of course it's ok. Great plan! I'd love a pint," said Charles, thinking the opposite. He'd prefer a stiff whiskey and his mind was on the untidy hedge at the bottom of Pearl's garden. It could do with a trim. If only he had his tools with him, but they were locked away in Windsor.

"Ah, that's not quite what I meant ..." said William.

Camilla said: "Go, Carl. See how their pork scratchings compare to mine."

In the sleeping area, the pile of clothes on the double bed grew. Kate discarded a sequin miniskirt, a chiffon blouse, a rara skirt and a pair of leggings. What was Pearl thinking? A convincing disguise was all very well, but was it necessary to compromise completely on taste? She had just had her most stylish year yet: she really couldn't be caught making faux pas now. She settled on stone-washed jeans and a V-necked frilly blouse. Her nose itched: she had taken it off for her nap and re-affixing it had been trickier than expected. Looking in the tiny mirror above the sink, she knew it wasn't quite right, but the glass was smeared across the middle, so it was hard to tell exactly how wonky it was. Never mind, she thought, pubs are dark, and a slightly off-centre nose would throw people even further off the scent. Smiling at the witticism, she collected a small, pleather bag from the sofa, scooped her arm around William's back, shouted 'goodbye' to the children and left.

Out on the pavement, there was a loud yell. Kate stopped suddenly. William swore.

"It's just some drunken youths," he said. "Don't be frightened."

"Come out from behind that dustbin then," said Kate, irritably.

William eased his way out from behind the galvanised steel wheelie bin. It stank. Newspaper liners would be advisable, he thought.

As the pair continued their journey towards The Swan, Kate hummed *Jerusalem* to raise her spirits. It was a revelation to have no bodyguards walking a few paces in front: she felt liberated, yet vulnerable: like a newly hatched fledgling. She gripped William's hand. Walking in Crocs was tiring. The nap had helped, but the mattress lacked memory foam and she had twisted and turned for ages before drifting off. The fairy tale, *The Princess and the Pea* had been one of her favourites growing up. Perhaps it was just that Pearl had left a dried legume in the bed by mistake. She cheered up: that must be it – no one would allow a bed to be so uncomfortable otherwise. She and Charlotte could have fun in the morning seeing who could feel the lump better.

William followed the small crowd of middle-aged people crossing the road in front of the pub. Some were wearing the same brand of tracksuit bottoms as him and several of the men sported hooded tops. William had a couple of these: one had been a present from President Obama with the slogan, 'Change we can believe in', the other a hand-me-down from his uncle Andrew. He hadn't packed them, of course, but he wondered now if that had been a mistake.

From inside the pub, the lilting melody of Coldplay's 'Sky Full of Stars' floated into the dusk. William's pulse quickened. If there was an opportunity for karaoke, he was up for it. Charles, a few steps behind as he had stopped to examine a broken fence panel which looked as if it had been hit by a moving vehicle, said: "I think I might be able to make myself quite useful around here."

Kate led the way into the pub. The smell of fried food and Issey Miyake hit her prosthetic nostrils as she approached the bar. Next to her stood a man with a honey-coloured arm and a near-empty pint glass of something pale resting on a beer towel in front of him. His hair rivalled her own, natural mane. It cascaded down his back in thick, luxuriant ripples, the colour of a rich chilli con carne. As he moved to make room for Kate's elbow, he turned and smiled at her vaguely.

"Sorry, love. Can you squeeze in?"

"Oh yes, thank you. Plenty of room," Kate said.

She roved the seating area behind her with her eyes and found William, Tess and Charles settling into a corner table. She mimed tipping a glass into her mouth and the word, 'drink?' William gave a thumbs-up, then held up two fingers and mouthed, 'Veuve.'

"Two bottles of Veuve Clicquot, please," said Kate to the bartender, a dour looking woman with blue hair and a tattoo of a small bird on her throat.

"You what?"

"It's, um, champagne," said Kate. "Do you have it?"

The bartender, whose name was Sally Haggan and who had never tasted Champagne, regarded her coolly. "We did have a bottle of champers once," she said. "But it was sold to Prince William when 'e came in 'ere at Christmas looking for another second 'ome."

Kate went cold. Sally made a noise between a snort and a small explosion.

"Only jokin'! Eh, Ted, only jokin', weren't I? Can you imagine! The Royals in 'ere?! 'They're a bit busy for that, I reckon. 'Specially as the little one's gone missing, I 'ere, wha's 'is name, Louis? Cava ok?" Standing on the toes of her Doc Martens, she reached to the top shelf and removed two dusty bottles of something dark green. She checked the label and said: "'s not cold, but it's 15% – more than the posh bubbles, I'll bet."

"Thank you," said Kate, quietly, trying to quell the hammering inside her chest. "I like your tattoo, by the way. The way the bird swoops across your clavicle... it's very romantic. Rather like a Manet. My father-in-law has several ... I mean, it's very artistic."

Sally's cheeks puffed with surprised pride. "It's a swallow, to remind me and everyone in 'ere how short life is. It's inspired by me grandma. She choked to death on a peanut five years ago."

Kate narrowed her eyes. Was this lady messing with her? The man turned twenty degrees and appraised her with an amused smile.

"Don't mind Sally," he chuckled, and stuck out a hand. "JD."

Kate offered her own. "Pleased to meet you. I'm Lizzie Mousor." The words felt alien in her mouth, like a dentist's X-ray contraction or the first time she said, "It's good news: I'm pregnant," in 2012 to William. If only she had tested both lines out in the mirror first, in each instance she might have felt less of a fraud.

"Pleased to meet you. You're not local, are you?"

Kate shook her head. "We're from up east. My husband and I, and my father-in-law – we're visiting the Oates."

"You're here to watch Dan? He's great, really talented, and always has the crowd in stitches. How long are you staying in Elderfield?"

Kate found the conversation increasingly difficult. She was used to asking the questions, used to smiling and nodding and holding the babies and pulling the pints. JD's intense gaze was disconcertingly critical. Squinting, she said something she had often dreamed of asking strangers: "Would you mind not looking at me quite so closely? It's making me feel rather uncomfortable."

JD's shoulders scrunched together in a shrug, like two small mountains. He had the grace to look faintly embarrassed but his expression was predominantly one of concern.

"I'm sorry. It's just, I mean ... is there something wrong with your nose? It looks, well, a bit *delicate*."

With a tiny squeal, Kate left the bottles of Cava on the bar and ran in the direction of the Ladies. Safely inside a cubicle, she locked the door, tried to block from her mind the almost certain presence of foreign bodies and reached into her bag for hand sanitiser and a pocket mirror. The reflection was distressing. Hanging by a thread, the top of the nose's triangular apex was threatening to break ranks with her face. A few seconds later, she realised with a shudder, and the nose would have dropped off entirely.

The main door opened and Kate heard Tess call in a low voice, "Um. Lizzie? Are you here?"

Kate eased herself out and stood, ashamed and furious, in the doorway.

"I can't go back out like this! What the hell am I doing? This is utterly ridiculous."

Tess steered Kate back inside the cubicle and shut the door. Kate's hands trembled as they tried to hold the nose in place.

"Oh dear." Tess tried to stifle a smile. "May I ..?" Producing a tube of medical glue, Tess swiftly affixed the nose back in place. She wiped Kate's eyes, then a droplet of something that may have been glue or mucus from her nose with a sheet of hand towel.

"Don't worry. It'll take a bit of time to get used to. You're doing brilliantly. No harm done. Was that JD you were talking to? He's a bit of a loose cannon, I'd watch him."

"He seemed nice. He warned me about my nose, I just hope he didn't suspect anything."

"He's usually a few sheets to the wind, and tonight's no exception," said Tess. "He won't remember. Come on, the drinks can wait. Dan's about to go on."

Joining Tess and Charles made Kate feel a little better. She gave JD a small wave and made an 'ok' sign to William, then settled into the overstuffed banquet, brushing a crisp off the seat first and trying not to think of the ketchup and mayonnaise grease stains that lay under her backside. At least, she hoped they were ketchup and mayonnaise.

The lights dimmed and the low roar of the pub settled down to a quiet murmur. Sally stepped up to the dusty stage and grabbed the microphone in one hand and the stand in another.

"It's great to see you all again. Wishing those of you without kids a very happy half term, and those of you with them the best of luck." She waited while the smattering of applause died away. "We have a real treat for you tonight, before we get stuck into our nineties classics. Starting with our very own ... Dan Oates. Ladies and gentleman, please welcome Dan to the stage!"

From behind a curtain, Dan's head appeared, followed by a black t-shirt and the mustard suit Tess recognised from the Briti-shots. He must have had it secretly dry-cleaned, she thought, fondly. He sprinted on, thanked Sally and launched straight in.

"Welcome, welcome one and all. Thank you. Being married with kids, I've got a lot of time on my hands. So I like to fill those hands with ..." There was a quiet titter from the audience, "... reading books in bed."

"What bollocks," shouted Arran Bindman, from the bar. Kate craned her neck to see who had the audacity to interrupt with such vulgar language and caught JD's eye. She blushed, though she would not have been able to explain why. William, puzzled by the lack of drinks, got up and made his way to the bar. "Your bedside table's never seen a book!"

"Oi, big nose!"

Kate, William and Charles all looked fearfully over their shoulders, exhaling with relief as they realised the comment was directed by Dan towards Arran.

"Mind your own business, and keep out of my bedroom!" shouted Dan, cheerfully. "As I was saying, I like to read. I've just finished this book: *The History of Glue*. I couldn't put it down."

The crowd groaned. William returned with drinks, putting a glass with ice, lemon and gin and a bottle of Slimline tonic on the table. Kate's smile flickered and died as Tess slid a hand over where the sapphire and diamond engagement ring should be. Parth had promised it would be stored safely with her Alessandra Richs. At Tess's suggestion, she had wrapped a hair band around her ring finger instead, and she twanged it now, trying not to think of Louis taking a ukulele lesson, which he would have done today.

"Thank you," she whispered to Tess, nodding towards the elastic. "It is doing something to help calm the anxiety."

Dan's act continued. JD slid over to stand next to Kate and

William, making Kate's hair band flicking speed up until she could feel a bruise starting to form.

"What do you think?" he asked, nodding towards the stage.

"Yes, yes. He's really much better than I expected," said William, rising to shake JD's hand.

"Aren't you an old friend of his?"

"Ah, yes, but we haven't seen each other for quite some time," said William, trying to remember how people stood in pubs. He settled on clasping hands over his groin, hoping it looked natural.

"Sorry about back there," said JD to Kate. "I must've had a bit too much to drink, or it was the light, or something - I hope you'll accept my apology."

Kate bestowed the smile reserved for small children holding bouquets. "Not at all, don't mention it," she said; the reply she often gave when she didn't, in fact, accept an apology. So far, not even the *Telegraph* had noticed.

Dan said: "I went into a bookshop to get another book; I asked if they had any on turtles. The shopkeeper said, 'Hardbacks?' and I said, 'Yes, and they have strong flippers, too."

"Are all these jokes book-related?" asked Charles.

Tess shook her head. "He'll move onto the recession soon."

"Ah, yes," said Charles, looking into his pint to hide his blank expression. He'd always got recession and depression confused; had never been quite able to work out which meant what. Luckily, neither had affected him in life so far.

William said: "My hairline is like the recession: receding. Oh, no. I mean ...my hairline is like the economy: recession."

Kate gave a weak smile. "Very good, Liam."

Charles, who had enjoyed the joke very much, said meaningfully: "You should get up there, too, Liam. You're a natural."

JD looked at William with interest. "You know, you'd suit being completely bald," he said. "I'm a hairdresser, by the way. I'd be happy to give you a quick shave while you're here?"

Kate's ears pricked up. She wondered if JD stocked the Argan oil conditioner she'd just started using on Princess Beatrice's recommendation. It might work wonders on the wig. The brand used kernels from a tiny farm in Morocco but it was worth asking. But her mouth curled as she remembered her beauty budget.

Dan's set finished to loud clapping. He made his way through the crowd and greeted Tess with a kiss, pausing to take off his jacket and hang it on a nearby coat stand with infinite care. He was ecstatic. It was an easy crowd, but it had gone incredibly well. He caught William's eye and glanced at Charles. The two future kings of England nodded approval and raised their glasses slightly. Dan felt dizzy with joy. He could now die happy.

Sally returned to the stage and thanked Dan. "Without further ado, let's hear some nineties dance anthems, shall we? Starting with a lovely warm-up classic, 'Everything But the Girl' and their hit, *Missing*."

As the chords started, Kate felt her throat closing again and a single tear ran down her cheek.

Could you be dead? You always were two steps ahead...

And I miss you, like the deserts miss the rain, warbled Tracey Thorn.

Could Louis be dead? He was always at least two steps ahead of everyone, often eight or nine. Oh Louis, where are you? What are you doing? Are you warm? Kate tried to take comfort from the recollection that alpacas were friendly and curious by nature and often preferred children to adults. Perhaps Louis was cuddled up with Orange right now. She hoped so.

"Shall we hit the floor, Lizzie?" The light in William's eyes was sweet, Kate thought, as she took his hand. The song faded, replaced with Ace of Base's *It's a Beautiful Life*. Kate flicked the hair band on her finger one last time and let her Crocs make some shapes.

23

CHAPTER TWENTY-TWO

Monday 29 May 2023, Elderfield, West Sussex.

Usually, Tess took the children to the library on the first Monday of school holidays but, as they were about to leave the house with - for once - every single overdue book in a bulging Tesco bag, Tess remembered that it was a Bank Holiday just as the doorbell rang.

It was Anastasia. She looked grey but serene. Tess took a deep breath, let it out slowly, told the children to play Minecraft for an hour and showed Anastasia in.

"I've resigned," said Anastasia, but she didn't seem upset. "I couldn't prove I didn't neglect Louis, and the writing was on the wall, but then again, Nanny didn't get a sick note for her tummy bug either. I've decided to go abroad for a while. There are lots of places that will appreciate someone with my level of experience. Anyway, I just wanted to say 'thank you' for sticking up for me at the Briti-shots. I won't say 'goodbye' to their Graces, but please give them my best. And these to the children." She handed Tess a multipack of KitKats with a smile.

Tess saw Anastasia out of the house and watched as she disappeared around the corner. She thought, there goes a girl with her head screwed on and a bright future. Rather like a light bulb.

Pleased with the analogy, she went back inside and turned on Radio Four. According to Woman's Hour, first-time shoplifting was on the rise. The cost-of-living crisis meant that even low-value items were being pilfered, often by women her age who – a year ago – wouldn't have taken a free wooden fork from a fish and chip shop.

Tess listened as she made a cup of tea.

"Theft, in any measure, is not something that can be condoned," said the Chief of Police.

"But people are stealing to eat," said Emma Barnett. "Inflation is at 10%. Doesn't that show that policy needs to change?"

Tess shifted uneasily on the kitchen bench. She glanced at the KitKats, knowing that even if she were offered one, she would refuse. Memories swirled and crystallised. "The best things in life are free," had been her plucky response to the wardrobe-shaped security guard who loped out of the Tottenham Court Road Tesco in the freezing fog and chaperoned her back inside. He'd led the way, wordlessly, to an interview room next to the charity bookcase. She remembered thinking she might take *The Great Escape* home if she left without arrest.

'Why these items?' the manager had growled.

Tess had eyed the pot of low-fat cheese and head of broccoli, nestled at the bottom of the plastic bag. She'd hung her head and muttered, "I just wanted to see if I could get away with it," which was, at least, partly true.

I'm in the grip of an eating disorder, which has warped my sense of right and wrong, would have been a more honest response.

Dan appeared in the doorway, dangling a new trainer by its laces. "I've only had these three days," he said. "Why is Rowley such a bandit?"

"He likes your smell," said Tess, rescuing the other trainer from under the sofa.

Dan pulled Tess towards him. "Is he the only one?"

The feelings of shame faded and the Tesco manager's voice grew fainter, overpowered by Dan's aftershave. Was it so terrible that she'd never told him? Would Mollie and Jack inherit her thieving ways? Tess drained her tea, put down the mug and solidified into the present.

"Are the children Minecrafting?"

Tess nodded.

"Don't forget we've got counselling up at the allotment this afternoon," she said, after they disentangled a while later. Relations with Dan had improved dramatically since his gig last night. They'd managed sex after the pub for the first time in several weeks and morning relations, albeit quiet and fast like today, hadn't happened for at least six months.

Dan's expression lost its shine. "Do I have to come?"

"It's meant to be about everyone's dynamics: not just the - er - Mousors' relationship with us, but you and me as a couple and, um, Liam and Lizzie, too."

"Why do Charles and Camilla get to skive?"

"Carl and Mills are fixing up the Shepherd's Hut," said Tess firmly. "They're doing Pearl a huge favour. Charles is making new seating, Camilla's taken on the soft furnishings and I think they're hatching a plan to get the electrics sorted."

Dan grunted. He didn't see the point of talking to a complete stranger about their private lives. And why did it have to happen at the allotment?

Mention of the Oates' small patch of vegetable garden was always a sore spot for Dan. He had taken on the lease as a birthday present for Tess a year ago, with every intention of rearing a handsome crop of super foods by this summer. It was looking as if they would be lucky to harvest a few strawberries and a handful of mint, as there simply hadn't been enough time to devote to the myriad tasks required of a gardener, but at least they'd managed to salvage an old trampoline from the dump a few months ago, so Mollie and Jack had somewhere to jump.

"The allotment is safe from earwiggers," said Tess, as if reading Dan's mind. "If not earwigs."

Kate and William were waiting outside The Nook. Kate wore a pair of dungarees and William a boiler suit given to him by Pearl.

"Jacob used to wear it. It suits you," Pearl had said. "He would be so proud to know it was being worn by a future king."

William's stomach flipped. It had been a big night at The Swan; he hadn't enjoyed himself so much since the days of Bodo's Schloss. The nineties disco had been a revelation: he had been able to perform the running man, electric slide and Macarena in public, in blissful anonymity. Never mind that he had an absolutely lethal hangover this morning; it had helped take his mind away from Louis for a few short hours, at least.

It was a ten-minute drive to the allotment. The Oates' Passat eased up the short slope to the padlocked gate where Dan had to look up the code. As they drove through the plots of dense, green potato leaves and chicken wire fruit nets, garden sheds puncturing the landscape, William said: "this reminds me slightly of home." He looked at Kate for a flicker of understanding, but she kept her eyes fixed on the broken mobile phone holder in front of her. Rose buds slicked the side of the car like lipsticks as it moved slowly along the dirt track. Early leeks sprouted like peacock crest feathers and a fine mist of hose water from earnest allotmenteers painted the air with an iridescent sheen.

Number sixty-nine stood defiantly bare, three of its beds overtaken by mare's tail and dandelions, the other three hosting plants in various levels and states of decline. The plot was surrounded by verdant raspberry bushes on one side and young lettuces like lime-coloured mop-headed puppies on the other. At the far end, nestled against an oak tree and a barbed wire fence that backed on to the main railway line, stood the shed.

"Want to see inside?" Dan asked. He unlocked another padlock, this time with a key, and reached into the gloom to turn the light on.

Unlike the shed at Buckingham Palace, Dan's was dull and dark. In just a few months, he had managed to fill most of the available space with offcuts of wood and old planks from allotment neighbours which were destined, he assured Tess, to become borders for raised beds. Spiders hung from the damp corners and the air was pungent with wood stain. A warped, plastic window which had once been clear but was now as opaque as a muddy puddle, let a cloudy light water the interior.

"Why are we *here*?" William said, wrinkling his nose.

"Jillian likes to meet somewhere earthy," said Kate. "Apparently, if you can breathe in soil and the smell of the planet, it helps emotions come to the surface."

Kate was feeling low. She'd slept badly, the prosthetic nose on the bedside table glowing faintly in the streetlight's diluted orange glare as she watched the seconds tick by on The Nook's alarm clock. Between two and four in the morning, she'd dreamt of being able to hug Louis, only to wake with the quilt between her knees and William's back alarmingly close to her. JD had also featured in her dreams, though she didn't want to linger on the images she'd had of his luscious hair becoming entangled in her own. She longed for the comfort of the Super King or Queen sheds or even simply her four-poster at home.

Her phone rang with a FaceTime alert. For a second, she believed it could be Louis and hurried to answer, before realising it was Jillian Cope.

Back in the early 1980s, Camilla had needed a friend. Events had become rather overwhelming for her at the time, what with one thing and another, and an old school friend of hers had come back on the scene. Jillian was a rock. A hugely privileged, slightly crumbling rock, with a smoking and drinking problem perhaps, but nevertheless, a rock on which Camilla had learned to lean periodically via the medium of conversation throughout her adult life.

Kate pressed the 'accept' button. Jillian's face sprang into high definition. "Hello, Jilly. How are you?"

"No, no, darling. I'm very well indeed, but you know the score: *I'm* the one who asks the questions." Jill's enormous mouth was puckered around the edges, to match the lines around her eyes. Her skin wore a dusting of powder and her eyebrows were groomed, but she required no other makeup to define a cast-iron bone structure.

Kate had worked with Jillian since her engagement to William. With a few years' marriage under his belt to the woman he loved, Charles had encouraged the two women to meet, saying, "Camilla and I would like to give you an extra wedding present: an afternoon of self-indulgence on the couch."

Not sure what to expect, and far too shy to enquire whether or not she should pack a little vibrator just in case, Kate had hurried to the Mayfair address. Jillian had been a breath of stale air, encouraging Kate to be herself, and to keep up with her own interests, whatever they might be.

Now, in the privacy of the shed, Jillian readied herself to get to the bottom of the current situation. She explained her experience and background, that she had signed a confidentiality agreement regarding the true identity of her clients, and set Kate and William's minds to rest in part, as she confirmed that clients' confidentiality and wishes were her main concern.

"Of course, there are limits to confidentiality but unless you wish your primary care physician or other family members to know that you are seeing me, I don't foresee it being an issue. Now, please introduce yourselves," she said, "and say a little about what the last few days have meant to you."

William cleared a space on an upturned wheelbarrow and perched on the wheel, his ankles crossed. He imagined he looked the spitting image of Pa at Sandringham. He looked Jillian in the eye.

"Whilst it has been and continues to be an undeniably scary time for me, I have been impressed, yet again, by the fortitude and resilience of my wife and the generosity of the community in which we live, in putting up with my rather eccentric ways."

Kate was puzzled. These were exactly the same words William said each time he made a birthday speech.

"LouLou means the world to us and we are desperate for a

line of communication, even if it is simply an alpaca snort," said William. "He is desperately missed, and while the rest of our family and I are certainly roughing it in rather cold accommodation, it's nothing to the discomfort and hardship Louis is bearing at this time."

Tess flinched at the words, 'roughing it'. Hadn't she brought over her own very best hot sauce to The Nook just that morning, knowing that William had forgotten to buy any? She cast her mind back to the Tesco shop they had done together on that fateful first day. After managing to extract a trolley from the queue after a tussle that had onlookers stepping back in alarm, William slid down the dairy aisle like a child, picking up flavoured milk, Tesco finest taramasalata and profiteroles. When Tess had reminded him of the seventy pound food budget limit, he had looked so sad, she had allowed him to keep a strawberry Nesquik and explained that food prices had risen, in some cases, by 80% in the last few months. William's blank expression and refusal to believe that Tesco did not stock Kaltbach cheese had infuriated Tess, who took charge of the trolley and filled it with own-brand staples: lemonade, milk, porridge, sliced bread, apples, pasta and tinned tomatoes. At the counter, she had again felt a pang of sympathy. It wasn't William's fault that Kate's favourite beetroot kimchi was also out of stock. It was a Tesco Local, after all, not an Extra. And he was used to a team of chefs preparing meals, so it must be quite a shock to have to choose his own groceries.

Her sympathy vein still throbbing, Tess had paid for the shopping using the allocated funds on Will's card, plus her own Clubcard points. The reduction of nine pounds eighty seven pence had brought the total bill to sixty-eight pounds and four pence. The triumphant look on William's face and his earnest request that she help him sign up for a Clubcard had been enough to see Tess through the journey home, even with *Now That's What I Call Music – Vol 15* pumping from William's phone through the Passat's loudspeakers.

But here in the shed was a different story. If William thought he could disrespect Pearl and Tess's domestic arrangements, he had another think coming.

"Excuse me," she said. "I beg to challenge William on the point he makes. Our house, whilst modest, is certainly not 'rough'. And neither is The Nook."

William had the grace to look embarrassed.

"We had our house painted only three years ago. It's small, but clean. None of the windows leak any more, as we opted to spend a couple of weekends fixing them ourselves in the early Spring ..." Tess looked at Dan kindly as she remembered the hours he put in, chipping away at the rotten wood and applying sealant, then filler, " ... and we keep the thermostat on low in the winter because fuel bills are absolutely insane, in case you hadn't noticed. The Nook, where the Mousors are staying, is cosy but warm, too. Well, warm to those of us who don't holiday regularly in Mauritius at this time of year."

Kate winced. Up until this point, she had managed a whole day without thinking of the bikini shopping she wasn't doing.

"Let's get back to the matter at hand, shall we?" Jillian looked stern. "Dan. Why are you seeking therapy at this time?"

"I'm bloody not," said Dan, kicking a tower of plastic plant pots over. "I can't think of much that I'd rather be doing less, to be honest. I'd promised Jack I'd take him to the motocross track this afternoon and now I'm going to have to work instead."

"Hm. I sense anger and frustration, am I right?"

"Gold star for you," Dan glowered.

"Do you resent the extra responsibility that's come your way since the Mousors moved down?"

Dan's eyes flashed. "To be honest, no. It must be horrific to have your son abducted. But the conditions of his return ... well," he glanced across at Kate and William. Kate gave a piercing look, and he was reminded of the gorgeous shots of her in a black face mask. But he had to say it.

"They don't seem to be trying very hard."

Kate made a sound like a kitten being kicked.

"Excuse *me*," said William. "We've succeeded in finding a home and sticking to the budget on our first food shop."

"With help from us," said Dan.

"Well, that's the point, isn't it?"

"Not really," said Jillian, cheerfully. "As I understand it from Parth, the idea is that you help yourselves to help ... yourselves. With a little support from the Oates, of course, but Trevor Malpas seems set on the test requirements being met, with at least the majority of effort on your part."

"How are we supposed to find jobs?" sniffed Kate. "We aren't allowed to work 9-5, being senior members of the Royal Family."

"The usual rules do not apply for this six week period," said Jillian, and Kate detected a note of smugness in her voice. "You are free to seek employment wherever you see fit."

"Well, I don't see what we're going to be able to find to do during half-term," said Kate. "With the children around our feet all the time."

William thought hard, rubbing his gold DofE badge between thumb and forefinger as he did so. Kate was right. It was much easier when children were in school, learning in their indoor and outdoor classrooms ... Suddenly, it came to him. That was it: DofE! It would get him out of the house, refresh his outdoor work skills, and leave him ready to tackle the Windsor rose garden on their return to normal life - and perhaps George and Charlotte might get involved. The problem was, where to find teenagers to sign up.

He suggested the idea to Kate. She looked briefly stricken, then brightened. "Tess! Can you ask at your academy trust? What's it called again?"

"TWAT," said Tess.

Kate flinched.

"I mean ... It's our acronym. The Wenceslas Academy Trust. I can ask my CEO, only ..." her saliva curdled as she thought of Enid's reaction. She wouldn't be able to hide it from her easily and Enid would go straight to HR to make sure they did twice as many safeguarding checks as normal if she knew William was a friend of hers.

"That's settled," said William, happily.

"What about me?" said Kate, wishing she hadn't. She sounded so helpless. Like Louis must feel, she thought. Powerless, vulnerable, exposed. At least she had the nose to hide behind. She was beginning to feel quite warmly towards it.

William nudged her. "Wallpaper!" he hissed. "Now's your moment. See if you can make a name for yourself, Lizzie!"

Kate stopped twisting a length of hose pipe around her wrists and thought. It was, actually, a very good idea. Very good indeed. The Briti-shot wallpaper had been much admired; she had heard the Bug Butter ladies talking about it backstage, though no-one knew where it came from. Perhaps the time had come to put her name to it, finally, but a nom de plume rather than her own. Yes! She beamed her famous smile, making it as wide as she ever had. The nose stayed put.

"Well," said Jillian, looking pleased. "I do wonder rather whether you needed to see me after all, but of course we haven't really even started. Tess, what do *you* want to get out of counselling?"

"I'd like to, um," Tess cast her eyes downwards. An old bulb bag displaying daffodils lay near her feet. Someone somewhere had told her they symbolised uncertainty. She picked it up and pushed it behind a box of tomato food. "I'd like to ask Dan why he thinks it's ok to flirt with JoJo Bindman."

A hush fell in the shed. Dan turned pale.

"I ... I don't flirt with her," he said quietly.

Kate watched with interest as Tess started to rummage in her rucksack.

"Then what," she said, producing two paper stubs, "are *these?*"

Dan squinted. "Er, two tickets to Mama Mia from last month!?"

"Exactly," she said, her eyes flaming. "You know I hate West End shows. I've seen you looking at her bum. And JoJo's been putting 'Dancing Queen' and 'Voulez Vous Couchez Avec Moi' on in gym class recently!"

Dan stared at Tess.

"Have you gone mad? Do you have any idea how crazy you sound?"

They stood, inches away from each other in the semi-darkness. Tess was seething. She felt wild, out of control. She hadn't imagined it, had she? The looks they gave each other? The way Dan mentioned JoJo's name before Arran's when they spoke about them both? The Lycra-clad pertness of

JoJo's bottom? She twisted the tickets in her hands until they tore, then ripped them into shreds, retrieved the daffodil bulb bag and stuffed it into her rucksack.

"I've had enough of this," she said, wrenching the shed door open. Outside, the cool air hit her face like a washcloth. She marched along the uneven ground, past the communal tap and over the discarded pallets on the corner of the entrance, without stopping to look back. She thought of the KitKats Anastasia had left for the children. Half of one wouldn't hurt. It would take at least forty minutes to walk home, so if she only ate two fingers, the calorie equation would work out ...

NO.

That way, Tess knew, madness really did lie. She stopped, breathed in deeply and looked back towards the allotment. If she carried on walking now, things would be much harder later on. Plus, she had the car keys. She tightened the rucksack's waist strap and headed back towards the shed.

24

CHAPTER TWENTY-THREE

Tuesday 30 May 2023, Paultons Park, Hampshire.

Ah, a day off, thought Dan, as he rolled over and opened his eyes. He shut them again and slept for another fifty minutes until Jack came and launched himself onto the bed.

"Paultons Park! Paultons Park! It's Paultons Park today!" Jack chanted, flumping around on the duvet and rousing Rowley, who lumbered up the stairs wheezing, and tried to join in. Eventually, Dan calmed the pair down and they all fell asleep for another ten minutes until Tess came up the stairs.

"If you fall asleep with a dog at your crotch and your mouth open, someone's going to take your picture," she said, surveying the muddle of limbs and hair.

Dan smiled weakly. He didn't want to argue. Last night, after the shed episode, he and Tess had been quiet but civil, eating cheese on toast with the children, putting them to bed together and using their usual 9 - 10pm TV slot to talk. They'd discussed grown-up issues like insecurity, resentment, over-work and money. They had admitted to each other that the strain of the Mousors was intense.

"It's like our old life has been smashed into by a car so hard, it's thrown us out of our shoes," said Dan.

Tess, who had also watched the Netflix series 'Hit and Run' with Dan on the sofa recently, said, "I know."

"Do they have to come to Paultons Park with us?"

Tess had shrugged, knowing full well that they did. It was one of Trevor's demands. Plus, as stressful as spending time with the Royal Family undercover was, she was quite looking forward to seeing Kate and William on The Storm Chaser.

Jack slunk off the bed with the duvet wrapped around his shoulders, leaving Dan and Rowley exposed and writhing like woodlice under a log.

"Up you get," said Tess, with forced cheer. "We have to drop the car at The Nook for William to drive, and pick up the Bindmans' Honda.

William was waiting outside the door as Dan drove up.

"Nice to have a bit more warmth in the end last night, eh?"

Unsure whether William meant the air temperature in The Nook or the atmosphere in the shed, Dan nodded and smiled.

George and Charlotte trooped out of the door. They wore black shorts and forest green t-shirts with a yellow embroidered emblem on the breast pocket.

"Isn't that ..?"

"Elderfield Primary PE kit," said William. "We didn't have anything suitable for them to wear, so Pearl raided her spare uniform store."

Dan was shocked. "You should have said; Mollie and Jack could lend you some clothes?"

"It's ok, they're dressed now," said William, cheerfully. It had taken far less time for his eldest children to get ready than usual, there being no starched collars to straighten, socks to pull up or enormous sports bags to fill.

"Well, if you're sure. Now, do you want to take her for a spin with me first? Have you used a manual before?"

"In Pa's fields," said William, looking serious, "we consult the manual each time the tractor breaks down. And, of course, we had plenty of manuals when I flew helicopters so, yes, I am familiar with such books. There's no need for practice. Kate's just coming, so let's kick the tyres and light the fires."

Dan walked towards the Bindmans' house feeling nervous. He stopped to stroke Billy the cat, who whined and curled herself around his heels. JoJo answered the doorbell on his first ring.

"Hey, Dan, I'll just get the keys, '' she said, but he didn't hear. He was taking in the pink and aqua sports bra, faintly stained with sweat at the top, and the damp tendrils of hair stuck to JoJo's forehead. And, as she turned to move back to the row of hooks that hung under the stairs, her peachy buttocks undulated like shiny, lilac clouds.

"Will you be back by six? I've got a class over at Monkton and I need the car for my equipment."

"Um, sure," said Dan. "We're going for the whole day but, um, Liam has a call at six thirty so we'll be back by then."

"A call on a day off?" JoJo looked sympathetic. "What's his job again?"

"I ... he ... he's in the public sector, but I'm never quite sure what it is exactly that he does," said Dan, quickly. "Thanks, JoJo. Give Arran my best."

He shot off. JoJo wondered what the matter was for all of a second, then headed back to her class of menopause movers and shakers.

Back at The Nook, George and Charlotte were fighting over which side of the car to sit on.

"Pops has really long legs, and I'm bigger than you, so I should sit behind Mama," said George.

"What's the problem?" asked Tess, patting her rucksack to check for water bottles.

"They're both a bit worried William might crash, and neither wants to risk a skull crush" said Kate. She was, in fact, quite concerned herself. Driving was second nature to William, but travelling with children and no convoy, in the back of a car which looked as if it might disintegrate at any moment – the oil, brake warning and engine temperature warning lights all shone yellow when the key was pressed, for goodness' sake – was a step into the unknown.

William stepped in and started the engine.

"See you there, then!" he said, and moved off.

"Wait!" Kate waved, "You forgot us!" She ran a few steps to gather George and Charlotte, who had started to walk back towards The Nook, and shepherded them in the direction of the car.

"Follow us as closely as you can," said Dan, "and if we get separated, it's exit 2 off the M27."

The car park was teeming with families and plastic. *How do people travel with so much clutter?* Kate thought, as she picked her way daintily through hordes of people with buggies, rucksacks, bottles, dummies and snacks. She had tried to pass the time in the car by imagining how her charities were getting on without her. The guilt weighed on her solar plexus like a particularly large meal at Balmoral. The parents whose hands she had not held; the children whose hair she had not patted and whose faces she had not smiled broadly into. There was a sunset-orange suit hanging in the dressing room at Windsor, ready for a scheduled visit to Birmingham tomorrow, which she hadn't even tried on yet and by August, it would be too late to wear it because, as everyone knew, the colour of autumn was moss green. At this rate, she might have to give it to Pippa.

Then there was, of course, Louis. Parth had been in touch that morning to say that Trevor wanted a call at six-thirty. She could hardly contain her excitement. They hadn't told the children, in case for some reason it fell through, like the last call. She fumbled in the polyester bum bag Tess had lent her for the photo of Louis that Parth had forbidden anyone to print, for fear of it being lost or falling into the wrong hands.

There he was, her baby boy. Trevor must have washing facilities, as Louis' shorts looked spotless and his hands were clean. He stood in the middle of a group of alpacas, his brow furrowed in concentration as he stared into the camera. The photographer side of Kate admired the composition: the framing was excellent and some sort of filter had been used to make Louis slightly pinker than he usually was. Or perhaps that was sunburn. Either way, Louis looked healthy and rather at home in the wild, thought Kate. She pushed it back into the pouch and hurried to join the others at the gate.

"Have you got the tickets?" asked William.

"Of course not," Kate said.

"Here they are," sighed Tess. She produced her phone and scanned the QR codes in for the group. The children ran straight through and started making a detailed itinerary via the medium of yelling.

"I want to go on the Cyclonator!"

"Flight of the Pterosaur!"

CHAPTER TWENTY-THREE

"Velociraptor!"

"Cobra!"

"Magma!"

Kate moved over to the large map. "Grampy Rabbit's Sailing Club looks fun," she said. "I didn't realise we were so close to the sea."

Dan looked at her with sadness. "Have you ever been to a theme park?"

"I inspired an adventure playground at Sandringham," said Kate, bristling. "They put a replica water tower in. I think I know fun when I see it."

"In that case, Grampy Rabbit's Sailing Club is not where you want to be," he said. "Why don't we all start off at the Auto Academy?"

"I think we've all had enough driving for now," said Tess, firmly. "Who's coming to Tornado Springs?"

"Definitely!" William sprang into life. George and Mollie skipped ahead, enticed by the smell of candyfloss and caramel and the sounds of screaming children.

"Wait, shall we go on Miss Rabbit's Helicopter Ride first?" George panted. "I know it's for babies but I've always wanted to drive one and Pops won't let me."

They shared a grin. Mollie clenched her fist. "Definitely!"

They sprinted through the crowds, dodging toddlers and greasy hamburger wrappers, until they reached Peppa Pig World. A straggly queue of mainly parents with small children moved quickly. George held the metal bar aloft as Mollie squeezed into the helicopter-shaped carriage.

As the Ferris wheel rose, the sound of the park's hubbub faded to a background murmur. Looking down, Mollie watched the colours blur and felt the open air around her feet. She stole a glance at the boy whose profile would, if things went according to plan, one day in her lifetime be on postage stamps. If, of course, postage stamps were still a thing in a couple of decades time. The Ferris wheel reached the top of its rotation and stopped. Mollie looked up and took a deep, cleansing breath. She felt she could do anything, up here on top of the world with her prince.

She became aware of a noise next to her. George was leaning forwards, his head in his hands, moaning softly. Dark brown hair dye had come off in the creases of his fingers, staining them like potter's clay. The wrinkles of his shorts scrunched back and forth under his elbows as he rocked.

"Do you feel ill?" Mollie put her arm around his trembling shoulders. "You silly. This ride is for children under the age of six. We haven't even gone on a roller coaster yet."

"No," he gulped. "I just ... I miss Louis."

Mollie felt ashamed. Of course he missed his brother. Up here, away from the chaos and the crowds, distanced from his parents and the new area he had had no choice in moving to, the feelings of despair were bound to overwhelm him. She hugged him into her side and offered popcorn from a rolled plastic bag she'd had since the start of the car journey.

"Mum doesn't let us buy snacks at the park."

"Why not?"

"She says it's extortionate."

George gave a small smile and pulled out a couple of kernels. "My mum says some people think we're extortionate."

Mollie considered how to answer tactfully. "I've had my doubts about your family, I'll admit. I don't think you offer value for money, really, given that you now have three homes, and insist on going everywhere in helicopters. But I like you, and I don't think your parents are bad people."

George smiled and gripped the metal bar. "Four. We now have four homes," he said, firmly. "Elderfield is our home for now and I'm going to do all I can to bring Louis back," he said. "I'm the eldest, so I have to set a good example for Lottie and LouLou. They need to see that I can take care of them - now and forever."

"Blimey," replied Mollie. "Good for you."

The wheel shuddered into life and started to move downwards. As they sank, Mollie held George's hand tight. His thumb rubbed hers. "Next stop, Cat-O-Pillar!"

After lunch, taken in light drizzle, in front of a jolly couple of pirates acting out a strange hybrid of musical, slapstick and tragedy, Kate turned to Tess and said: "I think I'd quite like to leave now."

Charlotte stood in front of her, two feet planted as staunchly as oak trees on the floor. "I. Refuse. To. Go," she said. "No-one is looking at me through their phones. I love it here."

"Darling, we've got a call with LouLou later."

"Not until six-thirty," said William. His mind had been utterly blown by the rides. The number of steering wheels he'd managed to commandeer in the space of a few short hours was exceptional. If only his mother could see him. Taking George and Charlotte on the log flume had been a highlight, transporting him back to the Loggers Leap Thorpe Park experience of 1991 with Diana and Harry. As water soaked his thighs, he clung to the plastic moulding, laughing joyfully into the wind and wishing Kate felt a little more secure about her nose. But she had stood there, waving at them animatedly, surrounded by flecks of confetti as a little girl's Moana balloon burst, wails drifting up through the sounds of excited giggles and squeals.

"Come on, it's time for The Edge," said Dan.

The group weaved their way to the flying disc, which swooped and spun like a drunken space ship above them. Jack looked warily at the camelback halfway along the track. He had been known to be sick on Viking Boat rides and Tess asked him whether he might not rather stay on the ground with her.

"No way, Mum. If Lottie can do it, so can I."

Standing in a line, William offered his hand to Kate. "If anything happens - to you or your nose - you know where I am," he said, softly. Gripping the hard, plastic handrail, he stared with determination at the country park beyond the amusement park. Hills the texture of the billiard table at Anmer Hall rose majestically into the cobalt sky. Early summer was his favourite time of year: Father's Day, his birthday ... his heart dropped briefly as the realisation hit. No at-home manicures this year. They would be in Elderfield.

The ride jolted, forcing William to check his phone was where it should be and that Charlotte had her eyes open.

"Here we go!" shouted a woman on the opposite side of the disc. William raised his arm in solidarity, causing his phone to drop with a thud out of a back pocket. It slid across the diameter of the circle and hit the back of the woman's heel, before slipping into the metal gutter with a soft clatter.

By now, the disc was gathering speed. William gulped and hoped Kate hadn't seen anything. He tried to get the woman's attention by wiggling his hands behind him but she was screeching and squawking at her neighbour, too involved in the ride to notice.

There was nothing to do but hang on and wait for the ride to end. As he twisted and swung, William considered hurling out of the seat belt and over to the other side, but realised quickly how unlikely that was to end well for him physically and how much attention it would attract. Eventually, the mechanical saucer slowed and the fog of confusion and nausea subsided. William fumbled with the metal clasp and staggered across the dimpled steel. He reached the woman just in time to hear the buzz of his phone.

"Someone's dropped this!" exclaimed the woman, "looks like a FaceTime coming in."

"Ah, I ... Thank you so much. It's mine." William reached out with a winning smile. His finger hit the 'accept' symbol as the phone passed into his possession. Louis's face filled the screen. William wobbled as everything dimmed, and he held on to the woman's shoulder for support.

"Are you ok? Oh, I say, there now - let me hold that for you ... put your head between your knees."

William steadied himself. The ground came back into view. He clung to the phone like someone drowning. Louis, it was Louis. He had to take the call. But first, he had to get off this thing.

"Do you know, your boy looks just like that little - oh, what's his name? - that young prince ..."

William pulled himself up. The woman's face swam before him. He glanced down - Louis was still there, looking cross.

"Thank you," he managed, "my godson. Yes, he does look rather like Prince in his Purple Rain days," and bolted towards the exit, holding the phone under his chin. "Louis! My darling boy. I'm just getting off this ride and as soon as I do ..."

"Having fun, are you? Glad to see you're taking my demands seriously. How are the queues? I hear half-term can be partic'ly bad."

A chill ran through William. He hurried to the shelter of an ice-cream kiosk and held the screen up, taking in Trevor's crumpled face with its wispy eyebrows and icy hair. The man looked deranged.

"How dare you!" William seethed. "What have you done with Louis? It's not six-thirty, by the way, and Parth said you'd call at six-thirty. I thought we had a deal!"

"Plans change. Times change. Something you and your family should be only too aware of. Times changing ... "

William felt Kate's familiar, calming fingers on his hand, which was rapidly turning clammy. Her face was naked without its signature 'public performance' makeup. She had foregone a smoky eye and pink lip in favour of a slick of Mollie's cherry lip balm and a dusting of blue eyeshadow Charlotte had found lodged at the back of a chest of drawers in The Nook. The blonde wig was becoming less of a shock each time he looked. Kate put one in mind, thought William, of a young Meryl Streep.

"Babe, you ran off. What's wrong? I thought we might take in the Victorian merry-go-round before we leave ..." Kate gasped and grabbed William's phone.

"You monster! Where is he?!" she cried. "Where's my LouLou?"

Louis appeared, looking smaller than usual against a skyline of towering, hairy beasts.

"I'm here, Mama."

"Darling! How are you? Are you alright? Pops and I are trying to find you and do all we can to bring you back safely. Are you warm? Are you eating? Have you made any friends?"

Before Louis could answer, Trevor took the phone and

pointed it towards a low, wooden building, barely visible on the horizon.

"This is where Louis is spending his time. He's absolutely fine. In fact, he's been very useful, helping with the important job of swimming instruction to our star herd. They'll be ready to head off before long, thanks to this young man's dedication to the cause. He's shaping up to be a real bastion of society. Unlike certain people I could mention."

"Let me speak to him again!"

"Sorry," Trevor's expression suggested the exact opposite. "No time. We're late for our push and glide session. Orange is hoping to get a merit. There's a letter on its way, though; Louis has been practising the trickier phonemes and had some success, I think you'll be pleased to see, especially with 'ough' and 'eigh'. I hope you're getting on ok with your tasks. Come on, Louis."

Kate and William watched their son disappear into a small, black square as Trevor ended the call. Kate sank to her knees and gazed unseeingly as an army of open-toed sandals marched past. Neon gel manicures and foot problems too ghastly to mention traversed the concrete, agitating sweet wrappers, bits of leftover food and juice-stained cling-film. The air felt oppressive. Rain was coming, Kate could feel it. Above, the cobalt sky had turned pewter and growls of thunder rumbled like William's tummy after a morning's gym training. She had to get out of here. Parks were for relaxing and this was as far away from relaxation as she had felt since ... Well, come to think of it, there had been too many unrelaxing incidents to count in the last few days. Mauritius, Mauritius, Mauritius. The squeaky white sands called to her like a siren.

Kate stood, helped by William and Tess, who had joined them

with water bottles and was trying to force a sip or two down her throat. Mollie and Jack stood awkwardly nearby, aware that Kate needed space.

"Would you like to hold my hand, Mama?"

George's heart ached for Kate. What could he do to ease his mother's pain? He offered his hand, as well as his last piece of watermelon-flavoured bubble gum.

"Where did you get that?" William demanded.

George looked at Dan but said nothing.

"Time to go?"

Tess's suggestion was heard and eagerly agreed by all except Jack and Charlotte who, sensing they would not be missed, were go-karting. Jack hurtled around a bend at top speed, closely followed by Lottie.

"You're so slow!" Jack yelled over his shoulder. "You're so slow, even a slug could catch up with you!"

"You're so slow, I could overtake you going backwards!" yelled Charlotte, as she crept up on the inside.

"You're both so slow, I could lap you," yelled a familiar voice from behind.

Cruising at a cool 20mph in a bright orange plastic car, his dark curls dancing like streamers in the wind, sat Malcolm Swift.

"Who's your friend, Oates?" he grinned, as he levelled with Jack. "Or is she your girlfriend?"

Jack pulled a face, which was met with a snarl and an engine rev. He knew, at that moment, that he had to beat Malcolm on this course if it was the last thing he did.

"Race you, then. Start on the next lap - first to do three circuits wins."

"You're on," shouted Malcolm. "Get ready to eat some

dust!"

Charlotte's adrenaline rose. This was more like it. Life so far in Elderfield had been, well, less exciting than she had thought spending time with commoners might be. She had enjoyed Paultons Park so far well enough, but to be truthful, most of the castle grounds of friends she had visited compared more favourably. But this was different: a real speed race with two boys who were not her brothers. She galvanised all her knowledge and experience of her John Deere days and committed to the task.

Malcolm got to the start line first. He tapped his forehead as Jack and Charlotte arrived. "You're both insane if you think you're going to beat me, by the way."

"Three, two, one, go!" Charlotte yelled, before Malcolm or Jack had a chance to decide on an alternative plan.

Jack was first off the mark. He put his foot down as far as it would go, keeping tight into the inside bend. He could sense Malcolm's presence on the periphery but it was easy enough to keep him at a distance while there were no issues with the road or the other drivers or ... suddenly, there was a bang. He was jolted to the right, his wheels spinning, and everything went upside-down. Then, as his vision returned, he realised he was facing the wrong way. Everything hurt. His knee was bleeding and the sole of one shoe was peeling off at the heel. It was brilliant.

"What happened ...?" he breathed, and watched as Charlotte careered away..

"He slammed you!" she yelled over her shoulder. "So I'm going to slam him back! Stay where you are!"

Charlotte gained on Malcolm like a cheetah closing on a gazelle. Closer and closer she grew, until there was little more than a car-length between them.

"Keep your distance!" screamed Malcolm. "You're going to bump me"

"Oh, like you bumped Jack?" Charlotte was full of rage. Rage against her brother's kidnapper, rage against her parents ... against the world that had taken her ballet lessons away. The track was a smear of grey as she closed in.

"Oi!" A man in a bright orange bib, waving a walkie-talkie ran alongside Charlotte's kart. "You're too young! Not allowed! You shouldn't be in charge of a go-kart! Get out! Get out now!"

Charlotte slammed on the brakes and watched Malcolm zoom away. The man approached, his hair slick with sweat.

"How old are you?" he breathed.

"Seven," replied Charlotte, calmly.

"You have to be eleven to ride, sweetheart," he puffed. "Where's your mum and dad?"

"Somewhere over there," Charlotte gestured vaguely. "My friend's only seven, too," she said, proudly. "He had quite a bad crash, but I think he's fine now. Do we get a prize, then, for being the youngest drivers?"

"ABSOLUTELY not. You should never have been let on to this ride. Do you realise you've broken the rules?" The man crouched down, putting Charlotte in mind of her parents' lecturing style.

"I don't think you're allowed to talk to me like that," said Charlotte.

"What? I ..."

"What fresh new hell is this, Tills? Can I help? What seems to be the problem?" William appeared at his daughter's side, like a friendly phantom. He took in the situation at once. It called for discipline, control and sensitivity, much like flying a helicopter. And he loved Charlotte more than helicopters, which was a lot.

"Are you this young lady's guardian?"

"I most certainly am."

"She's below age for driving; I'm afraid we don't allow children under thirteen on the go-karts."

"This is private land, no?" said William.

"This *is* private land, yes," said the man. "*Our* private land, or rather, the park's, so we decide what to do with it and we have public liability interests that prevent us from letting children under thirteen drive go-karts."

"Oh," said William. "Only that, where I live, if it's your own land, you can do what you like."

The man paused and scratched his chin. Something about this person was familiar. His eyes; the way they drew a line across the top of such a pronounced lower jaw. Where had he seen this face? A switch in his brain clicked into place.

"D'you know, you look awfully like ..."

William dropped to the ground. "Sorry, my shoelace ..."

Charlotte kicked the wheel hub. "You aren't *wearing* shoes with laces, Papa."

Kate hurried over as the first drops of rain plopped onto the dry ground.

"We must go, babe," she said. "We've got no umbrella people. What *are* you doing?"

"Never mind," said the security man, shaking his head and smiling broadly. "I thought for a minute you looked a bit like whatsisface, Prince William. But he's married to that dark-haired one, Kate Middleton."

"The Princess of Wales, you mean?" said Charlotte. "Titles

are important."

"They are indeed." The man pointed to upper arm. "If you're very, very good I might have something for you, missy."

Charlotte waited politely, like she had been told to do when faced with grown-up members of the public. She held out her hand. She knew the drill well: she held out both hands, ready for either a fluorescent pink flamingo or a couple of flower stems.

The man eased a rigid plastic armband over his elbow and down his forearm. It shone like a sea-washed pebble as he handed it to Charlotte.

"F.R.O.S.S" she read. "What does that mean?"

"First responder of site safety," he said proudly. "You can have that, though. I can see you're a spirited young lady but you should always keep safety in mind."

Charlotte was genuinely touched. Never before had she been offered something by a stranger because of her anonymous character. Here was a chance to wear something from the 'real world.' She wound it around her wrist twice, the elastic sagging even so.

"Thank you, I'll wear it all the time."

"Liam, darling, come *on*." Kate's eyes conveyed urgent irritation. Keeping his head down and his arm around Charlotte, William scooted past the Dragon ride and through the Chinese Garden to the exit, hoping that the F.R.O.S.S sign was the only Paultons Park takeaway.

25

CHAPTER TWENTY-FOUR

Tuesday 30 May 2023, Elderfield, West Sussex.

Rachel Swift was using a soft cloth to dust a handmade wooden Malagasy mobile when the doorbell rang. The wooden chickens nodded and clacked, their lurid orange beaks pecking the bottom of the bird in front. The chickens were her favourites; the hippos, that hung in Pearl's bedroom, always gave her the creeps.

"Why has Mrs Whitehead got so much hanging stuff?" Malcolm had asked when she had first started cleaning his headmistress's house.

"Because it all reminds her of home and the times she had with her husband. The embroidered cushions, the hanging tapestries ... the corkscrew carved in the shape of a penis."

They'd had a proper giggle about that. It wasn't often they shared a laugh any more and Rachel clung to the moments of joy, replaying them over as she lay in bed late at night, eyes closed but sleep still hours away. Malcolm had been such a happy young child. Aged four, his bright, olive skin and shock of curls marked him as someone 'cheeky' from the get-go and at Elderfield Primary, she had grown used to sitting in parents' evenings listening to the words, 'spirited personality' and 'lots of energy - we just need to find an outlet,' while the quality of work within the near-empty exercise books in his school bag belied the praise for Malcolm's 'enthusiasm in class.'

His Dad's departure was the catalyst for change. It had been a relief, really, to see Neil leave the family home after months of the affair with his colleague she'd known about and he'd denied. Months of keeping their arguments hushed so Malcolm wouldn't hear. She gave the mobile a last spray with furniture polish and went to the door.

"Package for you," said the postwoman. "Looks tasty!"

Rachel carried the monthly delivery of Fairtrade chocolates, made with Madagascan vanilla - Pearl's guilty pleasure - through to the kitchen, with two letters on top. She was about to turn her mind to de-lime scaling the bathroom plugholes when her eye was drawn to the address on the top plain, white envelope. It was written in joined-up, straggly writing:

The ~~Wales~~ Mousor Family (everyone except me)
The Nook
16 The Avenue
Elderfield
West Sussex
ENGLAND

The author had encircled the postage stamp with a wobbly, red heart and written the letters, G.A.n.G.A.n next to it.

Rachel was puzzled. It was halfway through half-term and The Nook was empty, as far as she was aware. Pearl paid her extra for cleaning the annex between AirBnB bookings but she'd mentioned nothing about any guests expected until the start of the summer holidays.

As she put the pile of post on the table, a loud rustling could be heard, as though a whirlwind was making its way through a forest. As Pearl entered the house, Rachel flinched. When she came into the kitchen, Pearl spotted the chocolates immediately and descended.

"My beauties!" She ripped open the box and seized the contents, opening them and selecting a vanilla caramel dark chocolate praline. She held it up to the light, as if examining a precious jewel, before inhaling its scent and popping it into her mouth. Rachel took a ganache, set it down on a plate and turned the kettle on, as was the custom. The kitchen counter was so full of tea caddies that the selection made her dizzy. She took a peppermint bag for herself and dropped a rooibos into Pearl's mug.

Above the sound of the kettle, Rachel said, "Did you get anything nice?"

Pearl put down a selection of six carrier bags, straightened her belt and sank into a chair. Once the tea was stirred and steaming, she began to list the arts and crafts items she'd purchased from Hobby Craft for the half-term ahead.

"Coloured A card, metallic alphabet cube beads, paint pots and stickers; brushes, pipe cleaners and felt tips. So many felt tips. On offer, too - you have to grab them while you can."

Rachel nodded; she understood. "Malcolm's got his recorder," she said. "Though I can't guarantee he will do what it's designed for with it."

Pearl put a hand over Rachel's and squeezed. She knew the forty-five-year-old's life was hard and she tried to find as much work as she could around the house for her, although as much of Jacob's possessions had been sold to make supplementary funds available for the students of Elderfield Primary after he died, there was less to clean. The Nook provided Rachel with a good supplemental income but, of course, she couldn't very well ask her to clean while it was occupied by the Royal family.

"Some other post came for you," Rachel nodded as she blew on her tea. "Looks like a child's writing. The address is a bit confusing, though. There's no-one in The Nook at the moment, I thought? And it's so funny - the letters around the stamp - did you know that the Royal kids' name for Queen Elizabeth is 'GanGan'? I read it in *Hello* at the newsagents. Imagine a child knowing that!"

Pearl looked at the envelope and pretended everything was fine. Then she glanced at Rachel's face. The drawn skin over the cheekbones; the deep greeny-purple bags under the eyes. The woman needed something else in her life to think about other than a delinquent son and whether the money would stretch to a packet of biscuits that week. Could she?

No, of course she couldn't breach confidentiality. Safeguarding concerns were paramount, not only as a Head Teacher but as a friend. And since George and Charlotte would be starting at Elderfield Primary next week, there was even more reason to keep their identity a closely guarded secret.

"Another chocolate?" she said. "The truffles are sublime."

Rachel smiled. "I'm all chocolated out, thanks: oh but, they're doing half-price chocolate oranges at Tesco."

She waited until Pearl went to wash her hands, then quietly took a photo of the envelope's front. She wasn't sure what compelled her to do this, but if pressed, she would have said there was something reassuring about seeing a child's handwriting that was worse than Malcolm's.

26

CHAPTER TWENTY-FIVE

Wednesday 31 May 2023, Elderfield, West Sussex.

Enid studied the man in front of her. Tall, bald and rather debonair. He was on the back foot already.

"You've been out of work for a while, Liam. How have you managed, financially?"

"I've had - ah - state support."

"You haven't tried to look for a job before now?"

"I've been actively engaged in some extremely worthy causes which have raised a lot of money."

"But you must have needed a significant income to support your wife, three children and - ah," Enid checked the application form on the desk, "four residences."

"My relatives help us out," William said quietly. "And I'm fortunate enough to have received an inheritance. But," he said, starting to feel rather bristly, "I'm not sure whether that's really any business of yours."

"Of course, of course. But you know this role offers a relatively modest salary? It's term-time only and, pro-rata, will work out at thirteen thousand, one hundred and fourteen pounds."

"Yes, and I think we'll be able to survive on that per week. I've done some sums," said William, proudly. He crossed his legs slowly and leaned back. He disapproved of this line of questioning and he was, to be frank, exhausted. After a compulsory sign-in process which felt like checking into Alcatraz, a man had appeared as a tour guide to the 100,000 square foot site. He remembered his work experience interview at Eton had been rigorous but it was nothing compared to this. So far, he had been interrogated about his love of the outdoors, commitment to young people and experience in something called bush craft.

"My wife and I enjoy monthly visits from an esthetician," he had said brightly, but Enid had not returned his smile.

"Hmm. If that's a joke, it's a risky one."

Now, she tapped the desk with a sharp fingernail. "Thirteen thousand pounds *per annum* - I assume you understand that? I do feel we're taking a bit of a risk generally with you Liam, to be honest, but I'm willing to give you a try until the summer. We're very short on the ground for adult volunteers, so that will be one of your first tasks – assuming you pass all the checks, of course." Her stiff but reassuring handshake put William in mind of his late grandfather and he said so.

"The grandfather who inspired you on your outdoor adventuring journey?"

"That's the one," said William. "You could always rely on him to create a bit of a stir anywhere he went with anything he put his mind to - and that's what I intend to do."

"Jolly good. Welcome, then," Enid managed a small lip curl. "And congratulations on your new role as TWAT's new Duke of Edinburgh coordinator."

William left Enid's office feeling as if the ground had dissolved and songbirds had arrived to carry him along. He was so proud, he could sing: if only his mother could see him now. Still, wait until Kate and the children got to hear about this, he thought. They'd have to have a celebration supper, of course. It was a shame there were no chefs around but The Nook might have a small barbecue in a cupboard somewhere – he would get some marshmallows on sticks going in honour of his incredible achievement.

Enid turned to the HR officer next to her. She said, with a stiff smile: "Let's set a slightly shorter probation time than usual for this one. We'll review things in a month's time."

27

CHAPTER TWENTY-SIX

Thursday 1 June 2023, Elderfield, West Sussex.

No-one made posters like Mollie. Sugar paper was her chosen canvas: rather than choosing one colour for the background and one to mount written work, Mollie preferred to cut shapes relating to the subject content and stick them on as a 'background with interest'. It took ages but, as she repeatedly told her teachers, it was worth it.

She sat cross-legged on the floor with George, snipping fragments of paper which scattered like confetti over the rag rug. Pearl had brought the rug through a political coup, holding it over her head like an umbrella as she fought her way through the crowds in Antananarivo. Kate sat in the rocking chair, watching them over a cup of chamomile infusion she'd found tucked in a suitcase pocket.

"We'll need a blue base and brown triangles cut out using this," Mollie said, thrusting a set square into George's hands. "Just trace around it. Then we'll need to make magma from this." Selecting orange and red tissue paper, she twisted them together to produce a dubious, passing resemblance to lava.

"Stick it on with PVA, it's the only thing that works."

George did as he was told. He was nervous about the idea of starting at a new school after half-term but he'd done it before. The move to Oscar's last September had been happy and relatively stress-free, thanks to William and Kate doing school runs when they could and being able to go to Nanny's house when Mama and Pops worked late or fancied spending time in the garden. It was just that he found himself feeling so painfully shy when asked to turn on the charm.

"Shall I write a bit about the pyroclastic current?"

"No, it's ok - I've covered that here," said Mollie, pointing to a piece of beautiful handwriting on the left side. George looked disappointed. "Could I just add a drawing?"

"Sure," Mollie beamed. "They'll want to see what you're made of, I expect."

The enrolment process had been smooth: simply a case of visiting Pearl at home, filling out a form and submitting it to 'county' - which Pearl said she would chase up.

"You can assume that George and Charlotte - sorry, Gee and Tilly - have places and as Parth will pull strings too, we'll see them on 5 June. I'll email you the clothing supplier link, but Tess and Dan may be able to lend you some of Mollie and Jack's uniform in the meantime."

Kate had balked at the suggestion. Second hand school clothes were not their style, as nice as the Briti-shot unicorn finalist had been. She'd heard how boaters carried head lice on the inside, and how could anyone abide wearing someone else's gym briefs? But the uniform list for Elderfield Primary was a refreshing one-sider and Charlotte had grown visibly excited at the mention of a hoodie.

"Where *are* the younger children?" Kate scrunched her lips

and checked under her cushion. "They were around here a minute ago."

Outside, at the back of the Oates' house, ran a narrow lane barely wide enough for the two children to stand side by side. The alley was lined with dustbins, hollyhocks and discarded tyres. Empty vaping pods lay at intervals between driveways and weeds filled the cracks, like twisted fingers reaching up in despair. Jack and Charlotte watched their domestic animals forage like wild tigers.

"Do you think they're friends?"

"Yeah. Like us."

Rowley and Tabitha studiously gnawed bones, looking in opposite directions to each other. Suddenly, Rowley's tail twitched. His head lifted and he let out a volley of high-pitched barks. Charlotte followed the dog's gaze to the top of a low, flint wall. Billy the tailless tabby lay along it like a stealth bomber, emerald eyes burning holes into Rowley's head.

"Hold onto Tab's lead," yelled Jack, as Rowley bolted towards the wall. "I can't handle both of them!"

Rowley's barks reached a crescendo. He pulled at the lead, as Billy miaowed and rolled over, pawing the air like an idiot.

"If I had to give you marks out of ten for control, I'd say … zero." Malcolm Swift came out of the shadows from the flats opposite, shaking his head sorrowfully as he sauntered towards them.

"Those dogs are a waste of space. They'd be better off dead. One bullet would do it if you were lucky." He aimed a phantom rifle in Rowley and Tilly's direction and mimed a shot, followed by a masterful duck of a non-existent ricocheting bullet. "Here with your girlfriend again, are you?" he said. "Aw. How sweet. He snorted. "You're not *living* together, are you?"

Charlotte flushed. She raised her fists and took two steps towards Malcolm. Tabitha bared her small teeth and growled. "Say that again and you'll be sorry," she said. "In a few years' time I could make your life *very* difficult."

"Oh, yeah?" Malcolm looked amused. "I'd love to know how."

"Let's just say I could make sure you never work again," said Charlotte, simply. "My parents are quite influential, you know."

"Tilly," warned Jack. "Leave it. Bye, Malcolm. We need to be going now, anyway."

"Let's hope you're going to training classes. I never saw anyone worse at managing their dogs than you two. I bet they don't do a single thing you say."

"They do so. Watch. Rowley, *come*," said Jack. Rowley gave a low growl, rolled over onto his back and started pawing at his nose.

"There!" said Charlotte.

"He didn't do what you said!"

"Tabitha, *sit*," said Charlotte. Tabitha trotted off in the opposite direction to Charlotte and started examining an empty chocolate bar wrapper.

"Absolutely hopeless." Malcolm scoffed. "I bet you couldn't even teach them to fetch."

Jack and Charlotte looked at one another.

"Rowley can't retrieve to save his life," whispered Jack.

"Neither can Tab - she chews things but only because I think she just likes the mouth feel," replied Charlotte.

"You're on."

Malcolm gaped at Jack, then doubled up in exaggerated laughter. "You must be mad!"

"*But* if you lose, you have to take on our challenge."

"Yeah, right. As if that's going to be in the slightest bit hard."

Jack and Charlotte conferred. Heads together, an idea sprang like a tiny mushroom in Jack's brain. What if ...

"You have to find us a skull."

"What?" Malcolm turned paler than the nightly milk Rachel made him drink, then quickly resumed his usual puce colouring.

"My sister and Tilly's brother are doing a presentation on Pompeii and they need a good prop. They're obsessed with what happened to people's skulls when Vesuvius erupted - they keep going on about it. And seeing as you're so tough and into killing things ..."

"You want me to find them a *real skull?*"

Jack nodded. Charlotte did, too.

"It might mean Mollie takes some notice of me," Jack said in a whisper.

Malcolm considered. It would be so easy to make fun of Jack's pathetic neediness right now. Look at that frizzy brown hair. Just crying out to be pulled. But, if he played his cards right, win or lose this bet, it might also land him with Mollie Brownie points.

"Fine. I'll do it, but you've got a month. That's it. *One* month, then I want to see both of these dogs fetch a ball and bring it back to you. Individually."

"Fine," echoed Charlotte. "You're so going to lose."

"We'll see. By the way," Malcolm scuffed the side of a bin with his Next shoe. His voice changed imperceptibly as he asked: "Does Mollie ever talk about me?"

One look at Jack's face gave him the answer. "Never mind,"

he said. "See you later, losers!" With a swagger, he disappeared down the lane, leaving a deafening silence, punctured only by Rowley's bum licking.

"What have we *done*?" Jack sank to the floor, flicking a piece of green glass out of Charlotte's way as she folded her skirt and sat down.

"We'd better start practising," she said, philosophically. "'*Cry havoc and let slip the dogs of war!*' After all, '*uneasy lies the head that wears the crown*'. Shakespeare," she said to Jack's nonplussed face. "We had to learn passages by heart in year two."

"I am so sorry. That must have been utterly horrible."

"I didn't mind it too much, because so many of the quotes made sense to me," shrugged Charlotte, looking every inch the young Marie Antoinette.

"We'd better start practising," said Jack, the idea that Mollie might see him as an equal, taking shape. Billy, the tailless cat, stared balefully out from under the car. Jack lobbed a ball in its direction.

"Fetch, Rowley!"

28

CHAPTER TWENTY-SEVEN

Friday 2 June 2023, Elderfield, West Sussex.

Rachel counted to ten before taking a deep breath and counting to ten again. She hated this bit. Steeling herself to choose her weapon of choice, she shut her eyes.

"You little darling," she murmured, facing the floor while reaching up and tickling the eye socket of a lamb skull with her duster. "What'd you do to deserve such a premature death?"

"It had, 'watery mouth'," said Enid. She breezed across the carpet, carrying a vase of flowers from the garden: a dozen blazing peonies. Strange, thought Rachel, how fond of the most beautiful flower on the entire planet Enid was. "They usually die within hours with, 'watery mouth'" she continued. "It's every farmer's nightmare."

Rachel's own mouth was watering as she moved quietly from the dining room to the kitchen, where wafts of boiled ham turned the air rich and meaty. Steam fogged the display cabinet above the hob. She reached under the sink for the wood glue: the unfortunate lamb had undergone over-enthusiastic peroxiding and bits of its forehead were starting to crumble away, like she imagined the wasting disease that was slowly taking her mother.

"Are you having people over?" Rachel asked.

"No, I thought I'd make an effort for my wife. We both like a bit of boiled pork."

"Delicious. Is it a family recipe?"

Rachel didn't care about the answer, but she did care about keeping Enid onside. The woman was notoriously fickle about her pay. One week there would be nothing on the mantelpiece, the next there would be a £50 note and a piece of paper reading, *change please*. Well, yes – Rachel *would* like change – oh, boy, would she like change! A mansion in London, perhaps? A few tropical holidays by the sea? Life was complicated enough, though, without having what Malcolm would call a 'glow up'.

"What compelled you to stay in the end?"

"I need the money," Rachel said, shortly. "Malcolm's got his leaver's disco coming up and he wants a new outfit." She didn't say: 'I also want to escape for a week in the summer sun together because I can feel him slipping away from me.' Her thumb had stroked Malcolm's back as they lay in bed the night before. She had felt his body rise and fall under her arm as they slept. Her beautiful boy: eleven years old but still her baby.

"And you love us, of course." Enid gave a short laugh that sounded more like a bark. The house was redolent of a cave. Deep red, inky curtains hung from the French windows and Rachel's furniture polish clung futilely to the deep scratches in the dining room table.

"Of course." Rachel gritted her teeth and smiled through the hoovering. Bloody Enid. She wished there was something to dangle in front of Enid's nose: something lucrative or desirable. A thought occurred to her: what if she showed Enid the photograph of the letter? Surely that would score her some points and let her foul boss see that Rachel Swift was someone to be reckoned with.

"I picked up something rather interesting," said Rachel, doing her best to sound nonchalant. "Something over at Pearl Whitehead's."

She dug her phone out from the pocket of her housecoat Enid insisted upon and scrolled through the photo album until the white envelope appeared. Thrusting it under Enid's nose, she crossed ankles.

"Pheee-ew," Enid wheezed. "What sort of cleaner have you used on the skulls today!?"

"Vapo-lene," said Rachel. "Did you look at the screen?"

Enid leant forwards. For a second or two she was silent, squinting like a myopic owl. Then: "Er, this reads very much like it's come from a young child. But what does that mean ..." She paused and took a long look at Rachel, who blushed and said,

"Don't you think it seems rather, well, um... regal in tone, too?"

"Are you suggesting this might have been written by ... *Prince Louis?*"

"Well ... I had that crazy idea, um, yes," said Rachel, yearning leaking from her eyes.

"But he was found! It was all over the papers after that spokesperson went on Radio Four and made such a balls-up. Whoever was responsible for that chap's media training has a lot to answer for."

Rachel nodded in agreement. "And whoever wrote this is obviously just winding Pearl up for some reason. The Nook's not even being used at the moment."

Enid screwed her face up, looking like one of the foxes she so liked to nail to her wall.

"Send that to me, will you? And then I need a drink. Fancy one?"

Rachel's heart flipped. "Sure," she said, trying to sound casual.

Over a bottle of red and a bowl of nuts and seeds, Enid and Rachel put the facts together.

1. Pearl must know there's someone in The Nook.

2. Prince Louis hasn't been seen recently, to our knowledge.

3. There's a suspicious resemblance to The Wales's in the family friends of the Oates.

4. There is money to be had if careful moves are made.

"Chinking glasses won't have felt this good since we landed tickets to the Commonwealth Games," said Enid.

Rachel smiled as if she knew what Enid was talking about. It was useless trying to follow sport on TV: she had enough sport at home.

"Are we agreed?"

"We are." Rachel felt as though the chink was a signature written in blood, but she thought of Malcolm and forced herself to accept a second glass.

29

CHAPTER TWENTY-EIGHT

Monday 5 June 2023, Elderfield, West Sussex.

Pearl breezed into the staff room and banged a coffee mug twice on the table.

Thunk. Thunk.

Paper shuffling and conversation lowered to a murmur. Around the walls, reminders of the funny things year R had said that term mingled with instructions on 'how to maintain your wellbeing'. A vase of chrysanthemums stood proudly near the sink, the flower water reminiscent of pond sludge.

"Welcome back, all," said Pearl. "I hope you had a restful and restorative break." She smiled broadly. This was her crew: her brethren. She lived for these people, and it showed - in the quality of the chocolate biscuits and the extremely low staff turnover. Resignation date for the summer term had come and gone, yet despite the lack of a pay rise, the faithful band of teachers remained. TAs were a different kettle of fish entirely, of course: many had been there for donkey's years and if Pearl were honest - as she was, nightly, with Jacob over a box of Prestat chocs and Netflix only a couple of years ago - she would like to sack the lot of them. They muddled on though, doing what was right for the children, thinking of the children and, every now and again, taking turns to be signed off with depression owing to the children.

"We've got two new students this half-term: a brother and sister. Class teachers have already been told. They're quite - ah - special students."

"They haven't *both* got EHCPs, have they?" Mrs Battersby's sloping chin dipped further into her handkerchief collar. She was not one of the class teachers – 'merely' a teaching assistant -Lat but there were so many absences, she knew the new children would come her way soon enough.

"No. In fact, they've had private tuition and an independent education until now."

There was a low murmur of derision and a whistle or two.

"Which one?"

"I bet it's Bishop's. Apparently, it's losing kids hand over fist because if you're scraping school fees together as it is, the climate now is forcing you to think again."

"It's not Bishop's," said Pearl, hurriedly. "They're from out of the area and the only thing we need to know, apart from them being siblings, is that they know Mollie and Jack Oates well and would prefer to be in their circle, if possible. So I am requesting that seating plans reflect this and they will be permitted to take an Oates child with them if they are unsure of their way around the site, for example."

There were noises of agreement and understanding. It was not unusual for a mid-term influx of students and the summer was the least disruptive time of year in primary schools.

Pearl wafted along the downstairs corridors, picking up lost property as she went. Jumpers lay on the floor at intervals like bright blue puddles, their peg homes so nearly the garments' final destinations but ultimately out of reach for owners lured by the break bell. Dumping them in the box by the school entrance, she side-stepped into her office and shut the door.

George and Charlotte weighed heavily on her mind. The whole situation was ludicrous. How had she managed to end up with a prince and princess, who might now have to take SATs at Elderfield? It was utterly ridiculous and frankly terrifying. 'Gee' and 'Tilly' seemed to have enjoyed their visit to the school but their questions had been disarming to say the least.

"There are quite a lot of trees for the bodyguards to hide behind," Charlotte had said, chirpily. "Not as many as at Oscar's, though."

"No room for a helicopter pad though."

"Silly. We don't need a helicopter pad here. We've got the Passat."

They had both collapsed into heaps of giggles then, rolling on the floor like puppies until William had jabbed them in the sides with his Sainsbury's own-brand trainer and told them to be grateful for what they had.

Pearl had come to the end of her usual last half-term briefing, ending with: "thank you for what you do and what you continue to do." There were glances exchanged by the TAs, who could generally be relied upon to find something to complain about, but the majority of staff beamed, gathered files, folders and highlighters and set off to teach their classes. Pearl teared up. She might not be able to pay the heating bill this winter and the classrooms on the ground floor might need to invest in air conditioning somehow to survive the increasingly hot summers but the current deprivation was nothing compared to Madagascar, where access to education was poor and literacy rate far lower than the UK.

There was a knock at the door and Mollie Oates stood, looking like a beady-eyed starling. Next to her stood Prince George, with dark brown paint in his hair.

"Gee wants to know where he should wash his hands," said Mollie.

Pearl was confused. "In the toilets, of course."

George spoke in a whisper: "I don't think I want to do that, thank you."

"Oh, darlin' I didn't mean wash your hands *in the toilets*," Pearl said hurriedly. "I meant ..."

George looked very much like he was going to cry. Now Pearl was slightly irritated: for goodness sake, this boy was going to be king of England one day. He was going to have to put up with more confusion than this in future.

"Malcolm's in there," said Mollie, shortly. "He's threatening to trap people's fingers in the cubicle doors."

Pearl stormed out of the staff room and rapped on the boys' toilet door. "Malcolm Swift, come out of there this second."

Malcolm emerged, looking like a dog caught eating homework. "Sorry," he mumbled. "I'm just feeling a bit depressed." This always worked with his mother.

But not with Pearl. "There is never an excuse for bullying," she frowned. "*Especially* on the first day back. What on *earth* were you thinking?" Beside her, Mollie's raised eyebrows echoed the disappointment in Pearl's voice. "I'd like you to come to my office." She dismissed Mollie and George back to class and they scampered like squirrels back up the stairs.

Taking their seats, Mollie whispered, "Don't worry. I'll do the talking if you get a bit nervous."

Mrs Buxey was feeling the strain of the new term already.

Pregnant with her first child, due at the end of October, she was already thinking about when to start maternity leave. She'd been told by colleagues and friends that the second trimester was better. It wasn't. So far, she'd forced down a boiled egg at seven am and a ginger biscuit in the staff room but could already feel the bile beginning to rise.

"Welcome to our new recruit, Gee Mousor," she said with a thin smile. Where was the waste paper basket? She would need it shortly, to be sick in the art cupboard while the children got on with their morning 'engagement' activities.

"Gee will sit with Mollie Oates. Gee, would you like to say a few words to introduce yourself? You can stay in your seat or come to the front, whatever you'd prefer."

George froze. He had not been expecting this. Though prepped by William and Kate the night before about his background story, the thirty one pairs of eyes that gazed upon him felt far scarier than the Briti-shots audience.

"My name is Gee," he said, in a small voice. "I'm friends with Mollie and I'm just here for ... I'm just here ..."

"He's here to experience the brilliant life of Elderfield," Mollie said. "His family wants to see what it's like living here for a few weeks."

"Thank you, Mollie," said Mrs Buxey, swigging from a confiscated water bottle. "I'm sure we'll all make Gee very welcome."

A small girl with pale yellow plaits stuck up her hand.

"Yes, Isla?"

"What does Gee stand for?"

George looked panicked. Mollie stepped in again. "It stands for 'Gorgeous,'" she said, smiling angelically.

"It's what my younger brother calls me," said George, so

quietly only Mollie could hear.

"Lovely," said Mrs Buxey, brightly, and got out a stack of lined paper.

"We'll start with English. Today - poetry. I'd like you to look at these examples and write your own version of a haiku, based on what you got up to over half-term.

After a lot of fuss with pencil sharpening, book opening and glue stick lid flicking, quiet descended across the tables. George sucked his pencil and thought hard. What *hadn't* happened over half-term? He sharpened his pencil, made a spider diagram like Mrs Buxey suggested, and got to work.

Adam Buxey was used to his wife's enthusiasm for her students' writings. Week day evenings, when they would share a sofa with mountains of marking, were occasionally punctuated by excited readings of Marie Curie diaries or stories with the title, 'Going shopping with Rabbity'. But tonight, she was quaking with excitement to share a haiku from the day.

"It's called 'Transition', by a young man called Gee who joined us today. She cleared her throat and read:

The way forward is
Paved with uncertainty but
We do our best best.

Adam blinked. "It's not grammatically correct, but, yes - I see what you mean. Very profound."

At the end of the week, George was delighted to receive a Head Teacher's Award for effort. "Thank you," he whispered, standing at the front in assembly. Seeking Mollie out from the rest was easy: her eyes radiated pride. Two rows back, Malcolm glowered at him. His face was obscured at intervals by Kelisha Taylor's high ponytail but he could still make out the words *You're dead.*

30

CHAPTER TWENTY-NINE

Monday 12 June 2023, Elderfield, West Sussex.

"D-Day comes around but once a year, but this year I hope that the celebrations of the bravery shown by our ancestors will last a lifetime in our memories."

The voice of TWAT's CEO, Steve Swan, was a little tinny, but audible. The lighting was good, the video conferencing background slide looked vivid and professional and Steve's bald head reflected the strip lighting that hung above his head like light-sabers, giving him an aura of near-divine authority.

"Oh, dear. We've been massively let down by the voice recording. What a shaame."

Enid's nasal voice whined in Tess's ear, making her wince. She knew that by 'we', Enid really meant 'I'. The implication being that Tess was to blame for the audio. She'd been a little distracted in the last few days, it was true, but recording the CEO's speech to all staff across the Trust about D-Day celebrations had been a job she'd executed without issue or complaint from Steve.

Tess turned and looked up. Enid's nasal hair bristled.

"The audio is perfectly fine," she said, trying to control her voice. For the first time, the usual resentment she felt building in her chest like a soon-to-erupt volcano threatened to show itself in speech.

"It's just irritating that we can't afford to pay for top notch technology and marketing support, I suppose," sighed Enid. Perhaps we can look at the budget and find something in the way of training for you, so the next time you have a simple task like this, it's not such a disaster." Her look challenged Tess to respond.

That was it. Like a cork from a bottle, Tess exploded.

"How dare you?" she seethed? "I work *sodding* hard at this job because I believe in what we stand for at Wenceslas."

"TWAT."

Tess glared. "Could *you* have done any better with the IT equipment we have? We're a group of state schools with a massively overstretched budget. We're *not* the independent sector. If you knew how damaging your words can be... I'd like to think you wouldn't use them, but you know what, Enid?"... She paused for breath while Enid's face slowly turned the colour of a vacuum-packed steak... "I think you like being mean to me. Let's call it what it is. Bullying. My husband has always been clear he won't tolerate bullies and now I'm finally beginning to see why his approach is better than mine. I'm calling you out, Enid Saunders. I don't care if it costs me my job, I'd rather be unemployed than worry daily about the snide comments you might make."

Enid sank back into her chair and picked up a TWAT branded pen. She twiddled it between two fingers and flexed her toes, thinking carefully how to respond.

"Well," she said, softly. "I'm glad I know where I stand. The thing is, I'm not sure you really mean that."

Tess's heart rate, which had begun to slow, started racing like one of Jack's maglev trains again.

"What do you mean?"

"I mean, I think there's rather an important secret you're keeping that would be of interest to - oh - just about the *whole world*."

She's obviously bluffing, thought Tessa, though her hands started leaking.

"I don't know what you mean."

Enid's eyes narrowed like a snake's. "Do the words, *Royal Family* mean anything to you?"

"Of course. Um - it's all become rather complicated in recent times," said Tess, trying to sound nonchalant. "I don't envy them one little bit. Lots of tricky things going on there, according to, um, the press, etc." She turned back to her screen, grateful for the distraction of an email inbox.

"Look at me when I'm talking to you," hissed Enid. Bloody hell, thought Tess, who did she think she was? "I've seen it. I've seen the letter."

"What letter?" asked Tess, genuinely puzzled.

"Just this one," said Enid, flashing the picture from her phone at Tess's face. Immediately, Tess recognised the writing from the invisible lemon juice note. The taste of morning coffee resurfaced in her mouth.

"Where did you get that?"

"Let's just say a little bird showed me," said Enid, pleased with her wit.

Tess thought hard. There was no way Pearl would have betrayed her trust - was there? Yet the envelope was addressed to The Nook, so how on earth had Enid laid her hands on it otherwise? And a Whitehead was a type of bird, wasn't it? She started to shake as the realisation of what this double shock meant.

"So you see, I don't think you *really* want to leave, do you? Not if you want 'Liam' to have a safe job here with us and for his family to enjoy a peaceful break in Elderfield without disruption." She laughed, warming to her subject. "I haven't the faintest idea why the Waleses are here, or why on *earth* they chose you and Pearl to live with - or where Prince Louis might be, by the way - but I've a feeling this might be the biggest story in the world right now - and you're going to tell me all about it. Once you've fixed that audio and made me another cup of coffee."

"Yes, Enid." Tess ground her teeth so hard, her jaw cramped. She hit 'Ctrl - Alt - Delete' and her screen froze, in a locked position. She knew just how it felt.

CHAPTER THIRTY

Thursday 15 June 2023, Elderfield, West Sussex.

JD's senior stylist was late again. Which meant the home-made cakes he'd promised to bring for the clients hadn't arrived either. Ordinarily, JD would have nipped to Tesco to buy a box of Mr Kipling's fruit cake and passed it off to the regulars jokingly as his own but this morning, he was buzzing with frustration and excitement. Lizzie Mousor, the lady from the pub, had called in the day before about an appointment to discuss a softer look. They'd agreed on a light balayage. As salon owner, JD took new clients very seriously: after all, repeat customers spent 120% more than new ones and it didn't hurt to have a pretty face in one of his chairs, either.

William had said, worriedly: "Can we afford it, babe? I've done the budget for this week and it doesn't include a three-hour cut and colour at the hairdresser's."

"Absolutely," Kate breezed. "JD's giving me a new customer discount. And if I buy a shampoo, it's redeemable against the cost of the hair cut."

Kate's understanding of domestic finances had improved dramatically since the family had moved. Instead of relying on other people to take care of bills, carpet cleaning and school uniform, she had become a dab hand with a Clubcard and Googling 'household money-saving hacks.' One in particular had caught her eye.

"Babe, look: after it tells you to save old toothbrushes to clean tiles, it says to use wallpaper as wrapping paper. What a superb idea!"

"The Nook doesn't have any wallpaper."

"I mean, when we're finally out of here, I can market my collection not just as high end interior design but gift-wrap, too!" Visions of chocolate boxes covered in her pregnant self being presented to dinner-party hosts gave Kate a shiver of pleasure.

She smiled shyly at JD now. The salon, Unbeweavable, was dimly lit. Entering, Kate couldn't help noticing the rather drab walls and faded red plastic chairs, sagging in the middle like sucked throat lozenges as she handed over her stonewashed denim jacket. Walking to a chair at the back of the salon, she felt the eyes of strangers watching in the mirrors.

"Just relax," said JD, encouragingly. "Would you like a cup of tea?"

"Not unless it's rooibos," said Kate, out of habit.

"Never heard of it, we have PG here."

Kate said: "We have PG at home, too, although I'm not allowed to tell anyone." She found, to her dismay, that this prompted a bout of hysterical giggling, followed by uncontrollable tears.

"Hey, I haven't even washed your hair yet!" JD looked

alarmed.

"I'm so sorry," Kate wiped her eyes with her cape sleeve. "I've had rather a trying week. I'm sure a cup of tea will help."

"It usually does. Now, let's get rid of this."

JD eased off the wig ceremoniously, revealing Kate's natural crown and gorgeous bone structure. Kate held her breath. She was having a good nose day, although she winced at the innumerable split ends in the mass of chestnut locks that tumbled from JD's hands as he combed out her hair gently. Worryingly, there were copies of *Hello* all over the place, her own face beaming back into the warm, dry room humming with the drone of hairdryers, where women of all shapes, sizes and hair colours waited patiently for roots to bleach and extensions to transform.

All JD did though, was make a quiet clicking noise with his tongue. "Honest to God. The condition of your tresses is just incredible. Why would you cover up a mane like this?"

"It's sometimes just easier," said Kate with a shrug. Seeing her tresses cascading freely was somewhat mesmerising. She'd forgotten the weight. The UK was jolly lucky to have her. She blew on the stewed liquid presented in a solid teacup by a child seemingly only a few years older than George.

"Do you read the magazines in the salon?" she asked JD casually.

"Never have the time, and they're not really my cup of tea." They shared a shy smile in the mirror.

"Why? Do you want to look at one? Sorry, I should have asked earlier." He stopped smoothing a paddle brush down Kate's back and started to move towards the basket of literature.

Kate was itching to read about the Marchioness of Wilbury

and her latest riding school but exercised restraint. "No. Thank you. It's all about the Royals anyway."

"Not a fan, then?" JD held a crocodile clip in his teeth and looked quizzical. He then told her to look down in a far more commanding way than she was used to, which was rather sexy in a primitive, cave mannish way.

"Oh, I think they're great," said Kate, to her chin. "To be honest, I think they're rather misunderstood and far too scrutinised in the press. It must be awful having the entire world interested in your parenting fails, or your next outfit."

"I can think of worse things," said JD. "Really not keen on them myself. Not sure what we get by having a Royal Family."

Under cover, Kate's eye roll escaped JD's notice but her stiff shoulders did not.

"All right under there?"

"Just a bit hot," she said. "May I go for a little walk once you've finished with the sweeping."

JD's voice was hurt. "I don't do the sweeping in my own salon, we have a junior to do that."

"Balayage means 'sweeping' in French."

"I'm impressed," JD stepped back to admire the application of colour on the back of Kate's head. "Of course, a walk's no problem but wait until I've finished. You've certainly got the natural assets here - I think we're going to end up with something rather special."

"You've got a lovely salon. Have you been here long?"

"Twenty years this autumn. Bought it with my earnings from selling subscriptions to WWF magazine. My parents were working-class and taught me there's nothing worth gaining unless it's through hard graft."

Kate tried hard to picture JD thumbing through centrefolds

of grey squirrels and jaguars basking on rocks. It seemed unlikely but the world was certainly proving itself to be full of surprises.

"How lovely. Charl... I mean, my daughter Tilly likes those World Wildlife Fund magazines, too. So does my husband."

JD gave an explosive snort. "Ah - no, no, it was WWF. World Wrestling, I mean. Though now I come to it, they go by WWE now. Think they had to change their initials for exactly that reason."

They sat in companionable silence. JD continued to paint rust-coloured sludge along separated strands. Then, impulsively reaching into his apron pocket, he pulled out a small, ring bound notebook, flicked a few pages forward and thrust it under Kate's shelter of hair.

"I don't normally do this but you seem like the trustworthy type. And you're out of the area, so I know there's no risk of you opening a rival salon," he laughed hollowly. "What do you think of my decorating ideas?"

Kate thumbed slowly through swatches of neon pink striped cotton and smears of yellow paint in a variety of hues. Wallpaper samples displaying black and grey abstract designs overlapped each other. It was a masterpiece in retro chic. It was pure, unadulterated nineties. If only Granny Diana could have seen this, thought Kate. Charles Worthington, eat your heart out.

"I *love* it," she breathed.

"Me too." Their eyes met in the mirror. "Sadly, I don't have the money to see through a transformation with the full works and I'm barely managing to stay afloat as it is with the cost of electricity, but I'm hoping in the next three years or so I'll be able to put in a perm station at least. I simply can't afford this gorgeous wallpaper, though." JD stroked a square of turtledove grey flock lovingly.

"What will you call it?"

"I don't know," JD pushed his lip out. "I adore *Unbeweavable* but I need something new. And all the good puns are taken."

"How about…" Kate paused for effect. "'*Cut and Di*', as in Princess Diana?"

JD's eyes lit up, but then he looked dubious. "'It's perfect. But do you think I'd get away with it? I mean, libel-wise?"

"Trust me," said Kate. "I know people who can advise. I'll help you all I can. What's more," she said, resting an arm on his, "I know where you can get wallpaper twice as lovely as that one, and for a fraction of the price."

CHAPTER THIRTY-ONE

Saturday 17 June 2023, Elderfield, West Sussex.

King Charles was struggling with a chicken.

It wouldn't go where it was supposed to. Despite being lured by worms, sprinkled with feed and clapped at, for some reason the small brown hen kept darting up the steps into the gypsy caravan and not into his arms.

"Darling, I'm going to have to give up," Charles said. He slapped his legs in exasperation and glared at the bird, which fled back down the steps and into the dense undergrowth of weeds.

Camilla, chopping onions inside, said: "What am I supposed to make you for Father's Day dinner, then?" Traditionally, she roasted a chicken with the full Monty, which they both enjoyed.

"That should be something William and Harry are thinking about," said Charles, sulkily. Despite living next door, he hadn't seen his eldest son properly for almost a fortnight, so enamoured was he with this new job doing something with the outdoors at a state school.

He walked up the steps and leaned into the door frame. Looking inside raised his spirits. From humble beginnings, the caravan had now realised the heights of... if not luxury, certainly colourful comfort. Camilla had recreated a Bauhaus-style collage of a castle from old copies of *Country Life*; a pleasing juxtaposition, she said.

"Form over function. It's how we all ought to live," she'd insisted, before getting up each morning to crack on. Gone were the lazy lie-ins and nail painting; she surfaced with the pre-dawn singers: blackbirds and thrushes warbling along to the sound of a sewing machine as Camilla's vision took shape. Foam was trimmed into ergonomic body shapes that just fitted the human figure. Counter tops were smoothed, cupboard corners sanded. Gone were the fluted gas lamps; in their place shone low energy, high beam spotlights. Happiness was beginning to edge around the corners of her days like the rising sun, illuminating everything with a mellow glow she hadn't expected to feel without the aid of good red wine. If only Charles were a little more relaxed.

"Plum, what have you *done* today?"

Charles thought. "I walked around the village and looked at some hedges. Many of them are in need of a good trim."

"Oh, for goodness sake. That won't get you anywhere. Do snap out of it, darling." Camilla banged the knife handle down. The flimsy plastic chopping board snapped cleanly in half with a crack.

"Oh, bugger."

"You just demonstrated foreshadowing superbly," Charles noted glumly. "Perhaps I'll write a book."

Camilla's jaw clenched. "Oh, please don't. We've had quite enough of those. Remember what your *strengths* are, my love.

You are a practical man. What inspires you around these parts? I know it's not exactly what we're used to, but there is beauty everywhere if you know where to look."

Charles lifted his head and gazed out across the tarmac drive. At the entrance, a stunning oak tree lay parallel to the pathway, toppled by a storm months ago. It made him sad each time he passed it, the majestic giant lying like a fallen hero. He made a point of stroking it daily, enjoying the sensation of its bark under his fingers.

"I'll go to Tesco for a hot chicken. But goodness knows where I'm going to find a nice wooden chopping board. It's hardly Neptune Kitchens territory around here," Camilla muttered.

Charles's ears pricked up. The tree. His wife's material needs. He had the time and the skills to attend to both. Thus, like an acorn, an idea took root.

33

CHAPTER THIRTY-TWO

Sunday 18 June 2023, Elderfield, West Sussex.

It was a world away from what he was used to but Kate had to admit that William was making the best of it.

For the last five Father's Days, three sets of small hand prints, eternalised in gold with large diamonds for the fingernails, had been presented to William at breakfast as solid tablets, cushioned in velvet, with hand-written vouchers for helicopter and horse riding sessions, football games and countryside trials for him to take one or other of his children on.

On the battered, multi-purpose, miniscule table, stood a bunch of blowsy roses in a Tupperware jug wilting in the heat and two handmade paper cards signed by 'Gee' and 'Tilly'.

"Happy Father's Day, Pops," George and Charlotte said gravely.

No-one said 'jinx'.

"Thank you, both," said William. "I'm so sorry your brother can't be here."

Kate looked away and blinked. It was intolerable to consider what Louis might be doing without them. He was the life and soul of breakfast: pancake demander, orange juice spiller, poached egg poacher. She hoped he was eating properly. And where was the promised letter? Trevor's last words rang in her ears: 'he's been practising phonemes'. It brought her slight comfort. Louis never practised phonemes at home.

Charles came into the room without knocking.

"I thought you might like to share breakfast on this auspicious day. Invented by card companies, of course, but nevertheless, worthy of recognition." He smoothed away space on the sofa bed and sat down.

"Of course, Pa." William set a bowl and a spoon in front of his father. "We're having microwaved porridge."

"Can I press the button?" asked Charlotte.

"It's George's turn this morning," said Kate.

Charles wondered if he might still be asleep and dreaming. Silence fell while they ate, until there was a knock on the door.

"Morning, all," said Dan. "Tess and I wondered if you'd like to go to the beach today. Take your mind off - well, other things, you know?"

"Oh, no, I ... that is," Kate smoothed a hand through what William called her 'Dulce-tresses' which didn't really work verbally or in writing, especially now she was a Princess and not a Duchess, even though he insisted on emailing Parth to see if he could secure copyright before The Mail.

"Sounds lovely," said William. "Just the thing - get a bit of air in the old lungs."

Packing took longer than it would with Anastasia at the helm. Despite there being only two children, Kate dawdled over George's jumper selection, finding it impossible to decide.

241

"Louis has the same one as this," she said in a low voice to William, holding up a red fleece with blue piping. "But if I pack it for George, I might call out 'LouLou' by mistake."

"You might call out 'George' by mistake too, my love," William pointed out. "Remember, it's Gee."

He was feeling quite shivery with excitement about the day ahead. There might be ice cream: something he hadn't eaten in public for quite some time, and the idea of being able to go for a swim in the sea without paps was exhilarating.

Dan loaded the car and a taxi swept up to take Camilla, Charles and the Mousors.

"See you there," Charlotte waved wildly to Mollie and Jack. From the boot of the Passat, Tabitha and Rowley gazed mournfully through the back window, dreading the thought of more training.

Elderfield beach lay like a wrinkled grey blanket draped limply over stones. Washing the shore, the pewter sea spewed foam onto black weed and gulls looped above the damp sand dunes, crying like bickering children. Overflowing bins shed chip packets, and wet dogs scampered off-lead, chasing each other and shitting with abandon while their owners battled the stiff, onshore wind.

"Not quite what I was expecting," said Kate, pushing Mauritius firmly behind her frontal cortex. "Still, I'm sure the sun will make an appearance soon. At least it's warm and a brisk morning outside will do us good, I'm sure. It's a bit like Norfolk."

Charlotte nudged Jack. "Race you to the dunes. We can do fetch practice - lots of cover," she shouted into his ear, nodding at Rowley and Tab, who were molesting a dead fish with intent.

"Shall we paddle?" said Mollie to George. "It's about the nicest thing to do here."

George looked at the waves with suspicion. In Norfolk, the sand was white. This beach looked as if it had been designed to swallow anyone who stepped on it. But Mollie's features were alive. She was already rolling up denim; within seconds, distant whooping trailed her like a kite tail to the water's edge.

"Sure." George stripped off his shoes and socks and scooted down the beach.

The wind whipped Kate's hair back and forth and tugged at her nose. Holding it on was impossible; without Anastasia, both hands were full with buckets, spades, a paddle board and various other beach paraphernalia borrowed from the Oates.

"Dump your stuff in this!" yelled Dan, wheeling what looked like a roofless golf buggy over the shingle.

Tess produced a woollen shape and pressed it into Kate's hands. "I always try to prepare for the British summer," she said with a smile. "Sun cream, loose change and balaclavas."

Mollie and George clambered through the dunes, dripping wet and giggling.

"Shh!" Mollie pulled George down next to her and pointed in the direction of a clump of seagrass. "Let's eavesdrop!"

Jack and Charlotte were hunched in a hollow. Beside them lay two tennis balls. A few metres away, Rowley and Tabitha, studiously ignoring each other, gnawed on sticks.

"... and so I was doing my poo and I just *imagined*, 'what if I did diarrhoea'," said Jack. "Then I imagined, 'and what if I did diarrhoea on a spider."

Charlotte gave a nervous half-laugh.

"And then," Jack lowered his voice. Mollie and George strained to catch the punchline. "... then, I just *narrowed my eyes and actually did do diarrhoea.*"

Charlotte's giggles bubbled up through the spiky grass. George and Mollie shared a look.

"Kids," said Mollie, rolling her eyes.

George said: "I despair for our future." He glanced at Mollie. "Shall we take a walk?"

Mollie said nothing but stood up and moved down towards the sea. They fell easily into step with each other.

"How's your dad's job going?"

"He kind of loves it I think." George screwed up his nose. "He seems happy, especially when he's allowed to make fires outside and use maps and stuff, but it's only been a couple of weeks."

"I'm glad he likes working there. My mum hates it," said Mollie. "She thinks I don't know but I hear her swearing when she comes off the phone a lot of the time."

"Why doesn't she leave, then?" George kicked a worm cast. The desiccated sand blew away almost immediately, grains scattered indiscriminately in the wind.

" She says she will, but I think she's scared of trying something different," said Mollie. "She was keen on a job at Oscar's, I know, but even if she'd got further I reckon she'd have found a reason to stay at TWAT. It's just easier for her 'time of life'."

Scudding across the sand dunes, Mollie's eyes fell on her mother's face. Fleetingly, Tess shot Mollie a look like a wounded seagull and then turned away.

"Oh my god, she must have heard us!" Mollie sank to the ground. "Urgh. Gee, what am I going to do?"

George had noticed that Mollie and Tess seemed less close than when they'd first met. It puzzled him. His mother's relationship with Mollie had improved, at least - but George hoped it wasn't Tess's loss and Kate's gain.

"Talk to her?"

"Yes." Mollie watched Tess join Kate and Camilla on the rippling sands. She started to sprint after them, calling over her shoulder, "thanks, Gee - catch you later."

George mooched over to Dan, Charles and William, who were picking up pieces of driftwood from the shoreline.

"What are you doing?"

"Finding stuff." William wiped his brow.

"Making stuff," said Charles.

"Wood stuff," said Dan.

"Good stuff," said George.

He bent down and picked up a wishbone shaped piece of detritus. The smoothness surprised him. It felt warm, too - he had a sudden urge to whittle it into something beautiful. He watched Dan rest a few pieces of driftwood together, forming a bench frame.

"Could we perhaps *sell* the things we make?"

William laughed. "Think we need to improve our technique a bit. And anyway, who'd buy things from us?"

"Um..."

"We'd need a customer base," said Dan, nodding thought-fully. "The best way of reaching people nowadays is digitally, of course."

"You mean like Instagram?" William asked, perkily. He was a whizz at social media. Well, Parth and his communications team were a whizz at his social media.

"Most of the well-known platforms are useful for selling.

YouTube is good for demonstrating, and tutorials. TikTok, too. We might get a few people interested that way. Disguises must be tip-top, of course."

"And there's Betsy," said William.

"Where?" Charles squinted into the horizon at weekenders wandering along the sands. "And who's Betsy?"

"I mean... Etsy," William mumbled. "I've heard of it, anyway. It's a place where people buy quirky homewares and presents and things."

"Let's do it!" Dan beamed.

"Do what?" Tess asked as the women arrived looking flushed and healthy. William filled them in. Kate's eyes grew rounder and, when Etsy was mentioned, skipped up and down on the spot.

"It's so funny you should mention it," she glanced shyly at William. "I've been testing out a rather outlandish scheme but it's one I feel very strongly about." Tales of wallpaper trials, sketching, testing and re-designing under cover of darkness followed. She watched the group's jaws sink lower, before hitting them with, "Etsy was the platform for me. I think, Camilla, if you agree, we could also make a formidable design team and, with the men, we might really be on to something."

"It'll be a marvellous fundraiser for the Shepherd's Hut," said Camilla quickly, before anyone thought to suggest such furniture reside in the hut and mess with her lines.

Charles's stomach tumbled like a washing machine. Hadn't he just come up with the idea of making wooden chopping boards from the fallen oak? This was a marvellous opportunity, he realised, to do something good and, crucially, *useful* for the people.

"I'm rather a good whittler," he ventured. "But I lack - er -

confidence and style in presenting."

"Mollie's your girl," said Tess, "though I'm afraid after the amount of effort given to George already, she's not for hire."

"How about me?" Dan ventured. "I'm pretty good in front of a camera."

The two men smiled slowly at each other as the significance of the idea grew. Of course, thought Charles. It was obvious: Dan had the wits, technological expertise, humour and sex appeal to lend to a wood whittling initiative.

"You're on!" he said, joyously. "This *will* be fun."

Rowley and Tab came hurtling out of the dunes. Kate and Tess reached for leads and yelled, "come!" only to watch with amazement as both dogs rounded on separate tennis balls. Having collected the balls, Tab shot immediately back into the dunes and disappeared. Rowley hesitated, taking a few running steps towards a seagull with a rotten cuttlefish in its beak, then galloped after Tab, leaving wet sand and a gaping crowd in his wake.

"Did you see that?" came Jack's triumphant shout. "We've trained them to fetch!"

34

CHAPTER THIRTY-THREE

Saturday 24 June 2023, Elderfield, West Sussex.

A week later, the grown-ups met in the shed for their second counselling session.

"Jilly, it's bloody great to see you again."

"Why thank you, your Maj... I mean, Charles - I mean, Carl. Very lovely to see you, too."

Jillian Cope scratched at a mosquito bite on her forearm and smiled into the camera. Charles seemed happier than she'd seen him in years, she noted with approval, and scribbled in her notebook. The shed didn't look any tidier but at least there were enough seats this time. On time, all of them, too: jolly good.

"Welcome, one and all. How have you been getting on since I saw you a month ago?"

Silence fell, and many eyes were on Tess. Even Jillian's piercing gaze seemed to burn Tess from the carefully balanced laptop on the wheelbarrow. Feeling the tension, Kate looked away and studied her nails, enjoying the 'Pink Flamingo' hue with flower nail art - a freebie from JD.

"Ok. Who would like to start first?"

Tess cleared her throat.

"I'd like to apologise for my behaviour last time we met. I'd had quite a lot on, as we all have, and I wasn't coping very well. I'm much - *we're* - better now."

Dan squeezed Tess's knee and mouthed, *thank you.*

William put up his hand.

"Yes, Liam?"

"I'd like to say that, thanks to this wonderful family, especially Tess, I have more job satisfaction than I have had in years. I feel my grandfather looking down on me with approval and my cockles are well and truly warmed."

Charles beamed at William.

"I'm fascinated," said Jillian, looking anything but. "Do tell me more."

Kate gave an audible sigh and settled more deeply into her compost bag.

"My first day was explosive," said William. "I was shown the outdoor classroom, introduced to a group of Duke of Edinburgh Gold Award winners and indoctrinated in how to use the TWAT Outdoors twitter account."

"Inducted," whispered Kate.

"Then we went out into the field to practise putting up tents and lighting fires."

"Why?" asked Jillian.

"Well, um, I can't actually remember *why...* "

"We had to take some new photographs for the academy trust website," explained Tess. "The Duke of Edinburgh's Award is always a winner for showing students that there's life outside school. Flames always look good online, too."

"Not that you encourage children to wag or commit arson, of course," said Charles, winking at William.

"Oh for heavens' sake, both of you, your comments are sometimes just a bit pathetic," said Tess, trying hard not to burst into tears.

Hunger was largely to blame. Although she'd managed not to touch more than a boiled egg and two oatcakes that day, after a week of stress eating. Prospectuses, promotional films and websites swam through her dreams, Enid appearing night after night in various guises: once as a dragon, once a penguin and once, most worryingly, as a new-born baby. She went to work each morning with a sense of dread, knowing that Enid knew everything. She still hadn't confronted Pearl about the letter! How much longer could this go on? she wondered. The only option available to her, she knew, was to do everything in her power to help the Waleses pass Trevor's test. Which meant sticking like Jack's disgusting chewing gum to them at all times.

"Don't speak to my husband and the King like that!" Kate's voice made everyone jump. She wore a pink, batwing cotton jumper with denim shorts and looked like an off-duty young Jane Fonda. For the first time in over a decade (to public knowledge), she was wearing coloured nail polish.

A cold atmosphere fell on the group. Charles twiddled with the belt loop on his jeans. William kicked the floor. Only Kate held her head high, meeting Tess's gaze before turning her focus to a spiderweb in the corner of the roof.

How irritating that she didn't have to worry about her figure, thought Tess, and immediately tried to block the thought. Images of low-fat yoghurt pots and frozen peas spun through her brain. *F off,* she urged. Another trip down the rabbit hole of food issues was the last thing anyone needed. She forced herself to come back to the present, where William was in mid-flow.

"There is one thing I'm not quite sure I know how to handle though," he was saying. "At work, there's a small man named Eric whom I believe has taken rather a shine to me."

Tess's ears pricked up. Eric was Steve Swan's PA. Sharp, gay, with a wicked party habit, it was well known amongst the tight-knit crew of support staff that Eric had recently split with his boyfriend and was on the lookout for new blood.

"He was keen to give me an *induction*," he said, pointedly looking at Kate, "into - ah - where all the WCs are."

"Good god," said Charles. "Are you really working in a place with indoor lavatories? You lucky sod."

"Steer clear of Eric," said Tess. She might not be in the mood for small talk but warning William was the right thing to do. Eric was a true drama queen. He had been known to take things extremely personally and was on to his fourth threat of resignation over a clash of personalities with an exam invigilator.

"Jolly good, will do," said William, with a smile. As long as he got to toast marshmallows and tell stories about helicopters he didn't mind what rules he had to follow. Although, as he remembered sadly, stories about helicopters were off the cards. Dammit.

"Tell me what you've been up to, Charles," Jilly said.

Charles looked at Camilla and Dan, who both gave nods of encouragement.

"I've become rather popular on TikTok," he said with a shy smile. "It appears that we're flying high in the hashtag wood tok universe."

"#WoodTok - it's the new #BookTok," said Dan, thrusting his phone near the laptop screen. "Do you see? We're becoming known as," he cleared his throat, "wooden influencers."

"What do you create?" Jillian's interest was piqued.

"Oh, everything from domestic kitchen accessories…"

"… chopping boards," said Camilla and Kate in unison. Nobody said 'jinx'.

"… to benches, and tables. But it's the personality we put into our videos that, I think, clinches our popularity."

"Do you have anything I could see?" asked Jillian.

"Sure." Feeling the heat flood his neck, but adrenaline pumping, Dan quickly scrolled to the most-viewed video on his channel, which he thought he had rather cleverly called, 'The Wood Wife' to demonstrate his commitment to his craft. Silence, again, fell.

Charles appeared in soft focus, smoothing a large piece of wood with a lathe.

"Where did you get the money for that?" hissed Camilla.

"Tell you later," said Charles, cheerfully.

"Now, boys and girls, I'm going to show you how to make a turned cap. Watch carefully, because remember - you're watching…"

Dan sprang into view.

"… The Wood Wife!"

"That's right," said Charles. Tess noticed the apron belonged to Pearl but it suited Charles perfectly. "We're here to show you how easy it is to turn your home into a castle fit for a king."

"Or Queen Consort," muttered Camilla.

They watched, as Charles mastered the art of turning a shapeless chunk of oak into a work of art.

252

"That one's going off to Paris. Someone's already nabbed it - for £200," said Charles, proudly. He looked at his wife. "Do you see, Mills? This really could be a boon."

35

CHAPTER THIRTY-FOUR

Thursday 29 June 2023, Spitting Water alpaca swimming school, location classified.

Louis was digging into a large bowl of porridge before sunrise when words on Trevor's newspaper began to form and make sense in front of him. The phonics lessons were working: he'd come on leaps and bounds and was enjoying his daily reading sessions to Orange more than he liked to admit.

Trevor grunted, stopped reading about a man in court being charged with the theft of a jewellery box and smoothed the paper out on the old picnic table. There was plenty of daylight by five am. The air was clear and quiet and held the promise of a scorcher to come. Breakfast outside was non-negotiable: it meant they could eat with the alpacas and Louis was getting much better at waking since he'd bought him a Spider Man alarm clock.

"What's that? Let me see."

The Elderfield Herald bore the headline, *Elderfield Primary students wow councillors with 'lava-ly' proposal.* A large picture showed the inside of a village hall. Along the table at the top of the room, four grown-ups in shirtsleeves stood with folded arms. One man, sporting facial hair that an alpaca would envy, smiled broadly. In front of the grown-ups, holding a large poster dotted with volcanoes, stood Mollie Oates and Prince George.

"Read it to me?" pleaded Louis. "It's about my brother!"

Trevor scowled, but he was, every other month or so, a kind man at heart. He cleared his throat.

"Two students from Elderfield Primary School have impressed local councillors with a red-hot proposal. Mollie and Gee, both aged nine, were fascinated and moved to learn about Vesuvius, a volcano which erupted in the town of Pompeii, Italy, in AD79. After researching the tragedy at school, the students were driven to campaign for a plaque to be erected in Elderfield village to commemorate the victims. They brought their proposal to a parish council meeting, and won councillors over with their enthusiasm and knowledge.

When quizzed on the relevance to the village, Mollie said,

"We all descended from Romans, so there's bound to be some relatives of the Vesuvius victims in our village. We should remember them. I think a plaque would look nice, too. Silver's my favourite colour but I think we should have gold."

Chair of Elderfield Parish Council, Ben Darke, said,

"We always welcome ideas and proposals from our community and were delighted with this suggestion from such young residents. This public comment will be discussed in full at the next Parish Council meeting, but it certainly gives us all food for thought."

Louis's head hung low. He scraped his bowl clean and said in a small voice, "George seems a bit busy. Do you think they've all forgotten about me?"

Trevor, who had been wondering the same thing, shook his

head.

"No, they'll be trying to take their minds off you, maybe, but no-one could forget about you."

Louis gave a watery smile.

"They haven't replied to my letter."

No, thought Trevor, they haven't. Which puzzled him, if he was honest. Why on earth wouldn't there have been acknowledgement of the letter, unless... no, he refused to believe the Waleses could have forgotten about the conditions of Louis' bail. It was only a couple of days until the test date. Parth had assured him the video conference meeting was set. He'd received a calendar invitation, for goodness sake.

"I'm sure they will." Trevor leaned over and ruffled Louis's hair. When the time came, he'd miss the boy, if he was honest.

If he was honest.

CHAPTER THIRTY-FIVE

Thursday 29 June 2023, Elderfield, West Sussex.

Kate, Tess and JoJo were in the Bindmans' bathroom, wearing face masks.

"I got mine from Boots," said JoJo, whose eyes and mouth were the only visible features on an otherwise wet, sheet-covered visage. "It's got coconut in it."

"Mine's Aldi," said Tess. "It's got as much vitamin C as a kiwi."

"Mine's, um, Selfridges," said Kate. "It's probably out of date." She knew it wasn't, and that it contained cerimides, hydrogel, soda bubbles, collagen and gold but there seemed no good reason to mention it. It was a shame the mask also contained flecks of diamond, but with any luck, no-one would notice.

"That one looks rather glittery. Was it *expensive*," Tess said, looking sharply at Kate. "Aren't you supposed to be on a beauty budget?"

"Oh, I've had this one for ages," said Kate. She wasn't lying. It was left over from Harry and Meghan's wedding; she'd been in the middle of breastfeeding Louis that morning before she realised the time. It was a choice between a face mask and finding Anastasia to spot-clean her cream outfit and she'd reasoned the television cameras would find a breast milk stain more easily than a slightly-less-than-glowing complexion.

LouLou. He was never more than five seconds away from her thoughts. Two days lay between now and the test video call with Trevor and there was one last thing the Mousors had to do. Kate felt quietly confident in how the family had coped over the last six weeks, but the lack of communication nagged at her like Tab's new-found love of a tennis ball. Parth had been unable to confirm contact with Louis in recent days, but the date for the test meeting was set. 1 July. She'd better see her lovely boy then.

"Do you mind if I borrow the car to take Tab to the vet this afternoon?"

"Of course, no problem," said Tess. "Do you want me to come with you?"

"It's ok, I have to stop in at JD's to take some photographs of the salon's reception walls on the way."

"You're really committed to the project, aren't you?" said JoJo, admiringly. She'd been following Kate's progress keenly. "Do you think you'll make a name for yourself one day?"

"I do hope so," Kate said, with a sideways look towards Tess.

"Shouldn't you get going? Isn't Rowley's vet appointment in half an hour?"

Kate blushed. Anastasia's lost presence was still keenly felt in terms of time keeping. The shared Google calendar Dan had set up wasn't really working; it was full of William's bush craft and forest school dates, making it look more like a tree surgeon's appointment book than a family schedule.

"We should. I'm picking them all up on the way after I've gone to JD's." At least I'll look good, she thought, not wanting to admit it might be for JD's benefit - though what did one wear to the vets?

Amanda Darling grew up in Scotland on a diet of fresh air and kedgeree. With aspirations to retire early and pound the length of the UK with her three huskies, veterinarian medicine was a passion she'd harboured, nurtured and grown for thirty years. Fixing broken bones, taking needle aspirations on every conceivable lump, constructing a fence around her heart when victims of road traffic accidents arrived and explaining patiently to children why removing a tumour from a mouse might not, on balance, end happily, was the breath of life to her.

She had been faced with whole families visiting with pets countless times but as she opened the consulting room door to this one, squeezed into the small waiting room with a nervous-looking dog that reminded her of Toby, her beloved childhood spaniel, something of her usual reserve slipped. She cleared her throat and checked the notes:

"Tabitha Mouser? Booster and three-year vaccinations? Step inside, please."

Kate, William, George and Charlotte shuffled into the consulting room. Tabitha, eyeing the rubberised examination table and smelling the unfriendly tang of disinfectant, crawled under a pair of plastic chairs. George and Charlotte bookended her, crooning gently.

"That's right; give her some love, poor wee thing. She looks a bit nervous but she'll be fine. Now," Amanda scrolled quickly down the screen. I see you're visiting for a few weeks - it's not altogether usual to vaccinate animals registered with other practices. May I ask why you wouldn't wish to wait until you're home to get this sorted locally?"

William glanced at Kate. "We've heard wonderful things about you," he said, using his very best garden party voice. "We felt we must come and see you for ourselves."

"We're friends of the Oates and their dog, Rowley," said Kate.

Amanda's face broke into a tight smile. "Lovely boy, Rowley. He once ate a fishing line - hook, weight and all. Given us a few frights over the years, that one. I remember there was an incident as a puppy with a punctured bottle of white spirit..."

She was interrupted by a series of gruff, defensive barks from the other side of the wall.

"Don't mind the noise; we've had a few vocal customers in today," she said cheerfully.

Charlotte screwed up her eyes. "I know that bark," she said. "It's Kayoss Swift. Malcolm's dog. Is she ok?"

Amanda looked at Charlotte, impressed. Rarely did she come across anyone with such an acutely tuned ear to the domesticated animal world.

"You're right, that is Kayoss." she said. I'm afraid he had an accident earlier today, running through a barbed wire fence after a tennis ball. Let's just say he's lucky to be with us. He's going in for surgery shortly but he should be out in a day or two."

"I wondered why Malcolm looked so weird this afternoon," whispered George. Charlotte looked pale. "Do you think... Do you think it's our fault?"

They shuffled closer to the wall, behind the chairs. George frowned. "How could it possibly be *our* fault?"

"I mean, Jack's and my fault," said Charlotte, quietly. She told George about the bet. "What if Malcolm was just showing off with Kayoss, trying to make sure he had more skills than poor old Tab and Rowley?"

George studied Charlotte. Her ginger hair dye was fading and her plaits, usually so carefully curated by Kate, were looking less Annie, more granny. Charlotte's tan - whilst not Mauritian, complemented the Titian. Smudges of grass stained her socks, knees, and elbows. Nanny would have a fit at her next visit.

"That's pretty brave of you - to take on Malcolm *and* try to train Tab and Rowley."

"As brave as Louis?"

George smiled, sadly. "As brave as Louis."

Shining like the sun through a rainstorm, Charlotte looked up at George and thought how lucky she was to have two such brilliant brothers. One at the same school; one who would never rule, but who were both super cool.

"We did it, though," she said proudly, feeling as bright as a rainbow.

They exited the treatment room. As they approached the reception desk, George spotted a familiar shadow in the corner, quivering.

"Hello, Kayoss," George said, gently. "We're so happy to see you. Are you going in to have an operation soon?A "

Ahead of him, having a conversation with the receptionist, his thumbs stuck into belt loops, was Malcolm. He turned at the sound of George's voice and stood, rocking on his feet like a 1960s policeman, looking choked and pale.

A veterinary nurse appeared and gently took Kayoss' lead from Macolm's fingers, then led the dog around the corner, giving Malcolm a reassuring smile as she went.

"He's going to be ok, isn't he?" asked Charlotte, quietly.

Malcolm nodded and fiddled with some woollen catnip mice on the reception desk. A tear slid down his cheek. George put a hand on Malcolm's arm.

"Where's your mum?"

"Cleaning."

Charlotte cleared her throat. "Would you like to come back to ours for a cup of tea?"

Malcolm raised his eyes and slowly nodded.

Flanked by George and Charlotte, Malcolm left the vets, casting a final glance back at the treatment room where his best friend would soon lie, with – Malcolm knew - his paws politely folded on the treatment table.

CHAPTER THIRTY-SIX

Friday 30 June 2023, Elderfield, West Sussex.

Pearl gazed through the window of her office at the entrance banner to Elderfield Primary, advertising forest school summer holiday sessions in Elderfield woods, a snip at only £30 per child per day. With three weeks until the end of term, the excitement amongst students and teachers alike was palpable.

"What do you do at forest school?" Emily, a small girl with pigtails in year two who was in Pearl's office for having told a boy he was stupid asked – in between slotting her finger up a nostril and eating the find. "Can we go camping?"

"May we. And don't do that, Emily, you'll get a nosebleed like last time. Nature walks, campfires, making friends and singing songs," had been Pearl's reply, immediately transporting her to the indigenous forests of Madagascar, where the memories of capoeira, rice and beans, and lifelong friendships huddled together like a warm blanket.

Had things gone according to plan, she would be on an aeroplane to Antananarivo in three weeks' time with Jacob, before boarding a cameo truck and heading back to the village of Agnena. They had saved for two years for the air fares, planning to go in 2020. Then COVID had hit; the travel agency had allowed a deferment... and Jacob had died, his stroke coming out of the blue; his demise mercifully short. Pearl had been granted a compassionate extension on the tickets and she had almost made her mind up to go alone, although the prospect made her insufferably sad. The affection and hospitality of relatives and the country in general was what kept her open to the idea, although there was something undeniably bleak about the prospect of boarding a plane without Jacob.

A knock at the door startled her. She gazed down at Emily, ruffled her hair, told her not to use the word 'stupid' again and set her on a route to get a tissue.

"Come in."

Malcolm sidled into the office. His hands were folded in front of his flies, his head bowed like a ministering angel.

"I've come to tell you something," he started, then faltered.

Pearl waited, holding her breath for the latest revelation from Malcolm's lips. Would it be the loss of a maths book over the fence bordering the train line? A broken chair, the result of a game of leapfrog? Experience taught her that silence not only saved one's voice but had the uncanny ability to coax confessions from children more effectively than even chocolate.

"I've come to say... um, that I actually *like* Tilly and Jack."

Pearl exhaled and nodded, slowly. "Oh, Malcolm. That's great. But why... why are you telling me this and not them?"

Malcolm looked up. Agony burned in his eyes. "Because I can *never* tell them that. We have a bet. They think I hate them. I said they wouldn't be able to teach their dogs how to fetch. But they did. And then, when Kayoss was at the vets, they were... really *nice* to me."

"Right..." said Pearl, not following. "Is Kayoss ok now?"

Malcolm sniffed and nodded.

"I'm so glad. So, what do you need to do?"

Malcolm whispered something under his breath.

"What?"

"I need to find a skull! It's too late to give it to them before their Vesuvius presentation but I still want to show them I care," he said, and collapsed on the floor in tears.

Pearl decided to go along with it, whatever the outcome of this latest adventure might be. It was, at least, taking her mind off missing Jacob and her end-of-year reports. Quietly, she slipped a piece of paper from a pile on her desk and began to make notes while Malcolm recovered himself and began to talk. After ten minutes, satisfied, she put her pen and paper away, told Malcolm she would see what she could do and escorted him to class.

On return to the office, she tapped in the surname 'Swift' into the school's information management system and picked up the phone.

"Rachel? It's Mrs Whitehead, from school. Nothing at all to worry about, Malcolm's fine; I just wondered if you had time for a quick chat?"

CHAPTER THIRTY-SEVEN

Saturday 1 July 2023, Elderfield, West Sussex.

Parth hovered in the driveway, a sturdy pair of Penelope Chilvers boots protecting his feet from the leaves, petals and general detritus of summer. In the early morning half-light, an unseasonable wind gusted warm rain and the faint scent of a full dog waste bin, blowing the roses around the perimeter fence to the Nook so that they resembled full-skirted Bo-Peeps having a little skip about in a car wash. He glanced at his watch: 4.51am. Trevor was running six minutes late.

Parth's preparations had been meticulous. From the minute Trevor's challenge had been issued, Parth had made a silent vow that 1 July would be the date that would elevate his service to the upper echelons of service to the Royal family. With King Charles's agreement, he had posed as a member of the constabulary, spoken to Elderfield council and informed them that the road to the Nook should be closed owing to special environmental circumstances. The vagueness of the vocabulary he had used had worried him to begin with but now he had greater fish to fry: not least, how to smuggle Trevor and Louis safely into the area without causing suspicion.

From around the corner came the sound of a dustbin lorry. It was Saturday: definitely not a day for rubbish collection. But at this hour, even with the sun now up and the birds beginning to sing, not a curtain on the street twitched.

Parth beckoned the driver forwards with a finger to his lips. Twenty seconds later, the lorry stopped, the headlights went off and a man and a small boy who appeared to be wrapped in a blanket jumped down from the cab.

Parth hurried up, opened a large umbrella and hustled them inside the Nook's front door. It was only when the latch was bolted and the curtain drawn across the threshold that he allowed himself to walk purposefully up the stairs and deploy the secret knock to the door. At once, it opened and the entire Wales family poured down the threadbare carpet and engulfed Louis with hugs, kisses, playful punches and (from Tabitha) licks.

"Can I play on my Nintendo Switch now, please?" asked Louis, ten minutes later.

Kate peeled herself away from his small frame and chuckled. "There's nothing like that here, darling. You can go and explore Grandpa Wales's gipsy caravan if you like, though?

"Not so fast." Trevor Crispin waved a cardboard folder in the air. "We have a deal, remember? I need to be certain that all the criteria have been met before young Louis here can be returned."

William rose from his place at the table, his face like granite. Kate noted his clenched fist and hoped he would refrain from banging it anywhere. The last time he'd done so, Charlotte's eggshell cress head had smashed from the reverberations.

"Now, look here. You've inconvenienced our family for far

267

too long already. What on earth makes you think we owe you anything?" He glanced towards Parth, who nodded minutely.

"At exactly six o'clock this morning, four plain clothes police officers will arrive to take you away," said William, enjoying the way the words, 'police officers' sounded on his lips. "Parth here persuaded me to give you the benefit of an hour to explain yourself to us, as a family unit, though I took some convincing, I can tell you."

"No!" yelled Louis. "Don't take him away. He's my friend!"

Trevor played with the zip on his canvas gilet and sniffed twice.

"I can't do that, I'm afraid. I've got 200 alpacas to see to."

"You should have thought of that before you kidnapped my son!"

"Our son," said Kate, gently laying her hand on William's arm.

"Now then," said Camilla, from the corner of the kitchen where she had been washing mugs. "Let's all have some coffee so that we might think about this sensibly."

"Quite right, my darling," said Charles. "Black, with a dash of that new type of cream for me."

"You mean UHT."

"Mmm," said Charles absently. "I'm getting quite fond of it."

Trevor looked at the King and Queen, and then Kate and William thoughtfully. He accepted the offer of a breakfast biscuit from the Queen and perched on a stool to enjoy it.

"I understand your need for retribution. But what do you say we see how you've got on, just for the hell of it? It might be fun."

"FUN?" William exploded, thumping his fist on the table.

"Do you think we've had *fun* living here in anonymity for weeks, not being able to look after Louis or go to any charity events..."

"... or do any public meet and greets," said Kate, picking up a felt-tip pen which had rolled off the table.

"... or wear shiny shoes and brush our hair nicely," said Charles.

"Actually, it has been rather relaxing," said Camilla, quietly. "Perhaps we could just see what's on Trevor's list and how we've got on... just out of interest?"

"Fine," said William, who - Kate was glad to see - had finally uncurled his fingers and was cradling a mug of milky coffee.

Trevor wiped crumbs from his mouth and reached into the cardboard folder. He opened his mouth to read from a torn and dirty scrap of paper, but before he had a chance to say anything, Parth stepped forward, holding a small iPad in front of him.

"Allow me."

He cleared his throat and began.

"Challenge issued to His Royal Highness, the Prince of Wales and Her Royal Highness, the Princess of Wales, on Thursday, 25 May 2023 - together with the results of said challenge on this day, Saturday 1 July 2023."

1. Find and live in a house no larger than 1,000 square feet, with no staff.

"How large is this place?" asked Trevor.

"A ridiculous size for a family of four," said Charles. "But certainly larger than our humble accommodation. My shed at Clarence House could fit four or five of our gipsy caravans inside."

"It is 996 square feet exactly," said Pearl, who had knocked lightly before entering the room. Her face shone with a newly-scrubbed look and she wore slippers with red, yellow and green tassels on the toes. She nodded at Trevor, who held her gaze for just a split second longer than he might have done.

"You've rather enjoyed the caravan," said Camilla. "We both have. It's been like a breath of fresh air, being able to really pare down our belongings."

"Yes. I suppose so," said Charles.

"Interesting," said Trevor.

Parth read on.

2. (Both parents) find and remain in paid employment for at least four weeks.

"Tick!" said Kate and William together, and smiled. Nobody said 'jinx'.

3. (Both children) attend a state primary school for at least four weeks.

"Tick!" said Charlotte and George together.

"Jinx!" said Louis.

4. Complete a weekly family food shop with a budget of no more £70.

"Easy," said Kate, blowing on her hand and miming a shoulder brush. "Last week I came back with four pounds change because the bagged salad was 30% off."

5. Take a day trip to Paultons Park in a 2007 Volkswagen Passat.

"Done," said the family in unison.

"Not fair!" said Louis. "Can we go again with me?"

6. Raise at least £100 for the local community.

"Yes, more than that, actually," said Charles, looking proud. "My chopping boards have gone down an absolute storm."

7. Take the family dog to the vet for its vaccinations.

Tabitha yawned and rolled over in her basket, showing her

tummy.

"She's wormed, too," said Charlotte, confidently. "In fact, we all are."

8. Manage on a budget of £10 per month for skin and haircare.

All eyes turned to Kate, whose complexion glowed like a peach, as if in denial of the question.

"Yes, I have. Honey and white yoghurt face masks," she said, simply. Then, seeing the sceptical looks on her husband and father-in-law's faces, "plus I *also* made jolly good friends with a hairdresser - and there were a few, erm, luxury treats I had in my handbag when we got here."

There was a peaceful silence. The grown-ups sipped their coffee, whilst the children shoved each other slyly.

"It's quite warm in here, darling," said Kate to Louis. "Take that..." she glanced down her prosthetic at what could only be described as a hair shirt, "top layer off, and we'll have some breakfast."

"What are we having?" asked Charlotte.

Louis slipped out of his coat, to reveal an impressive top physique.

"You've got muscles," said George, in awe.

"But I wanted lobster," said Louis, pouting.

William cracked a smile.

Everything felt surprisingly positive, thought Kate. Almost as if things were back to normal. There was a knock at the door.

"That'll be the police," said Parth, with satisfaction. "Let's go, Crispin."

Kate glanced at Trevor, finishing his coffee. She looked at Louis, who seemed to have acquired an aura of maturity she simply couldn't imagine him acquiring through nanny, nor a term at Oscar's. A sudden pang of sympathy for the alpacas and the man who had given her family freedom, of a kind, for almost six weeks, struck her in the heart.

"Wait," she said.

William, recognising the look in his wife's eye, sighed inwardly. Parth, recognising the tone of Kate's voice, sighed audibly as he imagined his 2024 New Year's Honours Royal Victorian Order slipping out of reach.

"Not so fast," Kate said. "There might be another way."

39

CHAPTER THIRTY-EIGHT

Sunday 2 July 2023, Elderfield, West Sussex.

William slowed to a jog and wiped his forehead with the front of his vest. He breathed in the morning air with relish. A fox peeped out from between two dustbins before scampering behind a parked electrician's van. In the top bedroom window of the Bindmans' house, he could just make out Arran's meaty shoulders working to pull on socks. He waved just as Arran looked up raised his hand in a salute.

It was surprising how little William missed his indoor gyms. He supposed all the lifting of Duke of Edinburgh expedition equipment was keeping his biceps in tip top condition; he certainly hadn't had any complaints from Kate on that score. Stretching his arms into the air, he rounded the corner into the road he'd come to think of as, well, home.

Trevor had returned to the alpaca farm yesterday, leaving behind a signed, watertight non-disclosure agreement and the promise that Louis would be welcome to visit his hairy friends at any time.

With the return to Royal life imminent, work preyed on

William's conscience. He was mindful that, with only three weeks left until the end of term, TWAT's Duke of Edinburgh expeditions might be complete but there was a lot of paperwork to catch up on. He winced as he remembered the conversation with Kate that morning, in which he had explained that he couldn't simply 'up sticks and leave' without making sure his students were properly looked after.

He stepped over two cardboard boxes, half-filled with the children's belongings, and walked into the kitchen, where Pearl and his wife were enjoying a break from packing, with a rooibos and lavender brew. Louis played at their feet with a set of dominoes, feeding them into a plastic Among Us figure and watching, mesmerised, as they were spat out of the toy's rear end.

"We were just talking about you," said Pearl. "I understand you're not keen to leave the fold yet."

"Honey, honey?" said William, picking up a squeezy bottle and adding a squirt in Kate's tea.

"Thanks, my love."

"Where are the other children?"

"Stripping their beds," said Kate, "and folding clothes, I hope - and then they're off to see Malcolm Swift about something."

Pearl turned her mug a full rotation before saying,

"He's starting to see the error of his ways, that young man. I think he has a bright future ahead."

"I hope so," said Kate. "Gee... I mean, George, said they had some business to settle but I know Tess has always been rather wary of him."

"I miss Trevor," said Louis in a small voice. "And my independence."

Kate and William exchanged glances. Kate hopped off her stool and took Louis's hands in hers.

"Aren't you happy to be back with us, darling?"

Louis looked at his feet. "It was more adventurous with Trevor. I had to get my own breakfast and feed the alpacas."

"We have chickens and Tabitha here," said Kate, tightly. "And hamsters and goldfish and all the animals in the petting zoo at Anmer Hall when we get home. They all need feeding."

"But we have people to do it *for* us," said Louis. "At the alpaca farm it was just, sort of, like living in the wild."

Pearl slipped off her stool to the floor. She watched as the Among Us character deposited the last domino and Louis touched the end brick with his little finger. It wobbled but stayed upright.

"Tell me what you liked most about being with Trevor Crispin." Pearl was aware that Trevor had undergone a safeguarding check shortly after his visit yesterday, but you could never be too careful, in her experience.

Louis's eyes widened. He didn't know this lady very well but he was quickly becoming used to grown-ups seeking his opinion. He shifted on his bum and turned his face upwards.

"He understands what it's like to feel a bit, I don't know, lonely but adventurous. Which is how I feel a lot of the time. I think I learned lots from him. More about alpacas than nanny's taught me, anyway."

With a decisive wrist flick, he pushed the dominoes over. The run, which wound in and out of stool legs and across the kitchen floor to the doorway, made a satisfying rattle as they tumbled.

"That's a good word, Louis," said William, licking a drop of honey from the countertop. "A great topple, too."

"The domino effect," said Pearl, gazing at Louis. "Look where it's got us all. But I can understand the mindset of which you speak, Louis."

"What will you do when we're gone," asked Kate.

Pearl shrugged. "Go to Madagascar alone, I suppose."

Louis's ears perked up. "Mama! I've seen *Madagascar*. There are penguins. I want to come with you. I want to go on an aeroplane again! I could come!"

"We've only just got you back, LouLou!" Kate spluttered. "And I'm hoping we'll be able to go to Mauritius very soon!"

"How much are the Oscar's fees?" whispered Pearl. "Because you might want to have a word with their Head of Geography."

To Louis, she said: "There are no penguins in Madagascar, my dear, but there are plenty of other exciting animals to see. Lemurs, crocodiles, snakes... "

"Alpacas?"

"No. Alpacas come from South America."

"But they're off to Zanzibar aren't they? Trevor's taking them."

William stood up.

"Lovely to chat but I've got some school work to attend to."

"Darling, we're supposed to finish packing, so that we can be on the road tomorrow morning. Have you done any?"

"I've plenty of time, and very few things to throw into a bag," said William, airily. "It'll take me all of half an hour."

Pearl and Kate looked at one another.

When he'd left, Kate asked the question that had been on her lips since the day before.

"Would you like us to put you in touch with Trevor? You two seem to be quite similar and at least you could compare notes on living with the nightmare Waleses!"

Pearl gasped. Was she that transparent?

"I... aren't you worried we'll talk to the press?"

"If I were, I wouldn't have mentioned it," Kate said, gently. "Have a think about it – you might not want to open that can of worms. Now, I really must go and pack." What does one wear, she thought, to leave a housing estate?

CHAPTER THIRTY-NINE

Saturday 15 July 2023, Windsor, Berkshire.

"Do you want to borrow a swimming costume?" asked Charlotte. "I've got about sixteen."

She stood, with Mollie, in her bedroom in Windsor. The sun streamed onto the carpet, highlighting the gold thread that ran through the pile.

"Yes, please."

Charlotte passed her a turquoise one-piece. Mollie took it to the en-suite to change. On the walnut vanity stand, stood a gold soap dish, with gold soap and a gold toothbrush mug with a gold handled toothbrush. Mollie picked it up and gasped at its weight.

"How do you clean your teeth with this every day?"

"I use two hands. Mama says it's antibacterial and it gives me a workout at the same time."

"You're lucky I'm not interested in you for your money."

"Ha ha," said Charlotte. "Did you get George a birthday present?"

"No," called Mollie, through the door. What did you buy a

prince who, now he was back in his normal surroundings, had everything you could possibly want?

"Good," said Charlotte, with approval. "He doesn't need anything anyway."

Mollie emerged and twisted her hair into a bun.

"You look really good, that colour suits you."

"I might be invisible once I get into the water."

"I'm sure George will still notice you," said Charlotte, giving a sly wink.

They made their way through the house to the swimming pool, where Jack and George lay on sun loungers, sipping milkshakes. Harry Styles blasted from a speaker and inflatables lay strewn across the ground.

"Has he arrived yet?" asked Jack.

George lowered his sunglasses and peered over the top. "Who?"

On cue, a loud 'woof' punctured the chorus of *As It Was* and a large dog hurled itself into the pool and started to scramble towards an inflatable ball.

"Kayoss!" shouted George, with delight.

"Happy birthday," said Malcolm, appearing with Tess and Dan from the house. "Um, thanks for inviting me." His eyes were wider than saucers. Under strict instructions from Parth not to disclose the purpose of his visit, he had only been allowed to tell his mother the true details of his day trip to Windsor.

"My birthday isn't until next weekend but I'm having three birthday parties, so it's the least I can do," said George, trying and failing to sound nonchalant. Never in his wildest dreams would he have thought that, aged ten, he would not only be able to speak with confidence in front of a crowd but have so many good friends.

Kate arrived, hurrying over to the edge of the pool, being careful not to dampen her new Fitflops.

"George, darling, there's a little surprise coming, remember? But you'll all need to get dressed for it. Shall we do cake and then head over to the track?"

Jack, who had popped up from an underwater handstand in time to catch the final word, said, "are we having a sprint race?"

"No," said Dan, grinning. "Better than that."

Thirty minutes later, Jack stared down at his hands, entombed in the softest leather, gripping a pair of handles. His eyes watered but the glass visor stopped him wiping away the tears of happiness.

"Go easy please," mouthed Tess, and whispered a silent prayer as Jack set his foot on the kickstarter, pressed firmly down and gave a whoop of joy as the motocross bike roared into life.

41

CHAPTER FORTY

Monday 17 July 2023, Elderfield, West Sussex.

With every whisk of the egg whites in the mixing bowl, Tess's upper lip became stiffer. She hadn't minded that George's birthday party had given her son the opportunity of a lifetime - a turn on the motocross bike had led to him meeting his greatest idol: Tommy Searle, who had offered weekly coaching, having seen Jack's raw talent. How could she begrudge something like that? She just wished she could have been the one to facilitate it, as well as afford it.

"What's cooking, babe?" Dan came wandering into the kitchen, tucking a couple of brown envelopes under his arm as he leant over to kiss Tess on the neck.

She kissed him back and nodded towards the envelopes. "Are those bills?"

"S'pect so. Energy's not getting any cheaper." Dan licked a finger and hovered it over the bag of caster sugar. Tess slapped it away.

"Don't eat that; it's for the meringues and chocolate mousse."

When will things get a bit easier? she thought, grimacing. She tried not to feel despondent. She knew how self-indulgent it sounded. Undoubtedly, the last few weeks had been the most incredible and surreal of her life but now, as the Waleses' absence made itself felt daily in the smallest of things she had begun to take for granted... no words of reassurance required for Kate's nose; Mollie no longer spending time trying to make Rowley curtsey... she felt the tiniest trace of despair and frustration.

Dan's demeanour, on the other hand, was decidedly chipper.

"Are they for my launch party?"

Tess nodded. One of the more pleasant hangovers from the Waleses' stay was that Dan had continued, with Charles, as the TikTok presenter for *The Wood Life.* Dan's star was truly on the rise. He had over 100,000 followers on Instagram and there had even been requests for interviews. It was all Dan had ever dreamed of. It was just a shame that Dan hadn't managed to monetise it. Yet, she reminded herself. Yet.

Tess's phone buzzed. Parth. She wiped her hands and answered.

Twenty minutes later, she was face to face with Kate on an encrypted Zoom call. Parth's name appeared in a window on the left, but he kept his camera turned off.

Back in her natural surroundings, Kate's skin seemed more luminous than ever. Her hair gleamed above a snow-white, high-necked blouse that shone like a laundry detergent advert. In the background, a George Stubbs hung majestically against a hexagonal print wallpaper, the mare looking down her nose. Inside the hexagons, Tess could just make out vaguely equine head shapes.

"Hello, your Royal Highness. Are they..."

"Alpaca heads, yes," said Kate, nodding. After all the, er, activity, I was inspired to create a range of domestic farm animal patterns. I took a chance, stuck them on Etsy and they've become popular - particularly with old people's homes. I have an exciting call with Habitat tomorrow."

Tess smiled warmly.

"But that's not what I wanted to talk about." Kate's tone became serious. "William and I received some devastating news earlier this week which, whilst turning our lives once again topsy-turvy, I must admit, has led to rather an exciting opportunity here at the Royal Household." She sniffed. "As you can see, I'm rather upset about the whole thing, so I'm going to leave it to Parth to take up the story."

Parth's face appeared. His forehead glistened with a faint sheen of sweat and his usual benign expression was strained.

"With much regret," he said, "I will be leaving my post with the Prince and Princess of Wales with immediate effect."

Tess tried to hide the surprise with a slow nod, but her wide, goldfish mouth belied her true feelings. "May I ask..."

"Why?" Parth bristled, but rallied. "Anastasia and I have decided to travel the world together."

"I see," said Tess, slowly. "So that means..."

"There is a vacancy," said Kate. "And we think you would be perfect as Head of Communications for the Prince and Princess of Wales."

Tess gasped. From behind her, she heard the bowl of meringue whites fall from some height.

"Dan!"

"Sorry, my love." Dan came over and peered at the screen. "Did I hear you correctly? You want Tess to fill Parth's boots at the Palace?"

Another black window appeared on the screen with 'KC3' in the middle. Charles's ruddy face, contorted with mirth, hove into view.

"Camilla's just been telling me a joke about a dinosaur," he said. "Terribly funny. Something about a small arms dealer. Hello, darling, sorry I'm a bit late."

"It's fine," said Kate, though Tess detected a trace of impatience. "We've just told Tess what's going on."

"Yes, of course. Darling Parth. Such an asset to the Household, but he seems to have come to the end of the road." Charles chuckled at his own wit.

"The lifestyle would require you to live on site, but it would be rent-free; we would see to it that the children's school fees would be covered, should you wish to provide them with a private education and we would, of course, reimburse you financially to the same level enjoyed by Parth."

Tess felt Dan's hand over hers. It was warm and rough. It would always be warm and rough, she realised, and she felt, suddenly, emboldened. Where had being nice ever got her, she thought. She had spent the best part of the last decade doing things for other people. Doing everything Enid asked of her. Looking after the children, the dog, the Royal Family... this was, admittedly, another caring job of sorts but she would be paid properly for it, be respected for her talents and skills and the children would have every opportunity she had ever imagined.

"You'll need to discuss it as a family, of course," said Kate. "And, of course, if you have any questions, you can text or call."

"I'll be sorry to see you go, Parth," said Tess. "I know how much you've done in your time."

With all due respect, you don't, thought Parth, but had the grace to smile and say, 'thank you.'

The call ended. Dan said, "I'll crack some more eggs, shall I?"

"You can't make an omelette otherwise," said Tess.

"I thought we were having meringues and chocolate mousse?"

"I think our plans might have changed," Tess said with a smile.

Dan, who wasn't a fan of double meanings, fetched another mixing bowl.

CHAPTER FORTY-ONE

Monday 17 July 2023, Elderfield, West Sussex.

Rachel let herself into Enid's house, took off her coat and shoes, and checked the place was empty with an experimental, 'hello?'. Receiving no answer, she tuned the radio to LBC and snapped on her plastic feet covers and rubber gloves.

She was halfway in to cleaning the kitchen sink when she heard a strange noise.

Squeak, *humph.* Then a pause.

Squeeeeeak, *humph.* Then another pause.

Rachel took off her gloves and cautiously climbed the stairs. "Hello?" she called again.

"In here," came a muffled cry. "I need some help. Please."

Peering around the corner of the spare bedroom, Rachel saw Enid's backside poking out from the underneath of the desk.

"I'm stuck," mumbled Enid, unnecessarily.

Rachel crawled towards the back wall. Enid's left sleeve was caught under the desk leg, and her right hand was bleeding from the palm, rendering her incapacitated.

Rachel reversed and lifted the desk a few inches. Freed, her boss quickly regained her composure.

"May I ask..?"

"You may," Enid's eyes lowered. "I dropped a round file. I was feeling around for it with the desk lifted up and I stabbed myself. I was using it to carve a bone pendant for a necklace. It's Marilyn's and my anniversary tomorrow."

Rachel tried not to show her surprise. In her experience, this was the first time Enid had shown any penchant for thoughtfulness. The piece of bone in question lay on the desk. It was curved, with wobbly edges but despite its crude beginnings, Rachel could make out the suggestions of the shape of a heart.

"Come on, let's get you patched up." Rachel led Enid to the bathroom, and reached into the cabinet for the First Aid kit. "We'll need to wash this first, but I don't think you'll bleed to death any time soon."

Enid lowered the lavatory seat, sat down and gulped. She wasn't used to this level of consideration from anyone other than Marilyn. "Are you sure you don't mind?"

"Not at all. Though in fact, this isn't completely selfless." Rachel took a deep breath. "There's something you can do for me in return. For my son, in fact."

Rachel began to explain Malcolm's predicament. Enid was quiet. Her hand throbbed under its plaster, a bloom of blood beginning to seep to the surface.

"... and although he seems much happier now, a skull would mean he could forget this silly bet altogether. He, Mollie and Jack are friends now. Did you know they invited him on a trip to Windsor? He never told me what they got up to exactly but I know they went to the castle," she said, not bothering to disguise the pride in her voice.

"There's a small badger skull I've been struggling to find a place for."

"Oh, I think that would be perfect!"

They fell silent, both in thought.

"Why don't you like Jack and Mollie's mother?" Rachel said, emboldened.

Enid took a sharp intake of breath. "What makes you say that?"

"Malcolm said Mollie told him. It must make things tricky, with you working together."

Enid kicked the loo brush holder with her toe. Rachel winced; she'd have to scrub the bathroom floor soon and it would help if the brush holder stayed upright.

"I don't dislike her," she said, softly.

"Sorry, what?"

"She's a good worker."

"I'd say she was a bit more than that," Rachel bristled. "She's done an awful lot for Wenceslas's reputation. I didn't know there were so many opportunities available for our children until I started noticing the social media posts and banners around the entrance of the school.

"She's very good at her job, then," Enid grimaced. "All right?"

"But why don't you seem happier about it?" Rachel was genuinely puzzled.

"Because I'm jealous!" Enid exploded.

"Ah."

"Ever since Tess Oates joined, she's made it perfectly clear that she's over-qualified for her position. She's always having fabulous ideas and, if it were up to her, she'd probably make Wenceslas stand out in our community as the best school in the area within a few weeks."

"Why on earth would that be a bad thing?"

"Because it's *my* job!" Enid said. "And I... I can't seem to do it."

"So ask Tess for help. Or promote her so she can do the job properly." Rachel was starting to feel irritated. Here was a grown woman, with a nice house and a good job, feeling sorry for herself because she had a great team worker by her side and couldn't recognise it.

The front door slammed. They heard Marilyn bang her bag down on the hall table and throw her keys in the bowl.

"She can't see me like this!" Enid put her head in her hands.

Rachel crouched next to her, like she used to when Malcolm was small.

"Listen. Marilyn loves you. You have everything: a nice home, a good job, you're a very talented woman. What is it, exactly, that makes you happy?"

Enid levelled with Rachel's gaze. "Making bone jewellery."

"Well," said Rachel, smiling, "if you ask me, to be honest, it wouldn't hurt to give it a real go. Seems to me you're pretty talented. But not before you tell those in your life that you value them - even that you love them."

Enid flexed the fingers of her right hand. "To be honest, or 'tibia' honest?"

"That's not in the slightest bit 'humerus'," said Rachel, smiling.

CHAPTER FORTY-TWO

Monday 17 July 2023, Witterings, West Sussex.

Tess, Dan, Mollie and Jack took turns to throw the ball across the beach, using Rowley as the 'piggy in the middle'. It was late in the evening, the smell of fish and chips lingering in the briny air; the tide miles out across the flat sands.

"To me!" yelled Tess. She turned her face at the last second, as the tennis ball sailed towards her forehead. "Hey, watch it, Jack!"

The children raced across the sand, away from their parents, followed by Rowley. Dan and Tess fell into easy conversation.

"Whoever would have thought we'd have the summer we did. I feel about a million years older, but it's all ended up working out rather well, hasn't it?" said Dan, tucking his hand companionably into Tess's armpit.

"Has it? What do you think about this opportunity?"

Dan's shoulders moved up his neck in a shrug, but Tess wasn't fooled.

"You think I should take it," she said, flatly.

"I don't think you *shouldn't* take it."

Seagulls circled overhead, wheeling in the inky sky, looking for a last snack of sandworm before retiring to bed.

"I'd miss this place. All our friends, I mean. And it's lovely to have our lives back – but it's true I feel a bit…"

"Stuck in a rut?"

"Well, yes."

Dan kissed the top of her head.

"We'll all be right behind you if you decide to go for it."

Tess looked out towards the horizon. "Let's do it."

44

CHAPTER FORTY-THREE

Tuesday 18 July 2023, Kensington, London.

Outside Kensington High Street station, Tess stumbled on the curb and, as she looked down the road, did a double-take.

"Did you see that man? I'm sure it was Prince Harry, getting into a car."

Dan squinted through the summer rain. "I don't think so, darling. He's safe with his family, enjoying life in the States, remember?"

Tess gave herself a little shake and let Dan lead her through the crowds to the Parisian Baguette, a cafe close to Kensington Gardens. They settled at a table and, seconds later, were joined by Kate and William, back in their Elderfield disguises. Two bodyguards hovered by the entrance, to be sure of no unwanted attention.

"We're terrifically glad you chose to accept," said Kate, after espressos and pastries had been delivered to the table.

Tess felt excitement fizz in the pit of her stomach. It was really happening. With the children safely deposited with Pearl for the day and a little white lie to Enid about a training session in London, the plan was to sign the job contract and get home for perhaps an hour of blissful peace.

William's phone buzzed. He glanced at it and immediately, his face became stony.

Kate leaned over his apricot twist. William held up the phone so she could see the screen. The colour drained from her cheeks.

"What on earth does that mean?" she breathed.

William passed the phone to Tess, solemnly. "A baptism of fire, I'm afraid," he said. "Your first assignment will be to kill this story."

Tess took a few minutes to absorb the text message's contents. It read:

With apologies, sir, but in Parth's absence, the Editor would like to speak to your representative about a story that will run in the Mail next week, regarding the Prince of Wales and a slur against his grandfather. We understand from a reliable source that the Prince of Wales has, recently, used the words, 'difficult' and 'in need of a makeover' to describe the late Prince Phillip. Call the Mail press office and ask for Ralph Pony to discuss further.

"We haven't even made my appointment public," said Tess. This was all becoming real rather too fast for her liking, although she felt a long-forgotten adrenaline surge through her veins. "I'm sorry to ask this, but… is there any truth to it?"

"Of course not!" William blew flakes of pastry across the table top. "I would never say anything against Grandpa." He looked genuinely upset. "I can't think where they've got this rubbish from."

"Leave it to me," said Tess.

"Would you like to come back to the Palace to see your office?" asked Kate.

Tess thought of Rowley. The dog walker would have left two hours ago; if they caught a train by noon, he wouldn't be alone too long.

"I won't today if you don't mind. As you know, I haven't actually resigned yet. I'll be doing that this week, as it's the last day of term, but I'd rather go home and study all of this new information a little harder. I've got the details I need. Don't worry," she said, seeing William's expression. "I'm sure we can get to the bottom of it."

Kate gave Tess an understanding nod. "Thank you, Tess. You haven't let us down yet. Please give the children our love. Gee is looking forward to seeing Mollie again soon. And, of course, before long, they'll be at the same school." She beamed. "That is, of course, assuming you have chosen Oscar's for your two?"

Tess smiled, non-committedly. "It's an excellent school," she said, "and I'm sure the children would thrive but we're still discussing it. Thank you for the drinks. I'll be in touch."

"Well, that was a bit rude," Dan said, as they exited the tube barriers at Waterloo.

"I know who it was," said Tess, rushing up the station steps.

"What?"

"Who the source revealing the slur against the Duke of Edinburgh was."

Dan stopped in his tracks. The guard on the platform blew his whistle.

"How on earth... how?"

"Let's get on this train and I'll tell you!"

45

CHAPTER FORTY-FOUR

Wednesday 19 July 2023, Elderfield, West Sussex.

With only two and a half days to go until the end of term, spirits were high at lunch time on Monday in the St. Wenceslas staff room.

"Anyone for ice-cream?" asked Enid, tentatively, draining her mug and rinsing it in the sink. "I'm going to the kiosk." She looked around at six blank faces. "It's on me."

There was further silence.

"A Mr Whippy for me, please, with a flake," said Tess, bravely making the first move.

All morning, Enid had been strangely pleasant to everyone. If Tess didn't know better, she would think there had been some kind of epiphany going on. But there wasn't time to worry about Enid's peculiarities; she had some sleuthing to do.

She found Eric photocopying - making booklets for Year Six summer camp in the resources room. They exchanged greetings and she nodded at the stapled A5 pile in approval.

"Those covers look excellent."

"Thanks. I used your Canva template."

Tess leant in what she hoped was a carefree manner against the enormous machine. "How are you getting on without your right hand man?"

She could have sworn Eric flinched.

"Liam."

"Yes, yes, I know who you mean. Um, well, his absence is a loss, of course. He seemed quite a natural with the ins and outs of Duke of Edinburgh... I mean, the Duke of Edinburgh"

Tess narrowed her eyes and said nothing for a few beats. Then she moved to close the door to the resources room softly.

"Eric," she whispered. "I know it was you. Who spilled the beans and briefed the press, I mean."

Eric paused his counting of booklets. He looked over his shoulder at Tess and she knew in that instant she had him.

"I..."

"Don't try to deny it. How did you find out who Liam really was?"

Eric lowered his eyes. "Not here. Everyone can hear. I'll meet you at the Queen's Head after school."

Tess spent the afternoon in a state of high anxiety. What if Eric tried to wriggle out of it? She'd never blackmailed anyone in her life - but the awful press comments that lay ahead for William if she didn't manage to nip this in the bud didn't bear thinking about.

Finally, four o'clock came around. With a glass of water in front of her, Tess sat down on a bench in the pub garden, took a breath and waited for Eric to come clean.

"Sibling rivalry," was all he said, then sighed deeply.

"I'm sorry?"

"All that stuff about Harry and William. I couldn't bear it.

296

When I found out who Liam really was, I felt such rage for how he put his brother through the mill like that - that I told my own brother. Little did I know that he was actually responsible for Liam being employed by our school in the first place." He sniffed and took a long slug of cappuccino.

"I'm sorry," said Tess again, shaking her head. "But I really don't see what that has to do with you?"

Eric looked hard at Tess. "My brother did the same thing to me that William supposedly did to Harry," he said, finally. "Bullied me and told me I wasn't good enough. We reconciled last year, though - but then I found out he had this little Louis plan up his sleeve."

"Wait. Your brother is *Trevor*... Trevor Crispin? The alpaca farmer?"

Eric nodded, miserably. "Trevor was always our mother's favourite. He inherited our alpaca farm when she died, so there was nothing left for me. He knew I was a massive Royalist and so, when it became clear that I was doing just fine on my own, when he was failing in his attempt to win the Briti-shots, he knew what would hurt me the hardest."

"But why..." Tess began to see things more clearly. "You mean... Trevor kidnapped Louis to get back at *you*?"

"That's right. Because I identified with Louis, you see. The misfit, the outcast, the youngest, the spare - like Harry."

Tess toyed with her glass, turning it around and around.

"So then... Why the DofE slur? Why bother blackening William's name? I don't see the point."

Eric shrugged. "It all seemed a bit hopeless once Louis had been returned to the fold. Trevor's been let off scot-free and Louis seems fine, but I couldn't get over my anger towards William. He thought he was so clever, all the time wearing those silly clothes, thinking people didn't recognise him. I saw through it at once, of course..."

"... well, you did have your brother to tell you," Tess pointed out.

Eric ignored her. "... but then, one day, he started going on about how difficult the DofE expeditions are. I thought I'd get my own back on him and brief the press on the fact that he..."

"... found his grandfather to be challenging," finished Tess. "A pretty low thing to do, don't you think?"

They looked around the pub garden. The smell of steak and chips from an adjacent table filled Tess's nostrils. Her mouth watered. Eric drained the last froth from his cup and stood up.

"This reminds me of a story Parth told me once," she said, looking up at him thoughtfully.

"Who's Parth?" asked Eric, innocence radiating from his eyes.

Tess looked at him witheringly.

"Ok, ok, I know who you mean."

"Parth used to work in Number 10," she said. "During the time of Boris Johnson. There was a cat there - the Chief Mouser. It was this cat's job to sniff out rats. And I think I might have done the same sort of thing in this instance, if I do say so myself."

"You see yourself as something of a 'Royal' Mouser, then, do you? I'm afraid I have always seen you as rather mousey. But perhaps I've underestimated you all this time. Perhaps we all have."

"Well," said Kate, standing and picking up her work bag. "I suppose I do, rather. Mouser, Mousor - I know which one I'd rather be. Goodbye, Eric."

46

CHAPTER FORTY-FIVE

Sunday 22 July 2024, Elderfield, West Sussex.

Sun streamed through the windows and highlighted smears on the glass of the cooker door. Unwashed school uniform spilled from the laundry basket onto the rug. A headless stuffed parrot lay in the doorway, its feet pointing skywards. Somewhere in the world, Prince George was turning eleven.

"Is that the end?" asked Mollie, as they sat on the kitchen floor eating ginger nuts and fending off an exuberant Rowley.

"Nearly, darling."

"Remind me. What happened next, then?"

"We went on holiday the following weekend, on George's birthday - the first weekend of the summer holidays like this, remember?"

"Oh, yes! We didn't go to Madagascar though, did we?"

"No. Although we went to Heathrow to wave goodbye to Trevor and Pearl, who flew to Zanzibar."

"The letter that Louis wrote was never revealed by Pearl, was it?"

"No," said Tess. "That was me jumping to conclusions. We

made friends again very quickly."

"Did they have a nice time together? Trevor and Pearl?"

"They did. And their alpaca farm is doing very well out there, too. They say it's the perfect island to help seaweed gatherers with their swimming. Even better, Eric went out at Christmas to see them, too."

"Didn't the Waleses go at Easter?"

"That's right! Well remembered."

"But last summer, we went..."

"To Greece. We stayed by the beach."

"Yes. And we swam loads, because we'd done all that practice at Windsor Castle pool."

"That's right. And then we had to get home."

"Yep, because you were starting your new job."

"Yes," said Tess. "Geddof, Rowley, that's my present from Enid!"

She brushed crumbs from her fingers and Rowley away from the handmade bone necklace that hung around her neck - and lifted her staff badge from her stomach where it hung on its lanyard. It read, Tess Oates, Director of Communications. TWAT.

"What does TWAT mean, again?" asked Mollie.

Tess smiled. "There we are, then."

She fell back onto the floor squealing with laughter and surrendered to Rowley's tongue.

Printed in Great Britain
by Amazon

25484870R00175